Kate Loveday

The
Trophy Wife

Kate Loveday

Contact Information: plover6235@hotmail.com

This is a work of fiction. Names, characters, places and
incidents are either the product of the authors imagination
or are used fictiously, and any resemblance to actual
persons living or dead business establishments, events or
locales is entirely coincidental.

Loveday, Kate
The Trophy Wife/Kate Loveday

ISBN-13: 978-0-646-93077-0

National Library of Australia Catalogue-in-Publication entry

Typeset in 12/16 pt. Garamond.

DEDICATION

For Gloria
Never forgotten

Other Books By Kate Loveday

Contemporary Women's Fiction

Inheritance
Black Mountain
Reflections
The Trophy Wife

****

Historical Romance

The Redwood Series
An Independent Woman
A Liberated Woman
An Ambitious Woman

****

ACKNOWLEDGMENTS

First I must thank my husband Peter for his assistance and support, as always. Without his help in formatting for publication, website management and other technical assistance, as well as his critiques, my life would be much more difficult.

Thank you also to Sally Sutherland, both Kay and Melissa Wood, and Jeanie Jackson who took the time and trouble to read this in its formative stages and offer their invaluable suggestions and advice.

CHAPTER ONE

Erin McDonald inhaled the incense that hung heavy in the air, trapped by the green velvet curtains that shrouded the windows. Was it the smoky atmosphere of the room making her light-headed, or the words of the black-clad woman opposite?

'I see great changes ahead for you. Your life will undergo a complete change.' The psychic's eyes narrowed as she studied the watch in her hand. 'I see your heart is aching. It is not a man who causes this sadness. No. You have lost someone very dear to you. Not long ago.' She lifted her gaze. Her black eyes bored into Erin's.

Erin's throat tightened. 'I lost my mother recently.'

'I see three. Was it three weeks...or perhaps three months?'

Goose bumps prickled Erin's arms. 'Three months.'

Grace stroked the watch. 'I see the Sydney Harbour Bridge.' She paused. 'You will go to Sydney, and live in a fine house. You will be buying clothes.

Beautiful clothes. And shoes. I see you trying on a shoe – a wonderful shoe. It has high heels and is covered with crystals.'

Her fingers caressed the watch again. 'Your mother wants you to stop feeling sadness for her. She has no pain now. She wants you to know she is happy. Yes. She wants you to get on with your life.'

Erin's blood chilled. 'You mean you can *talk* to her?'

'No. I have a message. I see a D, a big yellow D. Did her name have a D?'

'Yes.'

'What is it?'

'Deirdre,' Erin whispered.

'Yes. The message is from her. She wants you to know that you have a big future ahead of you. You will have troubles, but Fate will guide you, and you will find happiness.'

Grace sat back in her chair. 'That is all I have for you today. I hope it is a help to you.'

She handed Erin her watch.

Erin's head buzzed as she left. Part of her said it was all a load of crap. Very theatrical. But how could she know she'd lost someone dear to her? And that her mother's name started with a D. And the bit about seeing her trying on a shoe. Why shoes? How could she know she had a thing about shoes?

Could she see into the future? Could she get messages from the spirits? And would she really move to Sydney? How? Why?

As she let herself into the little flat she and Deirdre had shared Grace's words tumbled around in Erin's head. She'd said Deirdre was happy now – that she had no pain. She hoped with all her heart it was true. Her mother had been so brave, trying to hide the pain of the cancer from her only child. But Erin knew. She wouldn't bring her back again even if she could. Not to go on suffering like that. But how she missed her!

Grief filled her chest until she felt it must burst as great, wracking sobs came, tearing her soul. Grace said she'd find happiness, but right now it felt the furthest thing in the world from her.

Erin's friend Laura sat opposite her at the table in the staff room during their lunch break.

'So how did it go? What did the psychic tell you? Are you going to meet someone tall, dark and handsome?'Laura asked.

'Huh, no such luck. That's obviously not in my future. But she is pretty amazing, isn't she?'

'I told you! Come on – what did she say?'

'She knew about Mum. She saw a bit of stuff about that. And she said I'm going to Sydney.'

'A trip to Sydney. Lucky you. But what about your love life? What did she see about that?'

Erin gave a wry smile. 'Nada. Nothing.'

Oh, rats! Well, we'll just have to make sure you meet some new people. You've been so busy with looking after your Mum these last couple of years...' She broke off and leant across to touch Erin's arm. 'I'm sorry. I didn't mean to be insensitive. I know you're still hurting. But you must get out and about a bit. You've got to get on with your life.'

Erin's heart twisted. 'I know you're right. But I still feel so sad.'

'Of course you do. I know how close you and Deirdre were, it's only natural you miss her. But you dropped out of everything while she was sick and now you need to get out and meet people again.'

Laura was right. She couldn't keep sitting home forever. And she couldn't deny she was lonely.

'What you need is a romance. Something to cheer you up.'

'I don't know I'm quite ready for that yet.'

'Maybe not just yet, but you do need to get out. Look, I'm meeting Ben after work, and we're going for a drink and a meal. Just us, but you never know who we might bump into. Come with us.'

'Thank you, but two's company, three's a crowd. Besides, I'm not ready yet...'

'If you don't want to come to dinner, at least come for a drink.'

'I don't think...'

'Come on. Please. I really want you to.'

Erin took a deep breath. 'All right. And thanks.'

Erin hesitated as they entered the crowded and noisy pub, but Laura took her arm to lead her through the crowd. Suddenly Laura stopped, and her hand flew to her mouth.

'Oh rats! There's Troy...and Belinda. I didn't know they'd be here.' Laura cast an anxious look at Erin. 'Um. I don't know if you knew that Troy's seeing Belinda now?'

Erin's heart gave a little thump, but she kept her voice steady. 'I didn't, but it's okay. I didn't expect him to wait around for me after I let him down so often when Mum was sick.'

'Agh! I'm sorry... I should have thought...after all, you were more than just friends...'

'It's okay. Truly. Don't worry about it.' She nudged Laura forward. 'Come on.'

Ben turned with a smile on his face as Laura touched his arm.

'Hi lovey,' he said, squeezing Laura's hand and dropping a kiss on her cheek. 'And Erin. Good to see you. It's been too long.'

Erin returned his hug, conscious of Troy standing with his arm around Belinda's waist. 'Good to see you too.'

Troy and Belinda had been standing back but now Troy, who could have been on a poster for surfing gear with his bleached blonde hair, tanned face and blue eyes, stepped away from Belinda and touched Erin on the arm.

'Hello Erin.'

He'd once called her his 'pocket Venus with bouncy red hair'.

He dropped a kiss on her cheek. 'I was sorry to hear about your Mum.'

'Thank you.' Erin swallowed.

Belinda slipped her hand through Troy's arm 'Yes, me too,' Belinda said. 'Really sorry.'

'Thank you.'

Ben put his arm around Erin's shoulder. 'What'll you have, Erin? Do you still drink cider?

'Yes.'

Within a minute he pressed a drink into her hand. She sipped it gratefully.

'I haven't seen you around for a while,' Troy

offered.

'No. I've been busy lately. I haven't been out much.'

'Well, you know what they say – all work and no play makes for a dull day.'

She managed a smile. 'So Laura keeps telling me.'

'Well, I'm glad she brought you along tonight.'

'I'm glad I came.' The polite lie slipped easily from her lips.

'Why don't you join us for dinner? For old time's sake.'

Belinda tightened her grip on Troy's arm.

'Thanks for the offer, but I have something arranged. I just popped in to catch up for a drink.'

Erin stayed for another drink as they all started discussing the big game tomorrow, when the local Newcastle Jets were playing Melbourne City. Then she said her goodbye's and made her way home. The flat was very empty when she let herself in.

CHAPTER TWO

It was a few weeks later and the psychic's words had faded to the back of Erin's mind when the manager's PA gave her a message.

'Erin, the boss wants to see you in his office.'

'Do you know what it's about?'

'No.'

'Okay, thanks Sal.'

Erin gnawed her bottom lip. The firm was undertaking restructuring, as they called it, and one of the younger girls was given notice last week. Was this why the boss wanted to see her – to tell her she was no longer needed? He'd always seemed happy with her work, but a little knob of worry inside her whispered she'd been less than cheerful around the office recently, mired down in grief as she'd been. Perhaps he'd noticed, and felt it was bad for morale?

She took out her mirror and quickly checked her face, then smoothed her hands over her hair in case her unruly locks had escaped. She headed to his office and knocked on the door.

'Ah, come in Erin. Take a seat.'

Erin sat opposite Mr Hill, her hands in her lap, butterflies in her belly, and waited for him to speak. He took off his glasses and polished them before beginning.

'I understand why you've seemed unhappy lately, Erin. It's a terrible thing for a young girl like you to lose her mother, especially as you have no other family. I want you to know I feel for you, very much.'

The butterflies became a knot of tension. He was about to fire her. She sucked in a breath and forced words out. 'Thank you.'

'As you know, we've been restructuring things in the firm, both here and at Head Office in Sydney. Times are hard, and even an old established firm like ours is feeling the pinch, and we need to downsize.'

Erin clenched her hands together so tightly the nails dug into the flesh. It was her turn to go. Where would she find another job in these hard times?

The boss pulled a file towards him and opened it. 'I see you've been with us for four years now, since you were sixteen, and you've always performed very well. I'd be sorry to have to let you go, so I have a proposition for you.' He paused. 'I'm right in thinking you have no particular attachments here in Newcastle, aren't I?'

'Yes.'

'It so happens that our Sydney office is about to lose their receptionist, and I believe you would be ideal for the position. You're bright and outgoing, and I'm sure you'd fit in well. I think a change of scene might be good for you. If you like the idea, I'll recommend you, and arrange an interview with Mr Thomas.' He leant back in his chair. 'Now, how do you feel about it? It's a long way to commute, but perhaps you could move down there, if you wanted. Do you think you'd like to live in Sydney?'

Erin's hands unclenched as a surge of relief flooded through her. 'Yes, I've always loved Sydney. It would be wonderful.'

'Right. Then I'll go ahead and arrange an interview.'

Erin chose her clothes carefully for the interview, knowing a receptionist needs to look smart as well as capable. Finally she chose one of her favourite outfits, a plain white linen dress with a black belt and a short black jacket.

She caught the early train to Sydney to make sure she was in plenty of time, and she approached the interview with Mr Thomas, head of the firm, with twin measures of excitement and anxiety. What if he didn't like her? Would he think her capable of filling such an important position – the client's first contact with his business?

But if she got the job, working in the sophisticated metropolis of Sydney, how exciting that would be!

Shivers ran up and down her spine as she sat waiting in the outer office until Mr Thomas was ready to see her. What was he like? What sort of as boss would he be – if she got the job? When she was finally ushered into his office she found he was slim, middle-aged, with a pleasant face and a brisk, business-like manner.

He looked up from a letter he was reading. 'Ah, Erin McDonald,' he greeted her. 'Please take a seat.' He gestured to the chair in front of his desk.

Erin was aware he scrutinised her as she crossed the room to sit opposite him. He took in her looks – slender figure, deep green eyes with black eyelashes, and dark auburn hair.

'I've been reading your reference from our Newcastle office. John Hill speaks highly of you.

'That's very kind of him.'

'Do you think you'd like to work here, Erin?'

'Yes. I'd love to work here.'

'Do you enjoy meeting people?'

'Yes, I do.'

'I see that you took on the receptionist job in the Newcastle office when their regular girl was on leave. How did you find that?'

'It was stimulating.' She smiled. 'Meeting all the clients face to face. I enjoyed that. I'd love to do it permanently.'

'Then I would like to offer you the same position here.' He smiled at her. 'Will you accept it?'

The blood rushed to Erin's head. She gulped before she had breath to answer. 'Yes. Thank you. Thank you very much.'

When she walked out into the street a little later she felt as if she was floating. Receptionist at Atkins and Thomas, Chartered Accountants, of Pitt Street, Sydney. How good was that!

She bought a paper and carried it into a coffee shop. As she sipped her coffee she made a list of flats available for rent that were open for inspection today. The first four she viewed were dark and pokey, and she crossed them off her list.

The next one was a bed-sitter on the second floor of a building in Macleay Street in Kings Cross. When she climbed the steps to the door of 2A the agent was waiting to show prospective tenants through, and he invited her in.

The first thing that struck her was the sun streaming in through the double windows. She crossed the room and looked out. Opposite was the El Alamein fountain and the Fitzroy Gardens. She turned away from the view. The flat was bright and cheerful, and she fell in love with it. She went through the motions of inspecting the tiny bathroom and kitchen area, but she had made up her mind. She could be happy living here. She signed a lease right away.

She moved her belongings in the next weekend, and settled to life in Sydney. Just as the psychic had predicted.

Erin had been in her new job three weeks when she met Giles Brightman. A long-time client of the firm, he'd come in for a meeting with Mr Thomas. A striking figure, tall, dark and solid looking, without an ounce of fat on him. He exuded self-confidence and power.

'You're new here, aren't you?' he asked her, his eyes assessing her as he spoke.

'Yes, Mr Brightman,' she replied, smiling as she did at all the clients.

'What's your name?'

'Erin McDonald.'

That's Irish, isn't it?'

'Yes. My parents came here from Ireland.'

He nodded, but said no more as he went through to the offices. When he came out from his meeting he stopped by her desk.

'I'd like to take you to dinner if you're free tonight, Erin. Are you?'

Erin's tummy fluttered. Fancy this imposing man wanting to take her out.

'I…well, yes Mr Brightman, I am.'

'Good. Call me Giles, and write down your

address for me. I'll pick you up at seven thirty. And leave your hair down,' he added as he left, nodding at the barrettes she used to keep her hair tidy at work.

Erin looked Giles up on the internet later. He was forty one years of age. Divorced from model Megan Andrews three years ago. No children, and...Wow! He was one of the richest men in Australia. He owned a huge conglomerate with interests in hotels, real estate and property developments all over the world.

Why would he ask her out, when he could probably have his pick of the society beauties around town?

As Erin prepared for their night out she looked at her wardrobe. Giles was probably used to escorting lavishly dressed women when he went out. She owned nothing glamorous enough to compete. But her mother always managed to look stylish on her secretary's pay. 'You can look good without spending heaps,' she'd told her. 'Buy quality over quantity. Make sure you always have a little black dress and one really good pair of shoes. Then you can go anywhere.'

So she wore her little black dress, and her best shoes. And she left her hair down.

A lift whisked them up to the eighty-eighth floor of the Sydney Tower in Market Street. A muted buzz of voices and soft music greeted them as Giles escorted Erin into the restaurant. Erin drew a quick breath as she viewed the scene before her.

Diners sat at tables set with gleaming cutlery and sparkling glasses, talking and laughing as waiters in formal attire glided to and fro taking orders or serving meals. Discreet lighting threw a soft glow over everything, and the floor to ceiling windows that curved around the perimeter of the room cocooned them all in a haven of indulgence.

The women among the diners looked expensive. There were probably enough designer labels here to fill a store. It was a far cry from the bistros and pub dining Erin was used to back in Newcastle.

Giles was obviously well known at the restaurant, for the maitre d' bustled forward to greet him by name, and led them to seats by a window.

'Champagne cocktails to start?' he asked Giles, as a waiter held Erin's chair for her.

'Is that all right with you?' Giles asked Erin. 'Or would you prefer something else?

'No, that's fine.' Erin took her seat by the window, wondering what a tycoon liked to talk about when he took you to dinner.

Their cocktails arrived almost as soon as she settled. Giles smiled and raised his glass. 'Here's to a very pleasant evening.'

'To a pleasant evening,' she repeated, raising her glass. As she sipped her drink Erin glanced out the window and almost spilled her drink as she took in the dazzling panorama below. Night had fallen, and lights blazed from city's skyscrapers. The suburbs beyond stretched in velvet blackness, speckled with a million pinpoints of glittering light.

'What an amazing sight.'

'Do you like it?' Giles asked.

'It's fabulous. Look, there's the Harbour Bridge. And the Opera house.'

'Yes. We'll see the whole city as we pivot right around, and come back to this point.'

'So the building revolves right around?'

'Just this outer part of the restaurant.'

'It's wonderful.'

'I'm glad you like it.'

He sounded pleased with her enthusiasm, and Erin relaxed.

'Now, what would you like to eat? How about some oysters? And maybe lobster to follow?

'Yes, to both.' She smiled and raised her glass again. A taste of luxury really was wonderful.

'So tell me about yourself, Erin,' Giles said, when the waiter had taken the orders. 'Did you always live in Newcastle before you came to Sydney?'

'Yes, always.'

'I suppose you have family back there?'

'No. My father died when I was young, and I lost my mother recently.'

'I am sorry. Do you have any brothers or sisters?'

'No.'

'So you're all alone in the world. Is there a boyfriend?'

'Not really. I go out occasionally, but no-one special.'

'So you really are all alone.' He gazed at her with thoughtful eyes. 'That's very sad, and surprising for a beautiful young woman like you.'

Erin's throat tightened. 'That's what happens in life, and there's nothing to be done about it.' She paused for a second before continuing. 'How about you? Have you always lived in Sydney?'

'Yes. I grew up here, and my business is here. I have a brother who manages the New York office. We're not all that close. We catch up when I go to visit, or on the rare occasions he comes here.'

'And your mother?'

He sighed. 'I lost her three years ago.'

Erin's heart went out to him as she put her hand on his arm. They shared a similar loss. 'I'm sorry.'

He placed his hand over hers. 'As you said, that's life.'

Over dinner Giles proved himself an entertaining companion. He regaled her with amusing stories of mishaps in places he'd been or things that had happened to him, and wanted to know about her life in Newcastle, and how she liked living in Sydney.

They chatted easily while Erin watched the whole three hundred and sixty degree view slowly reveal itself.

They lingered over the wine Giles ordered to go with the lobster, and when the waiter returned to whisk away their plates and offered them the dessert menu, Erin shook her head.

'I couldn't manage dessert.'

'Then just coffee? And perhaps a little chocolate?'

They lingered longer over the coffee.

'Have you enjoyed tonight?' he asked, as they were almost ready to leave.

'Yes, it's been wonderful.'

'Do you like the ballet?'

'Yes, I do. I haven't seen many, but those I've seen I really enjoyed.'

'The South Australian ballet company has a

production of Swan Lake on at the moment. Would you like to go?'

'Swan Lake? Oh yes, I' love to go.'

'Then that's settled. I'll pick you up again tomorrow night. All right?'

She was breathless as she answered. 'Yes.'

Erin wondered about Giles' intentions as they drove home. What was he going to expect in return for all this? She wasn't going let him stay the night.

When Giles dropped her home to the door of her little bed sitter he kissed her chastely on the cheek, and arranged to pick her up again the next night.

As she readied herself for bed she thought back over the night. It had been wonderful, but why would this powerful man want her company, when he could probably have his pick of the models or socialites around town?

The next night Erin sat enraptured by Tchaikovsky's sublime music, and the dance of the two swans, white and black, and their prince. She was aware of Giles sitting in the seat beside her, but he made no attempt to take her hand or touch her.

When interval came Giles took her arm to escort her to the foyer.

'Are you enjoying it? He asked, smiling down at her.

'Oh yes. How could anyone not enjoy it? It's wonderful.'

'Would you like a glass of champagne?'

'Yes please.'

As Giles threaded his way through the throng near the bar Erin cast covert looks at the groups standing around, drinking and discussing the show. All ages were represented, with most of the older patrons dressed in smart evening clothes, but several of the younger ones were more casual in chic casual wear. She'd rung the changes with her little black dress by adding different jewellery, and she didn't feel she looked out of place, but now she had a little more in her pay packet maybe she should consider buying a pair of designer jeans.

Giles was back in minutes with the champagne.

'Here's to your company,' he said, looking into her eyes and raising his glass.

'And to yours,' Erin replied. She was startled by the phrase, but realised she was enjoying his company too, now she wasn't so much in awe of him.

They chatted about the show until the bell sounded and they made their way back to their seats. As the show resumed Erin was again lost in the magic of the story unfolding on stage, and the beauty and grace of the dancers. Finally the last scene was over as Odette and her prince sailed away in their boat. The tumultuous applause dragged Erin back to the present. She clapped so hard her palms stung.

Giles turned in his seat and smiled. 'I can see you really like ballet.'

'It's just wonderful. What dedication and years of practice it must take for them to be able to dance like that.'

'Indeed it must. Now I must get you home, or you'll be tired for work in the morning.'

Erin floated downstairs on Giles' arm, still in the thrall of the performance.

He escorted her to his waiting black Jaguar saloon, and held the door open for her. She inhaled the scent of leather as she sank into the soft seat. It was a far cry from her mother's little old Toyota, which she now drove.

Again she wondered about his intentions as they drove through the night, and again he left her at her door with a brush of his lips across her cheek. He was a most unusual man. Or was she thinking that because she'd only been out with boys before?

Giles took Erin out every night for the rest of the week.

They dined on pasta in a little Italian bistro with checked red and white tablecloths, candles in Chianti bottles, and photos of Venice on the walls.

They went to Doyle's at Watson Bay by water taxi, and ate mud crabs.

They had Sunday lunch at Pilu in Freshwater and shared a platter of crisp-skinned suckling pig while they looked out over the beach.

Giles dated Erin three or four times every week over the next month. He took her wining and dining. He sent her flowers and chocolates. They saw the latest shows at the Opera House, complete with champagne during the interval, and the view of the city lights. He took her dining on board the Captain Cook on Sydney Harbour.

He told her how wonderful she was, and generally swept her off her feet. She felt like the princess in a fairytale.

Still he asked nothing more from her than the pleasure of her company. Could he be gay? The thought made her frown, for she knew she had fallen in love with him.

One Saturday afternoon they drove up to the historic Newport Hotel and listened to a local band.

'I'd like to take you to see my home tomorrow, if you'd like to come. Would you?' he asked her later, as they sat eating pizza and looking across the water.

'Of course I would.'

'Good. I'll pick you up in the morning. Will ten o'clock suit you?'

'Yes. Where do you live?'

'Point Piper.'

Of course. She should have guessed.

That night, when he took her home to her door, he put his arms around her and kissed her on the mouth. As he pulled her to him, she felt the hardness of his body against her. He wasn't gay! Erin felt a stirring of passion, but he dropped his arms and stepped away.

'Good night. I'll see you in the morning. Sleep well.'

CHAPTER THREE

Erin's breath caught in her throat as they pulled into the forecourt of a white mansion perched on a slope above the waterfront in Point Piper. She'd expected something grand, but this was incredible.

Giles came around and opened the door for her. As she stepped out she caught the tang of salt in the air. It reminded her of the air at Bar Beach in Newcastle, and of sitting on the sand with her mother, eating fish and chips and flapping her hands at the squawking seagulls as they jostled each other in the hope of a tidbit. She turned and looked across the water. The view here was nothing like that at Bar Beach. The Opera House, the Harbour Bridge, and the city of Sydney lay just across the water.

Giles took her arm and led her past an expanse of lawn and up three steps, then ushered her through a heavily carved timber door into an entrance hall. A painting hung on the wall opposite the door. Its vibrant colours dominated the room, glowing against the plain white walls, its colours replicated in the rich rug on the polished timber floor.

A severe-looking, rather prim woman dressed in black came forward to meet them.

'This is my housekeeper, Mrs Winter,' Giles introduced her. 'I'm going to show Erin around, and then we'll have lunch on the terrace.'

The woman nodded and withdrew.

Giles took Erin's elbow and steered her towards a room leading off the hall. Shade from the balcony above shielded the room from the brilliant sunshine that poured onto the terrace beyond the open glass doors at the front of the room.

Erin walked across to the doors, and her gaze swept over the sparkling blue sea of Sydney Harbour. The white sails of yachts skimmed along, water taxis darted to and fro, and a myriad of other small craft dotted the water. And the view across to the Bridge and the Opera House, with the city skyline beyond. Fancy living with this view!

Giles led her over to the edge of the terrace and she looked down to a wide sweep of lawn bordered by trees and shrubs that led down to the water. A small building nestled at the water's edge next to a jetty, and a motor cruiser rocked gently in the water alongside.

'That's the boat house down there, with the jetty beside it.'

'And is that your boat tied up?'

'Yes. Would you like to go out in the cruiser some time?'

'I'd love to.'

'Then we'll arrange it sometime soon. Come and have a look at the rest of the house now.'

They went back into the sitting room; a symphony in white. White walls, white rugs scattered over a timber floor. Two white leather Chesterfield couches and white armchairs formed a seating area around a central blond ash coffee table. The only splashes of colour in the room came from turquoise cushions and several modern paintings on the wall. A chandelier hung from the ceiling.

'What do you think?'

'It's beautiful.'

'I don't spend a lot of time in here. I have a study

that's more homely, and a sunroom at the back, by the pool.'

Giles took her hand and led her through the rest of the house – dining room, library, a music room with a grand piano, and a home cinema for television. Upstairs were five bedrooms, each with its own bathroom.

After a delicious lunch, served by Mrs Winter, they stood on the terrace looking out over Sydney Harbour. He reached across and took her hand.

'Do you like it here?'

'Yes, of course, how could anyone not like it? It's amazing.'

'You can be here all the time if you want.'

The blood rushing to Erin's head made it spin.

'What…what do you mean?'

'I'm asking you to marry me.'

'To marry you?'

'Yes. You funny little thing. Did you think I was making you an indecent proposal?'

'I…I..no, that is…I didn't know what to think.' Surely he was joking. This wonderful man couldn't actually want her for his wife.

'Well, now you know, what do you say? Do you want to marry me?'

Erin gazed up at him with her heart hammering. A little smile played around his lips. He raised his brows.

'Well?'

'Of course I want to marry you.'

All of a sudden she wanted to laugh out loud. Giles meant it. He really wanted to marry her. She threw herself into his arms, hugging him close.

'Giles, darling, I never thought for a moment that you loved me. I thought it was all one-sided, I never believed you could love me.'

He bent his head and gave her a swift kiss. 'Well now that's settled, let's go and tell Mrs Winter, and start making arrangements for the wedding.'

The next day Giles gave Erin a Platinum Amex card, and told her to go shopping for clothes.

'You have good dress sense,' he told her, 'and you always dress nicely, but as my wife you'll accompany me on many social and business occasions. We'll often be in the company of high profile members of society, and I want you to always look stylish as well as beautiful. You need to go to the designer boutiques and buy a complete new wardrobe, including a wedding dress. It doesn't matter how much you spend. Don't stint yourself. You have unlimited credit on that card, and my accountant will take care of the bills.'

Erin went on her first spending spree.

At first she hesitated to pay the high prices for designer clothes, but then she remembered Giles' words and let herself be seduced by the exquisite materials and attention to detail in high fashion. What a delight to be able to indulge her love of beautiful clothes and shoes.

It was as she browsed amongst the shoes in a smart shoe shop in Double Bay that she saw a shoe that took her breath away. It was a pale satin *Gianvito Rossi* high-heeled pump embellished with crystals.

The price was two thousand five hundred dollars. What an obscene amount of money to pay for a pair of shoes. Then she remembered Giles' words not to stint herself. They were the most beautiful shoes she'd ever seen. As she tried them on the psychic's words came back to her. She had described these shoes. An icy chill touched Erin. She'd been right about her coming to Sydney, too. It was eerie, how could she possibly know? Was life really pre-destined? Was it all Fate? She shook her head and pushed the thought away. And bought the shoes.

Erin and Giles married in a lavish private ceremony in the garden of Giles' country house in the Southern Highlands. They drove down from Sydney the day before the wedding, and as they entered the long driveway flanked by towering elm trees, the lovely old colonial homestead came into view. Erin gasped in surprise and delight.

'Do you like it?' Giles asked her.

'It's beautiful.'

'My great-great-great-grandfather built it. He came out to Sydney with the British military in 1820, and a few years later he was granted a thousand acres in recognition of his services to the colony. While he devoted his time to farming the estate, his wife devoted her time to establishing the gardens.'

'She did a wonderful job.'

'Yes, she did, and over the years both the house and garden have been added to, so we're very comfortable here now.'

Giles drove onto a parking area behind a terrace at the side of the house.

'This is where we'll have the ceremony,' he told

Erin as they stepped onto a terrace covered by a pergola dripping with wisteria blooms.

'It's a lovely setting.'

'And you'll make a lovely bride. Now, let's go inside and have an early dinner so you can get a good night's sleep.'

On her wedding morning Erin dressed in the beautiful full-length gown she'd chosen from a bridal boutique in Double Bay. She twirled in front of the mirror, and smiled. She actually looked pretty! The white silk dress skimmed her body, flaring out at the hips to swirl around her legs. It was saved from total simplicity by a bodice encrusted with crystal beading. She left her hair down, and adorned it simply with a band of dainty white roses. And she wore the *Gianvito Rossi* shoes.

As she took a last look in the mirror tears pricked Erin's eyelids. If only her mother could be here today to see her married. They'd always been close, being just the two of them. But during the two years of Deirdre's illness they grew even closer as Erin supported her mother through the terrible days of chemotherapy. If only she could be here to see her so happy, and marrying such a wonderful man. She shed a few tears in the bathroom, not wanting Giles to see. Then she splashed her eyes with cold water, fixed her face, and walked out with a smile.

A large contingent of Giles' friends and business colleagues was present, but only Laura and Ben were there for her. A crowd of paparazzi milled around outside the security-controlled gates, and a helicopter flew above, all hoping for photos of the happy couple.

A wave of panic overcame Erin at all this attention, but Giles ignored it.

'You need to get used to being in the spotlight,' he told her.

'Will this sort of thing happen often?'

'Yes, but only when they think they might get a good news story. Once they're used to you, they'll ignore you. Unless you do something to draw their attention to you.'

'I'll make sure I don't.' Erin shuddered.

'Good girl.' He squeezed her hand.

All such thoughts went from her mind as they repeated their vows.

As Giles slipped the ring on her finger Erin's heart nearly burst with love. She was so happy she floated through the rest of the day.

After the reception they retired to what Giles called "the bridal suite". It was a bedroom with king-sized bed, a bathroom, and sitting room.

Erin's pulses beat faster than normal as she entered the sitting room, wearing the lacy *La Perla* night chemise with its matching robe that she had chosen for her wedding night.

Giles sat waiting for her with a bottle of champagne in a silver ice bucket.

'Ah, my beautiful bride.' He patted the seat beside him. 'Come and sit here, and we'll enjoy a glass of bubbly in peace, after all the hullabaloo.'

Erin's hand shook ever so slightly as she accepted the glass.

'So here we are on our wedding night. You're not

nervous, I hope?'

'I...I'm not a virgin,' she blurted out.

Giles raised an eyebrow. 'I didn't expect you to be, but I do expect to be the only one from now on. I won't play around, and I don't expect you to.'

'Of course not. I wouldn't dream of it. I love you, Giles. There'll never be anyone else for me.'

'Good. Now let's enjoy a glass of this very nice *Dom Pérignon*, and we'll go to bed.

Erin was relieved, but she still felt a little apprehensive. She wasn't very experienced, and the sexual encounters she'd had, had not been great experiences for her. But she need not have worried. Giles was a skilful lover. He awakened passions in her she'd not known were there. In the end it was all very enjoyable.

CHAPTER FOUR

Their honeymoon was magical. They flew in Giles' private jet to Paris. Erin gaped when she saw the comfortable bed on board. She was sure she'd never be able to sleep for excitement. But it seemed that no sooner had her head touched the pillow than they were landing. She was in Paris!

They were whisked through customs and ushered to a waiting limousine that deposited them at the Georges Cinq Hotel, just around the corner from the Champs Elysees. Giles took her arm and led her through the entrance door.

Erin stood still as they entered the lobby. She had never seen so many flowers outside a flower show. Flowers dominated the lobby. Clusters of blooms were massed in the middle of a circular area under a glittering chandelier, and all around the foyer. Everywhere you looked you saw flowers. The best flower show in the world wouldn't be able to compete. Everything else was marble and gold – sheer opulence. It took her breath away.

When they were shown to their suite the elegance continued. It was a symphony in cream and gold.

Erin went immediately to the sitting room window. The Eiffel tower dominated the view over the rooftops. A tall church spire nearby pierced the blue sky. She was in the most romantic city in the world.

'What do you think?'

Erin tore herself away from the window to answer Giles.

'I think you'd better pinch me to make sure I'm not dreaming this.'

'Wait till you see the rest of Paris. Do you want to come for a stroll?'

'Yes please. But I'd better unpack first.'

'Leave it. It will all be done when we get back.'

Erin wanted to skip as they walked along the Avenue George V. 'I can't tell you how much I've always wanted to see Paris. I always thought, maybe, sometime in the future. And here I am. It's hard to believe.'

'Spring in Paris. The poets all rave about it. I thought you'd like to see it.' Giles smiled indulgently down at her. 'We'll do all the touristy things. And you can do some shopping too. It's the home of the high fashion boutiques, this area. You must buy some things to take home. That's what your Amex card is for.'

'I don't want to go shopping and leave you. And you'd be bored to come with me.'

'I'll have to make phone calls.' He waved a hand airily. 'You can go then.'

'Oh. All right. But I do want to see all the sights.' She stopped and clutched his arm. 'Oh look! There's a hop-on hop-off bus. That'd be a good way to see everything.'

Giles laughed down at her. 'You are a funny little thing. A hop-on hp-off bus? I don't think so. The concierge will arrange a car and driver for us. Much more comfortable.'

Erin's hand dropped from his arm. 'Yes. Of course.'

That night they dined in Le Cinq, the three-Michelin-starred restaurant in the hotel.

'You'll never taste better food than here,' Giles told her.

'What?' She flicked him a smile. 'Better than Mrs Winter cooks?'

He laughed. 'Much better. You'll see.'

After the meal she had to agree. The Tower restaurant was good, but this was sublime. She was gaining an appreciation of this fine living. How lucky she was to be married to Giles.

Over the next few days they saw all the sights. They wandered the city, visited the Eiffel tower, the Louvre, and took a boat ride on the Seine. They visited Montmartre, and had their portraits sketched by the artists in the Place du Tertre. They took a drive to Versailles and Erin marveled at the extravagant palace and the manicured gardens of the former royals.

'But you've seen it all before,' Erin said. 'You're probably not enjoying it that much.'

'I never tire of whatever Paris has to offer. So don't worry, you just enjoy yourself.'

She knew he was indulging her, but she was having too much pleasure to worry about it.

The day before they left Giles told her he needed to make several phone calls, and urged her to go shopping. She wandered along the beautiful tree-lined Avenue Montaign, home to many famous names in the fashion world.

Erin's head whirled with the offerings on display in the elegant boutiques. When she returned from her shopping spree her bags bore famous names. She unloaded them and spread the garments on the bed to admire.

A glorious full length gown, pale blue, with slender straps and a floaty gauze overskirt sparkling with sequins, from *Valentino*. Another in sophisticated black silk that clung to her figure, with a draped front extending to a wide strap over one shoulder, from *Christian Dior*. Both for the formal occasions Giles had told her they would be attending when they returned home. A suit of creamy raw silk from *Chanel* for elegant day wear. And a pair of *Manolo Blahnik* shoes, because she fell in love with them.

She must be the luckiest girl in the whole world.

All too soon the week was over and they flew home to Sydney and the house in Point Piper.

The next morning Giles sat at the breakfast table reading the paper as he ate, while Erin sat opposite, wondering if he read at the table every morning. She didn't like to chatter while he perused whatever it was he was so interested in.

When he finished he stood and dropped a kiss on Erin's head.

'I'm off now. Busy day ahead. Enjoy yourself. Mrs Winter will fill you in on anything you want to know. If you're bored, go and do some shopping. Or go out for lunch. Use your card for anything you want. I might be late home tonight, so don't wait dinner for me.' He dropped a set of car keys on the table beside her. 'These are for your new car. You'll find it in the garage, where your old one was.'

Erin stared at the keys in amazement. Before she managed to utter a word, he was gone.

She gulped down the rest of her toast, stood, and

picked up her plate, cup and saucer.

Mrs Winter appeared at her side. 'I'll do this,' she said, taking the plates from Erin's hands.

'I don't mind helping.'

'Oh no. There's nothing for you to do. I attend to all the duties in the house. With the staff to help me, of course. We know exactly how Mr Brightman likes things done. But you can let me know if there's anything special you'd like for meals. If it's for dinner that night, I need to know in the morning, so I can prepare.'

Erin swallowed. 'Of course.'

She picked up the car keys and hurried down to the garage. When she saw the sleek, red Lexus coupe sitting there her heart somersaulted. She ran her hands over the gleaming surface with something akin to reverence. Opening the door she slid inside. The driver's seat wrapped itself around her, and the 'new' smell took her breath away. She checked everything. She adjusted the seat, turned the radio on and off, tried out the automatic locking doors, and slid the windows up and down. And when she opened the glove box she found papers inside that listed Erin Brightman as the owner.

Erin spent most of the day driving, letting the GPS guide her through unexplored parts of Sydney.

She couldn't wait to thank Giles for the car.

It was almost midnight when he arrived home, and she stayed awake, reading in bed, to greet him. When he climbed into bed alongside her she turned, threw her arms around him and kissed him.

'My new car is wonderful. I've been driving all over Sydney today, and it's just perfect. I want you to know I'm over the moon with it.'

'Good.' He accepted her thanks with a half smile and a nod. Then he patted her head, slid down in the bed, and turned his back. He was asleep in seconds.

'We always dine at seven thirty when Mr Brightman is at home,' Mrs Winter told Erin the next day. 'I hope that suits you.'

'Yes, of course.'

Erin spent the morning wandering around the house, inspecting the different rooms. When she went into the kitchen Mrs Winter looked up from writing at the kitchen table. She put down her pen and stood up.

'Can I help you, Mrs Brightman?'

'No. I'm just looking around. But I might take a cup of coffee out into the sun.'

She moved towards the coffee maker on the bench, but Mrs Winter intercepted her.

'I'll bring it to you. The sunroom is very pleasant at this time of day.'

Erin thanked her with an inward sigh. It seemed she was allowed to do nothing in her new home.

After the coffee she strolled down to the water's edge. She peered down into the water that lapped the piles, then dangled her legs over the edge of the jetty. How she'd envied Giles this view over the water to Sydney's metropolis when she first visited the house. She could hardly believe this was her new life. The psychic had certainly been right about the big changes.

When Giles came in that night he tossed his briefcase onto a chair and stretched.

'Hi, prettyface.' He dropped a kiss on Erin's cheek. 'What a helluva day I've had. With what I pay them you'd think they'd manage to get it right if I'm away for a few days, wouldn't you?'

'What's wrong?'

He grimaced. 'Ah, everything. But don't you worry your pretty little head.' He took her hand. 'Come on, let's have a drink before dinner.'

He led her out onto the terrace. The sun had set, and the light was dwindling. The sea was no longer blue, but lilac. Strata clouds of mauve and pink and amethyst highlighted the translucent sky. Giles flicked a switch and lights came on, spilling their soft radiance onto the terrace. He flicked another switch, and soft music filled the air.

He poured them a drink and sat back, glass in hand.

'Ah, that's better. I feel like a quiet night at home for once. What would you like to do? Sit here and listen to music, or watch a movie?'

Erin opted for music. So after dinner, served in the dining room by Mrs Winter, they came back on to the terrace and listened to music until bed time. Erin had never been happier.

CHAPTER FIVE

'We're going out tonight,' Giles told Erin at breakfast a few days later. 'A dinner at Four Seasons for the spina bifida foundation.'

'Will there be anyone there I've met before?'

'A few who were at our wedding. We'll be sitting at a table that includes Laurence Harvey and his wife Bobbi. Do you remember them?'

'I think so. Was she the pretty blonde woman with an older husband?'

'Yes. Though Laurence wouldn't be happy to hear you describe him as old.'

'Then I'll be sure not to tell him.' Erin smiled.

'He's a friend, as well as a business associate, and we'll be seeing them often, so I'd like you to get to know them. I've arranged for them to be seated with us.' He paused, 'It'll be a dressy affair, so you might want to wear one of those dresses you bought in Paris. The blue one, I think.'

'I think perhaps the black one...'

'No, the blue.'

Erin opened her mouth to protest, but closed it again without speaking. What did it matter? He was concerned that she should look her best to meet his friends, and if he liked the blue better than the black, did it really matter?

'And leave your hair loose,' he added as he left the table. 'Be ready by seven.'

Erin brushed her hair until it shone, and took extra

care with her makeup. She chose diamond earrings and a thin diamond bracelet as her only jewellery. Her skirt was sparkly – she didn't want to look like a Christmas tree.

Giles smiled as he looked her over when he came home to change. 'You look beautiful, as always. There'll be some envious glances tonight at my pretty little wife.'

His words gave her confidence to hold her head high as she walked into the crowded room on his arm. Although she was becoming used to being in posh places now, she felt a little flutter inside as she checked out the stylish crowd mingling in the foyer. She recognised some of the faces from the society pages in the papers and magazines she'd started to read, hoping to become more familiar with this new set of people she was now part of.

Giles steered her towards a couple she recognised from their wedding. The woman, a blonde with long silken hair, bright blue eyes, and a doll-like face, wore an elegant white satin gown.

Giles introduced them as Bobbi and Laurence Harvey.

Bobbi gave Erin a warm smile with her greeting, while Laurence, a grey-haired man with a creased face and intelligent eyes, took her hands and kissed her on both cheeks.

'I'm very pleased to meet you, my dear.' He stood back, still holding her hands. 'Ah yes, you're every bit as beautiful as I've been led to believe. Well done, Giles.'

Giles dipped his head, smiling, and took Erin's arm again to lead her in to dinner.

The dining room was filling rapidly, and they made

their way to a table set for four. Erin was seated opposite Giles, with Laurence on one side of her and Bobbi on the other.

As the two men launched into a business discussion, Bobbi turned to Erin.

'Did you enjoy Paris?

'Yes. I loved it. Have you been?'

'Yes. Laurence and I had our honeymoon there too, three years ago. He's promised to take me back again one day, but I'm still waiting.' She shrugged with a slight smile. 'So tell me, what did you do? I suppose you visited the Eiffel tower, and all those wonderful sights?'

Erin relaxed. Bobbi was easy to talk to. 'Oh yes. We did all the touristy things, but there are still heaps more I'd like to see.'

'Me too. Did you go to any of the fashion houses?'

'Yes. Aren't they amazing? I have to admit I'm just getting used to spending such huge amounts of money on fashion, but I do love the couture clothes.'

In between dinner, and listening to speeches – many of which were long and boring – and occasional words with their husbands, who seemed to have endless business to discuss, Erin and Bobbi got to know each other. They talked about Paris, and fashion, and the charities that Bobbi supported. Erin learned a lot about society life in Sydney. They arranged to meet later in the week for lunch, and by the end of the night Erin felt she had a friend.

The days were long. While Giles went on with his work, Erin spent her days wondering what to do all day. She spent so much time driving around Sydney that she was sure she came to know it better than some taxi drivers. She looked forward to the nights when Giles came home in time for them to dine together. Then she was in heaven as they had a drink before dinner, and afterwards listened to music, or watched television.

'Just like any old married couple,' he joked one night. 'We mustn't become too staid.'

But there was not much chance of that. It seemed that his work often extended into the evenings. 'Meetings,' he would explain, or just, 'a heavy workload.'

Erin spent many nights alone at home, with a book, or watching a movie in the home cinema. She welcomed the nights when they attended a glittering function, for then she was sure of spending time with Giles.

She was glad of Bobbi's friendship. They often lunched together, and sometimes watched a movie. They shopped together, and she came to know all the best boutiques, and to gain a real appreciation of fashion.

Some weekends they socialised with Giles' business acquaintances. If the weather was fine they often took guests out on the harbour in the motor cruiser, and Erin supervised the luncheon that had been prepared by Mrs Winter. But he often worked at weekends too.

As the months passed Erin got to know the other society wives. Somehow she adapted to her life of lunches, shopping, and being roped in to help with various charity projects by other women who were as bored as herself. She made friends easily enough, but it was Bobbi, who was only a few years older than her, who became a true friend; one she could exchange confidences with. As they got to know each other well, the two young women realised how similar their lifestyles were – in marriages with older husbands who spent little time with them. Husbands who regarded them as decorative and obedient, but as air-heads, and good for nothing else. It formed a strong bond between them.

Erin enjoyed her new life for the first year. Giles was attentive and loving to her in a playful way. But his business took most of his time and interest. He made frequent overseas trips, flying off in his private jet.

'Perhaps I could come with you,' she suggested after his fifth trip away.

'No. I'll be tied up with business all the time, and you'd be bored. Much better for you to be here at home, in comfort, and with your friends.'

'But I wouldn't be bored. I love to see new places, and I'd be quite happy to wander around on my own.'

'Then I'd be worried about you all the time, and I wouldn't be able to concentrate. No. It's out of the question.'

She had to accept it, but she longed for something to fill her days. If only Giles would agree to her doing something meaningful, rather than spending her days in a senseless round of shopping and lunches and charity do's. Or spending a day a week sorting the used clothing at the local Salvo's depot. Worthwhile, she was sure, but hardly a stimulating task. But Giles wouldn't even listen when she broached the subject of getting a job.

'Your job is to look after me,' he told her. 'That and to keep yourself looking as beautiful as you are, and to be my hostess and companion when I need you.'

As the time passed Erin realised that Giles wanted nothing more from her than to look beautiful, to be compliant and ready to accompany him whenever he wished, to be charming to his business associates, a good hostess, and ready to accommodate him in bed whenever he felt so inclined. In return she got to live in a magnificent waterfront home in Point Piper, and an unlimited Platinum Amex card. She was an attractive addition to her husband's possessions, to be used and displayed as he wished, and ignored for the rest of the time.

Sometimes they slept together in the big bed in the master bedroom, and sometimes Giles slept elsewhere, and offered no explanation for his absence. She began to wonder if he was seeing other women. If so he kept his dalliances well hidden.

She tackled him about it one night, keeping her voice calm.

'You're spending a lot of nights away from home lately. I'm beginning to wonder if you're seeing another woman.'

His face hardened. His eyes were like flints as he replied, his voice harsh. 'Don't be ridiculous. You know I keep a bed at the office for when I have to work until all hours. Working so I can give you all the luxuries you enjoy, I might add. And I don't take kindly to being accused.'

Her stomach tightened. 'Then if I'm wrong, I'm sorry.'

'I should think so. After all, I don't ask you what you do with yourself all the time you have to yourself. For all I know you might be meeting other men while I'm working.'

'You know I wouldn't do that.'

'Nor would I.'

Erin had to accept his word. She had no way of finding out, and she remembered his words on their wedding night – surely he wouldn't go back on that. But the thought lurked in the back of her mind.

Giles spent less and less time with her. She tried to make allowances for him. Such an important man, he was so busy. And when a little voice whispered that he'd made time for her before they were married, she pushed it away. Surely that showed how much he loved her –he'd wanted her for his wife.

They were dressing for a gala dinner in aid of the Fred Hollows Foundation when Giles showed a side of him that Erin had never suspected.

He uttered a curse as he struggled with a cufflink.

Erin picked up the other cufflink, her hand reaching for his arm. 'Here, let me do that for you. They're so fiddly...'

Giles batted away her hand, his mouth twisting. He struck her a back-handed blow across the chest.

'What do you think I am? An imbecile? I can manage my own dressing. When I need your help I'll ask for it!'

'Yeow!' Erin staggered and clutched her chest. Tears sprang to her eyes. She hurled the cufflink at him. 'Here! Do it yourself!'

'Don't be childish.' He bent and picked up the cuff link. 'I didn't hurt you,' he said stiffly. 'I don't want you fussing round me as if I'm a child. I don't need it after a day's work. I work my guts out for you, you know. It takes a lot of damn hard work so you can have all this.' Giles swept his arm towards her walk-in robe, packed with designer clothes.

Erin drew a deep breath, her lips set tightly. Yes, this wardrobe was what she got for being his obedient little wife. Do as I want and I'll give you luxury. Was this what their marriage had become? You scratch my back and I'll scratch yours?

Giles finished doing up the cuff links and looked at his watch. 'Now hurry up and finish getting ready. It's time to go.'

A slow burn began inside Erin as she picked up her purse. When he took her arm to lead her down the stairs she shook his hand away.

For the rest of the evening Giles acted as if nothing had happened. Erin did her duty – she smiled, and charmed those they met. She spoke to Giles only when necessary.

The next day a huge bunch of roses arrived. The accompanying card had one word on it, 'Forgiven?'

That night he came home early. As he bent to kiss her she stepped back and turned her head.

'Come on now, don't be like that. I'm sorry for my bad temper. I had a bad day, but I shouldn't have taken it out on you. Surely you can forgive me?' He reached for her hand.

She swallowed a sharp reply and let him pull her to him. What was the point of continuing an argument?

'Please. Tell me you forgive me.'

'All right, I forgive you this once. But I hope you never think you can hit me again.'

'Of course it won't. Now, give me a little kiss.'

She returned his kiss reluctantly, but it seemed enough for him.

'That's my girl. You'd better go out and buy yourself something extra nice, to make up for my bad temper.'

CHAPTER SIX

As time passed Erin became more miserable. She longed for them to have a child. As an only child herself, she'd decided at an early age that she wanted a bevy of children. But Giles didn't want fatherhood. He wasn't ready for 'a bawling kid around the place'. Perhaps sometime in the future, he promised.

That time seemed to recede further away with each passing year. But Erin clung to the hope that, as the years passed, Giles would spend more time at home, and they could find again those happy days of their honeymoon and their first year of marriage.

The day of their fifth wedding anniversary was only two days away. At breakfast Erin broached the subject with Giles.

'Have you thought about what you'd like to do on our anniversary?' she asked him as she buttered her toast. 'Five years is a significant number.'

He lowered his paper and looked at her, still half absorbed in what he was reading. 'Five years?' he said vaguely. 'Yes, I suppose it is. Remarkable. Hmm, yes, I suppose we should do something to mark it.' He put the paper aside. 'A special dinner, perhaps. Where would you like to go? To Quay maybe?' He raised his brows. 'Or would you prefer a special dinner cruise on the harbour – Sydney Harbour at night? We could invite Laurence and Bobbi, you'd like that. But I'll let you decide. What would you like to do?'

'We go out so often, perhaps it would be nice to

have a quiet night at home for a change. Just the two of us. We don't eat at home alone very often. I could arrange a special dinner; that roast duck with orange that you always enjoy. Would you like that?'

Giles gave a little laugh. 'You are a funny little thing. Stay at home for a celebration? You'll probably be bored with just me for company, but if that's what you really want...?' he shrugged and let his voice trail away.

'I think it would be lovely.'

'Then that's settled.'

At that moment Giles' phone rang and he answered with his customary greeting, 'Brightman.'

As Erin began to plan a romantic evening, just the two of them, she saw Giles scowl as he listened to the caller. He turned away.

'You're sure he's the best?' he barked into the phone. He frowned at what he heard. 'Then give the bastard what he wants, this is too important to fuck with. You know what's at stake. You tell fucking George he better be able to come up with the goods or it'll be the worse for him. Fix it, whatever you have to do.' His face was like thunder as he clicked off his phone.

'A problem?' Erin asked.

Instantly his scowl disappeared, replaced by his usual urbane countenance. 'No, no. Just a business matter, nothing for you to worry about. Now, what were we talking about?'

'Our anniversary.'

'Yes, of course. Well, we'll have it home here if that's what you want.'

'I think it would be lovely.'

'Then you go ahead and make your arrangements.'

As he left the table Erin continued to make her plans. She would speak to Mrs Winter and arrange a delicious meal. They would have champagne, and then, maybe, they could just sit and talk, and listen to music. Something they hadn't done since that first year.

On the morning of their anniversary Erin reminded Giles they were dining at home tonight.

'Will you try not to be too late? Do you think you can be home by seven?'

'Yes, yes. I'll be home by seven. In plenty of time for a cocktail before dinner.'

He hadn't mentioned their anniversary, but that didn't matter.

Erin hummed to herself as she made her arrangements. She didn't care if he didn't have a present for her, she just wanted his company.

That night she took extra care with her appearance, and came downstairs at half past six to check that the table was set with a low bowl of roses in the centre, that the crystal glasses shone and the *Mumm cordon rouge* was cooling in its silver ice bucket.

Then she settled in the lounge with a book to wait for Giles to arrive home.

She waited – and waited – and waited.

At eight o'clock she tried to ring him, but his phone was turned off. She paced up and down, biting at her knuckle. Something might have happened to him.

She tried to settle to her book again, but after reading the same page twice and unable to remember what she'd read she put it aside. She tried his phone again. Still turned off. Her stomach clenched. Surely he would've called her if he was just running late? She paced some more, checking her watch every few minutes. He didn't call.

The night wore on. Ten o'clock. She would have heard by now if there'd been an accident. He wasn't coming. He didn't care enough for her to spend their anniversary together. Or to even bother to ring her with an excuse.

She picked up her book and threw it savagely to the floor, then kicked it the length of the room. She had no appetite left. She called Mrs Winter.

'Don't wait any longer. You go to bed. He's obviously been detained.'

'Very well.'

At ten thirty she climbed the stairs with an aching heart. She threw herself down on her bed, and cried into her pillow. How could he do this to her? He obviously cared nothing for her now. Had he met someone else? Someone he cared for more than her?

Giles did not return until ten o'clock the following night. He was in a surly mood as he entered their bedroom and pulled off his tie.

'I was disappointed last night,' she told him, her voice cold. 'In case you've forgotten, we'd arranged to have dinner together to celebrate our anniversary.'

'Something came up.'

'I think you could at least have called me.'

'You do, do you? Well I didn't, did I? So get over it. Go buy yourself some new clothes. Use your Amex card. It seems to be the answer to all your moods.'

Erin's lips tightened. 'I'm not just in a mood. I think I have a right to be upset.'

'Oh, you do, do you? Well maybe this'll give you something to be really upset about.' He bunched his fist and punched her in the solar plexus.

Erin gasped for air and fell to the floor, doubled up with pain. Tears sprang to her eyes. She struggled for breath.

Giles gazed at her as she lay on the floor, then turned and left the room. Seconds later the door slammed in the adjoining bedroom.

When her breath returned Erin dragged herself on to the bed and lay there, trembling with fear that he might come back and hurt her more. Slowly the pain subsided. When she felt a little better she undressed, and climbed between the sheets.

Rage burned inside her. He didn't love her. She doubted he ever had. He'd only wanted her to show off at his functions and to act as his hostess. He'd seen she was inexperienced and naive; a young woman with no family to interfere. He'd realised he could mould her to suit his own requirements. Well, she was older now, and wiser. She'd learned a lot about life in these last five years. Their marriage was a sham. What a fool she'd been to think he would ever change. Why was she staying here? She would leave him. Leave him and make a new life.

The next morning Giles told her he was sorry. 'I didn't mean to hurt you. Everything just got to me. I'd had a bad day, and a helluva meeting last night. And a bit too much booze. It finally caught up with me. Can you forgive me?'

Erin gazed at him as he stood there – his face so open, his eyes so sincere – and her resolve faltered.

Their marriage was disintegrating; there was no doubt about that. Should she try to save it? Should she give him another chance? She couldn't understand why she still felt even a flicker of love for him after what he had done, but she couldn't help it, she did. Yes, she must try. She drew a deep breath.

'Very well. But if it happens again...'

'I won't, I promise.'

He reached for her hand, but Erin turned away.

'It's time for breakfast. We don't want to keep Mrs Winter waiting.'

She accepted his apology, but it was an uneasy acceptance.

For the next few weeks Giles became more attentive, and spent more nights at home. Erin believed he was truly sorry. She felt happier than she had for a long time. It seemed their marriage was improving.

Until the night he came home late, unsteady on his feet and smelling of drink. When she remonstrated with him for driving after drinking, he slapped her.

Over the next weeks Giles hit her several times. He always said afterwards that he was sorry, but she stopped believing him.

Her dream of leaving hardened into reality as her love faded with his ill treatment. But he wouldn't let her go easily. She needed a plan.

CHAPTER SEVEN

At first she thought only of escaping away somewhere on her own and getting a job in an office. But then she realised that life with Giles had given her an appreciation of the finer things in life, and she would no longer be content living from week to week on a meagre pay-packet. No. She wanted more than that. Not a life of wealth and luxury, but independence. A better life than her mother knew as a struggling single mother. The way to do this was to have a business, but that seemed unlikely. Until the day she had her idea.

It was a simple idea. It came to Erin suddenly as she stood in her walk-in wardrobe. Everything was tidy and orderly, as usual. But the wardrobe was becoming overcrowded. She would soon have to cull some more things and send them to the Salvos.

She looked at the clothes hanging there; dresses, coats, jackets, evening gowns, pants and tops, all arranged in orderly groups according to style and colour. A bank of drawers for underwear, and another of shelves for shoes and bags. So much money tied up in here. Clothes, bags, shoes. Especially shoes. She loved shoes and could never resist buying something special.

She picked up the *Gianvito Rossi* high-heeled pump embellished with crystals, and turned it around. She would never part with this – it was one of her favourites. Putting it back on the shelf next to its mate she drew in a deep breath. What a disgrace to have spent so much money on a pair of shoes. But, she had time on her hands, a husband who expected her to be always immaculately groomed and gowned, and an unlimited Amex card. The bills went straight to the accountant to pay and there was never any criticism of her extravagance. It was part of Giles' reward to her for being 'a good girl', as he put it.

As she gazed at the racks Erin had a flash of inspiration. Could she turn her unwanted items into actual cash?

Cash was something she never had. She had unlimited credit on her Amex card, as well as a Visa, the use of Giles' charge accounts at all the best restaurants, and a taxi charge card. But never any cash. When she'd broached the subject with Giles he told her she had no need for cash. If she needed some for a specific purpose she could come and ask him for it. It was another way he exercised his control over her.

Erin had little money of her own – just a little nest-egg that came to her when her mother died. She hated having to dip into it. As she looked now at all the wonderful clothes hanging around her, her mind wandered back to her mother. Deirdre had been resourceful. She'd always found a way to overcome a problem. What would she do in her position? Taking a deep breath, Erin considered her idea again.

'There are plenty of women out there who would love to wear designer clothes but can't afford them,' she told Bobbi. 'I'm sure if I could offer them these clothes at a reasonable price, they'd sell like the proverbial hotcakes.'

'It sounds a good idea, and I'd be happy to come in with you. We can be partners. But how could we finance it? We can't just ask our husbands for the money.'

'No, what we have to do is sell as many of our own clothes and accessories as possible, and save the cash until we have enough capital to go into business, with an exclusive boutique selling recycled designer labels. We'll set it up like a fashion house, all classy and glamorous.'

'Won't it take an awful long time to save enough money for that?'

'We need to up our purchases, so we keep having more things to sell.'

'I see.' Bobbi grinned. 'So, more spending sprees? Sounds like fun. But are you sure we'll be able to sell enough?'

'I'm going to have a trial run tomorrow morning. I've picked out a shop over in Manly to start with, where I'm not likely to be recognised. Can you meet me for lunch at Catalina's after, to see how I go?'

'You bet!'

Erin approached the shop with a nervous flutter in her stomach. Her step faltered as she glanced around. Was anyone watching? No, no-one seemed to be taking any interest in her.

She'd been so nervous about being spotted here that she'd been unable to eat breakfast this morning. She'd toyed with a piece of toast while she reviewed her planned itinerary. She'd decided to use public transport instead of driving. She'd take a train into Circular Quay and then the ferry across to Manly.

None of her acquaintances used public transport.

Even choosing Manly was a considered choice – very few people from the eastern suburbs of Sydney bothered to cross the bridge to the northern beaches. No, she'd been fairly confident she wouldn't be recognised on this side of the bridge. Besides, who'd suspect Mrs Giles Brightman of what she was about to do?

Erin sauntered past the shop and looked into the window at the mismatched array of garments and shoes on display. Huh, she could do better than that. She went a little further along the Corso, then turned and walked back at a relaxed pace.

'*Recycled Threads*', she mused, pausing to read the name on the window before entering. She placed her carry bags on the glass topped counter. The saleswoman gave her a smile and a quick, 'I'll be with you in a minute'. She continued attending to a young woman with long brown hair and a butterfly tattooed on her arm, who was dithering over two jackets.

Erin gazed around as she waited. It was a large shop. Its walls were adorned with articles of clothing – mostly women's evening wear, ropes of beads, hats and various accessories. And a shelf full of shoes. Fairly ordinary shoes. All a bit of a mish-mash, really.

The saleswoman finalised the sale to the girl with the tattoo, walked over to the counter and put money in the till.

'So, what have we here?' she asked Erin, gazing at the bags.

'Would you be interested in these?'

Erin removed three pairs of shoes from the first bag, followed by three dresses, an evening gown, two jackets, a velvet evening wrap and sundry tops from the other bags.

The woman's brows shot up. She drew in her breath as she picked up one of the black pumps with soaring heels and turned it around, scrutinising it carefully. Then she did the same with a black and white sandal.

'*Jimmy Choo's*?' Her voice reflected her surprise.

'Yes.' Erin waited while she examined the rest, piece by piece.

'Do you think you can sell them?' she asked, when the last piece was put aside.

'Oh yes, I can sell them.' The woman gave her a piercing look. 'Do they all belong to you?'

'Yes.'

The woman's eyes raked her up and down. How good she'd worn her *Lagerfeld* pants and top, and the *Jimmy Choo* sandals.

'They're all designer garments.'

'Yes.' Erin's heart picked up a beat. This was the crunch. Now she would find out if her scheme was feasible. 'How much are they worth?'

Erin waited, scarcely breathing, as the woman picked up a pen and itemised each piece on a docket, jotted down a figure alongside it, and totalled the column. Turning the pad towards Erin, she pointed to the bottom line.

Erin released her breath. 'Okay. I'll take it.'

'Good. I'll write you a receipt for the goods.' The woman took a book from a drawer beneath the counter. 'What name?' she asked, her pen poised above the page.

'Jane Smith.'

'And the address?'

'Hornsby will do.'

The woman pursed her lips, and seemed about to say something more. But she wrote it down without a word. When she finished she added the amount of payment at the bottom, took the money from the till and handed it to Erin.

'Just sign here to acknowledge payment please.' She handed Erin the pen.

Erin put the money in her purse, took the pen and signed, J Smith, with a flourish.

'If you have anything else to sell, I'll be only too happy to take it, Mrs Smith.'

If only she could see her wardrobes at home. After all, who really needs fifty three pairs of shoes?

'Then I'm sure I'll see you again.'

As she left the shop and headed down to the ferry it was all Erin could do to stop herself doing a happy dance along the way. It had been so easy. She had cash now, nestling alongside the Platinum Amex card in her purse. Onboard the ferry for the ride back to Circular Quay she didn't go inside the cabin. Instead she stood outside near the stern, where she could feel the breeze blow through her tumbling mane of hair, careless of its disarray. When the swell picked up and the ferry started to rock and roll as they passed the gap between the Heads the wind whipped her cheeks until they tingled. She threw back her head and laughed with the sheer exhilaration of it.

Erin simmered with excitement as she followed the waiter to her table in Catalina's restaurant. She smiled and nodded to some of the other diners she knew as she walked through; an ageing socialite lunching with her latest toy-boy, a fashion editor lording it over her usual crowd of hangers-on, and a gossip columnist in a huddle with a stick-thin model. Many of the other diners were socialites easing their boredom with another ladies' lunch, and a sprinkling of business men with expense accounts.

She looked out over Sydney Harbour while she waited. It was a sight she never tired of. Today it sparkled. Brilliant spring sunshine danced off the choppy wavelets. With spinnakers filled, yachts chased each other towards the Heads, crews straining on the ropes. Small crafts criss-crossed the water. As always, the harbour buzzed.

Erin knew many here today envied her position as wife to the eminent and wealthy Giles Brightman, but she was sick of her futile life. As long as she remained with Giles she would never be more than a trophy wife, being his gracious hostess and hanging on his arm at social events. She wanted to do something useful with her life. And now he was showing the violent side of his nature she had lost her regard for him. Could she really go her own way, and make a new life for herself? The psychic had said she had a big future, but was that possible? And what did it actually mean?

Erin snapped out of her reverie as Bobbi sat down opposite her.

'So how did it go?' Bobbi asked.

'Without a hitch.' Erin grinned.

They were interrupted as the waiter arrived to take their order, but after ordering they returned to their conversation.

'Do you think you were recognised?'

'I don't think so. I didn't see a soul I knew, and I doubt the woman in the shop cared enough to question me. She was just interested in the goods.'

'I bet her eyes popped when she saw the Jimmy Choo's.'

'She positively drooled over them. Anyway, she said to bring in anything else I might have to sell.'

'So she might see you quite often, huh?'

'It's quite possible.'

They both laughed. Suddenly the smile slipped from Bobbi's face. She reached across and flipped aside Erin's scarf to reveal a bruise.

'Don't do that!' A hot flush flooded Erin as she pushed the hand away. She straightened the scarf. 'There are eyes everywhere here. There's Evie Tate, the columnist. She'd love to get hold of a juicy bit of gossip.'

'Might do him good for others to know...'

'No!' Erin's throat tightened. 'Do you think I want the humiliation of anyone else knowing my husband hit me?'

Bobbi's eyes narrowed. 'When did he do that?'

'Last night.'

'Bastard!'

'All the more reason to continue with our plan.'

'Yes but...'

Erin shook her head and swallowed the lump in her throat.

'Forget it.'

'All right.' Bobbi glowered. 'But one more thing to add...'

'Enough, let's move on. Have you had a chance to speak to anyone else yet?'

Bobbi took a breath. "Yes. It seems several of the girls aren't averse to earning a little pin money by lightening their wardrobes. So I've told them to let me know and I'll arrange it for them.'

'Good. And you just brought it up casually?'

'Yes. Just dropped it into the conversation, you know, just told them how I'd picked up a bit of cash money by selling a few clothes and things I'd grown tired of. Some were interested, some weren't.'

'And those that were?'

'I told them to bring anything they want to get rid of to me, and I'll do the deed for them.'

'So we'll take the things and sell them, keeping a percentage for ourselves for our effort, and giving them a fair price.'

'Yes. Of course, there are some who shrugged it off, saying they always give theirs to charity.'

'Of course. And that's up to them.'

Their lunch arrived at that moment, and over their meal they continued to discuss their plan.

Erin had to be careful about smuggling clothes out of the house. The staff had all been with Giles for many years, and she didn't want to arouse any suspicions about what she was doing. On her initial trip to *Recycled Threads* she'd managed to slip from the house with her bags without being seen. But she realised this was too risky, so she started carrying a large handbag or tote with one or more items stuffed inside whenever she left the house. At her first stop she then secreted the bag in the boot of her car until she had sufficient for another visit to the Manly shop, or one of the other stores she'd begun to frequent.

As their savings started to grow Erin had another idea. She put it to Bobbi.

'If we had somewhere to store the things we could build our stock with our own clothes, instead of selling them for someone else to make the profit.'

'Of course, but where could we store it?'

'We could rent space in one of those self-storage places where you rent by the month. I had a look online, and a small space won't cost much.'

'That's brilliant. Then when we buy something that we don't really want it can go straight there, without even taking it home.'

'Yes, and so we don't have all the same sizes, you keep on collecting as much as you can and we'll pay for them out of our kitty. And when we buy something, we can always buy in a different size by saying it's for a gift.'

'You've really got a good head for business, you know. I think we're going to be successful.'

'I'm determined we will.'

The next morning Erin went to a large self storage facility in Chippendale. She rented a space in the name of Jane Smith, and paid for it with cash. Then she drove to David Jones store in Chatswood, where she made her way to the women's fashion floor and browsed among the designer clothes.

In the *Chloe* section she picked out a black and white spotted dress, then checked the price tag. Two thousand five hundred and seventy nine dollars. That would do nicely.

A saleswoman came up to her. 'That's lovely, isn't it? Would you like to try it on?'

'Yes, thank you.' Erin handed her the garment and followed her to the change room. The assistant hovered outside, waiting while Erin tried on the dress. She turned this way and that in the mirror, inspecting it.

'How is that, madam?'

'Yes, very nice, I'll take it.' Erin took off the dress and handed it out to her before dressing and leaving the cubicle.

'While I'm here I want to pick out something as a gift for my mother.'

After browsing some more she chose a black crepe *Carla Zampatti*, two sizes larger than her own size, and priced at just under a thousand dollars. She added a ruffle top with a removable scarf, again by *Chloe*, for thirteen hundred dollars.

'I hope your mother likes her gifts,' the smiling assistant told her as she took her Amex card. She completed the sale, folded the garments with tissue paper, and slid them into bags with the distinctive DJ's pattern.

'If not, I'll bring her in to exchange them, but I think she will.'

'She's a lucky mother.'

Erin smiled as she took her purchases and headed for the shoe department.

Here she purchased a pair of *Ginger & Smart* high heeled sandals. Four hundred and eighty dollars. She added an *Emilio Pucci* envelope clutch adorned with crystals, at two thousand and forty nine dollars, and carried her purchases back to her car.

She slid behind the wheel and totted up her purchases. A bit under seven and a half thousand dollars. Not bad for a morning's work, even if they would only bring about half that when resold. She drove straight to the self storage complex and placed the two bags containing the 'gifts' into their space, and added another three bags that she removed from the boot of her car. The other purchases would be added in due course, after she'd worn them a few times.

As she left the storage complex and headed for home she switched on the radio. The car filled with the sound of Britney Spears singing. Erin laughed out loud as she thumped the wheel, and sang along with her, 'You might think that I won't make it on my own, but now I'm stronger than yesterday. Now it's nothing but my way. My loneliness ain't killing me no more, I, I'm stronger.'

A few weeks later Bobbi called Erin to arrange lunch at Catalina's again. When Erin arrived Bobbi was already seated at a table waiting for her, gazing out of the window with a faraway look on her face.

'You look miles away,' she told her friend as she took the seat opposite her.

Bobbi snapped out of her reverie, and smiled a greeting. 'I was, rather.'

'So, what's up? You're either excited or apprehensive.'

'A bit of both, I suppose. I guess you could say I've got good news and bad news.'

'Have you now? Tell me.'

The light shining in Bobbi's eyes made it plain she was happy, yet there was a hint of anxiety there too as she drew a deep breath.

'I'm pregnant.'

Erin's heart leapt. 'That's wonderful! Congratulations!'

Bobbi laughed, and her face lit up. 'It is exciting, isn't it? Laurence is over the moon, and he's changed so much since I told him, you wouldn't believe. He couldn't be more attentive and caring. He can't wait to get home now, and he talks about the baby all the time.' The smile left her face. 'But I'm afraid it does change my plan of leaving him. I couldn't take a baby away from him. At least, not while he continues to be so considerate.'

'Of course you couldn't. And perhaps this is just what he needs to make him realise that a happy family life is what he really wants. And to appreciate you.'

'I hope so.' Bobbi's voice was wistful. 'His first wife was never able to have children, and it seems he's been secretly hoping it would happen. So now he's treating me like a princess. He can't do enough to please me. I'm so happy.'

A surge of pleasure filled Erin. 'I'm so pleased for you. I know how much you've always wanted a baby.'

'But it does change my plans somewhat,' Bobbi added hesitantly. 'However, I've been thinking about it, and I'll still continue to collect as many clothes as I can, like always. Maybe I can be a silent partner, doing just that? At least for a while, until I see how things go.'

'That's up to you. I don't want you to do anything that doesn't feel right to you.'

Bobbi twisted one of her rings, her face sober. 'It won't make any difference to you...to our friendship...if I can't go ahead, will it?'

Erin smiled. As if that would affect her feelings for the best friend she'd ever had. She reached across the table and touched Bobbi's arm. 'Of course it won't. Friends forever,' she assured her.

Bobbi relaxed. 'Friends forever,' she echoed.

They ordered lunch and settled down to discuss

the coming baby. Erin was delighted for her friend, but how much harder would it be to achieve her goal alone?

As the weeks and months passed Bobbi kept her word and delivered more garments to the storage area, including two parcels of stylish maternity clothes.

Perhaps this would be a whole new market, together with baby's and children's outfits. All have their own popular designers. Maybe the business could become a store selling pre-loved designer clothes for the whole family.

CHAPTER EIGHT

Erin was sitting at her dressing table brushing her hair as she was getting ready for bed when Giles entered the room. He stood inside the door, swaying slightly, before crossing the room to stand alongside her.

'Well, my pretty little wife.' He slurred his words as he leant forward and slid his hand inside her satin nightdress. He squeezed her breast. 'Aren't you a sight for sore eyes? I must say you look quite delectable sitting there like that. Good enough to eat, in fact.' He laughed, squeezing harder.

'Ow!' Erin gasped at the pain of his rough grasp. She dropped the brush and shrugged free of his hand. 'You hurt me.' She sprang to her feet and turned to face him.

'Now, don't be like that, I just want to feel those gorgeous tits. After all they belong to me.' He laughed, grabbing her arm and pulling her to him. 'Come on now, give your husband a little kiss for starters, then we'll go to bed and I'll give you much more. I've got something here you'll love.'

Erin's lip curled as he pulled her to him and she caught a strong smell; a mixture of perfume and sex mingling with the whisky fumes on his breath. She pushed her hands against his chest, and tried to wriggle free of his grasp.

'You're a pig! Coming here to me like this when I can smell another woman on you. You didn't even have the decency to shower first. Get away from me!'

'Don't come that stunt with me, you bitch. You'll

do as I say.' Giles shook her. 'And right now I'm going to take you to bed.'

'No! Let me go!'

He shook her again, until her teeth chattered. She struggled, her heart racing as he tried to pull her towards the bed. But to no avail. He held her tighter, hurting her arms.

He shook her again. Fear stabbed her as his hands went around her throat. His thumbs pressed into her windpipe. Cold sweat ran down her spine as she clawed at his hands, struggling to pull herself free. But she was no match for his superior strength. His hands squeezed her throat. Black spots swam before her eyes, and his face distorted with frenzy. Erin couldn't breathe. His fingers tightened, pressing, pressing into her throat. A roaring in her ears blotted out any other sound. Her heart pounded. Her chest burned. Her legs buckled beneath her. Her strength was ebbing away, and she couldn't struggle any more. He was going to kill her.

Erin let her body go limp. She slumped to the floor as her dead weight forced Giles to drop his hands. She lay there, gasping for breath, her throat on fire. Every pulse in her body throbbed.

Giles bent down and picked her up. She flopped like a rag doll in his arms. He carried her across to the bed and dropped her. She stayed where she fell, her breath coming in tortured rasps. He stood by the bed, staring down at her. He turned and left the room, slamming the door behind him.

Erin remained where he dropped her. Every tendon in her body screamed. When she gathered enough energy she crawled beneath the bedclothes. She lay there, curled into a ball, trembling, terrified.

Giles had tried to kill her. Was he about to come back and finish what he'd begun? Why had he done this? Surely it wasn't just because she'd tried to resist him. Did he want to be rid of her? Had he met someone else? Fearful he'd return, wishing she had some way to keep him out, she finally drifted into an uneasy sleep.

When she woke at daybreak her throat throbbed, and she had trouble swallowing. Her body ached all over. She turned her head to look at the other side of the bed. Thank God she was alone. She moved carefully and found the rest of her seemed all right, except for her arms that pained where Giles had grabbed them. When she looked she saw dark bruises. She caught a faint odour in the air. Stale alcohol and perfume. She trembled as the terror of the night before flooded back, and she tried to come to terms with what had happened. If she hadn't let her body go limp, Giles would have killed her. Or would he have realised what he was doing, and let her go? There was no way of knowing. Would he try again?

Erin slid her legs to the floor and tried to stand, but they threatened to give way beneath her. She swayed, and sat on the edge of the bed, shivering, as she took deep breaths. Her strength gradually returned and she stumbled into the bathroom.

Leaning on the counter she looked in the mirror. An ashen face stared back at her. She touched the purple bruises that stained her throat, and flinched at their tenderness. The rest of her seemed to be all right, but her legs felt as if they had no bones. Nausea made her head swim. Was she about to faint? No, she mustn't. Giles could come back at any moment. What then? She gripped the edge of the counter. She must get away. What should she do? She needed time to decide.

Who could she turn to? Bobbi? Bobbi would want to help, but it wasn't fair to inflict this on her, when Giles and Laurence were friends. She could go to her old friends, Laura and Ben in Newcastle, but she didn't think she could drive so far today. Tears pricked her eyes. She stroked her throat where it hurt. She should probably have it looked at...

Her doctor! Of course! Her doctor would know what to do – Doctor Irene Leclerc, who specialised in women's health. Perhaps she might have somewhere she could suggest for Erin to go. The thought gave her strength

CHAPTER NINE

Erin showered with shaking legs, her body trembling. She let the hot water run on her throat and her bruised arms for a long time. It eased the pain a little. She dressed and picked up her handbag with quivering hands. She checked to make sure she had her keys, some cash, and all her identification.

When she left the room Giles was nowhere in sight. He probably hadn't woken yet. She hurried down the stairs, hoping to avoid being seen, but as she crossed the hall Mrs Winter appeared.

'I'm going out,' she told her, her voice coming out in a croak.

'But you haven't had your breakfast yet.'

Erin shook her head and flapped her hand at the startled woman, and continued out through the door and to the garage.

In the car she rested her head against the steering wheel for a moment, taking deep breaths to steady herself. She mustn't waste any time in leaving. Giles might wake up and come after her. Her hands on the wheel shook as she eased the car out into the street. She drove carefully and steadily the short distance to Edgecliff, to the doctor's rooms.

It was still too early for the clinic to be open so she parked her car in the multi-storey car park and sat in the car, taking deep breaths until she felt calmer. He would never find her here. Finally she locked the car and made her way to a nearby coffee shop. She ordered coffee and a croissant, and pretended to read a newspaper while she slowly drank the coffee and took a bite out of the croissant. She checked her watch every few minutes until it was time to go.

She was waiting outside the clinic door when it opened. The receptionist took one look at her and disappeared into the doctor's room.

'Doctor will see you now,' she told Erin when she came back, and a few minutes later the doctor came to the door and called her in.

Dr Irene was a tall woman in her mid forties. Her dark hair was twisted into a knot at the back of her head, held firmly in place with a tortoiseshell comb. Her dark brown eyes gleamed shrewdly. She had a no-nonsense air about her.

Gesturing Erin to the chair alongside her desk she sat down.

'Now Erin, what can I do for you?'

Erin trembled again, and the tears came as she told her story. She fumbled in her bag for a tissue, but Irene had one in her hand before she could find it.

'I'm sorry,' Erin sniffed, drying her eyes and blowing her nose.

'There now, a few tears won't do you any harm. Helps relieve the pressure a bit. So first of all let me have a look at your throat.'

Irene stood up from the desk and turned Erin's head from side to side to check the bruises on her throat. She examine each one, her lips set, then inspected those on her arms.

'Open your mouth wide now,' she told her, taking a light from her top pocket and shining it down Erin's throat. She moved it this way and that, her face grim, then snapped off the light.

'All right, just relax now.'

Erin sank back in the chair as Irene opened a

drawer and took out a camera. She took several shots of Erin's throat, turning her head to show all the bruises. Then she did the same with her arms.

'So your husband, Giles Brightman, did this to you last night?'

'Yes.'

'I have it all documented here. Now, let's check your blood pressure.'

'It's up a little,' she said as she checked the reading, 'and your pulse is a bit fast, but that's natural under the circumstances. I don't think there will be any lasting damage to your throat. No thanks to him.' She sat back in her chair and gazed at Erin.

'How are you feeling in yourself, apart from the pain from your injuries?'

'I feel...shaky, I suppose you'd call it.'

'You're suffering from shock. I'll prescribe something for that, and you need to have a few restful days.' She paused. 'What do you want to do Erin? If you want to lay charges against your husband, I have your injuries documented.'

'I...I don't know. I just want to be somewhere by myself for a while. Somewhere safe, away from everyone for a while, just for two or three days.' She paused for a second. 'Is there somewhere...do you have a hospital or something...' Her voice trailed off. What should she do?

'There are shelters for women who've been victims of domestic violence, but they're over-taxed. There are always more women in desperate need of a bolthole than there are refuges.'

Erin's heart gave a little thump. Was that what she was now? A battered wife? Tears sprang to her eyes.

Irene smiled sympathetically. 'I don't think that's

quite what you want, Erin. How about I book you into in a small private hospital, one that's used mainly for recuperation, for a few days?'

'Could I have a private room?'

'Yes. And while you'll have nursing staff on hand, you'll be left alone when you want it. There's a counsellor there when you feel you want to talk to someone. I'll make the arrangements for you, if you like.'

Erin let out a sigh as relief washed through her. 'Yes, that sounds ideal. That will give me time to think what to do next.'

'Good.' Irene picked up the phone on her desk and made the arrangements for Erin to be admitted immediately, writing on a pad as she did so.

'That's all arranged,' she told Erin as she finished the call and tore off the sheet of paper and handed it to her. 'They're expecting you this morning. You don't have to worry about anything. You'll be able to purchase toiletries and anything you need there, so you can go straight from here. You can stay as long as you need, but I'm guessing three days will probably be sufficient for you. I could arrange an ambulance to take you, but I don't think you need that. A taxi will be sufficient.'

'My car is in the car park...'

'Leave it there. It'll be quite safe until you collect it. You're in shock, I don't want you driving. I want you to rest and try and calm your mind over the next few days. I'll call in to see you before you leave.'

'Thank you so much, Irene. I just need a few days by myself.'

'I know. By the way, don't pay your bill on the way out. I'll send it directly to your husband. It's important he knows you've been here to have medical treatment this morning. And that he knows, that I know, what he did to you.'

CHAPTER TEN

When Erin arrived at the hospital she was given a white cotton gown and a towelling robe, and put to bed in an airy room with a window that looked out over a green lawn bordered by rose bushes, with large shady trees beyond. A small bathroom adjoined, and, when she asked about toiletries, a young aide came to take her order, and returned a little later with her purchases.

She spent most of that day, and the next, lying in bed or sitting in a chair by the window. She slipped in and out of a drowsiness that was partly induced, she knew, by the medication she received. She was glad of it, for it enabled her to push aside her troubles. Thoughts of Giles came and went. She was too tired to worry about him or their marriage.

On the third day Erin woke with a clear head after a restful sleep. She felt strong again. Leaving the bed she slipped on the robe and padded to the window to look out. A stiff breeze whipped the leaves of the trees in the garden. A purple carpet lay on the ground beneath a Tibouchina tree. No one was about at this early hour. All was quiet and peaceful. She watched a small bird as it hopped about on the lawn, pecking among the blades of grass in its search for worms.

As she gazed at the tranquil scene Erin sighed, and wrapped her arms around herself. A sweep of melancholy overtook her as she reviewed the distressing ending to the marriage she'd entered into with such joy. Her mind turned to their wedding day. How happy she'd been then.

But now their marriage was over. Of that she had no doubt. Giles was not to be trusted when he got into one of his rages. But even before this, his indifference to her, unless it suited his purpose, had been apparent. Oh yes, he still wanted her on his arm at his functions. Still wanted to show her off when it suited him. But that was all. Any affection he'd felt for her hadn't lasted beyond their first year of marriage. She must accept that, much as it hurt. The years of disappointments, and hurts, had lessened her love. His attack killed it. Now she just wanted to go her own way.

How she missed her mother. How comforting it would be to have her to talk to, to turn to for help and reassurance. But she was not here. Again she thought of phoning Bobbi. Her friend would want to help. But there were only a few weeks to go before the baby was due, and she didn't want to cause her any hassles because of the two men's friendship. And when she thought of calling Laura she cringed at the thought of having to go through the humiliation of admitting that her husband had tried to strangle her.

Better instead to think of her plans for a business. Her bank balance was growing slowly, but Fate had pushed her into moving forward now, rather than later. She would just have to manage as best she could.

Her musings were interrupted by the arrival of the breakfast tray. She was hungry; she'd eaten little for two days. She tucked into a breakfast of juice, fruit and yoghourt, toast, jam, and coffee. As she finished the door opened and Dr Irene came in.

'How are you feeling this morning, Erin?' Irene asked as she pulled up a chair and sat by the bed.

'Very much better. My throat's still sore, but I can think clearly now. I've just been lying here thinking about what I'm going to do.'

'And have you come to any decisions?'

'Yes. I'm leaving Giles, right away.'

'Can I ask you how your marriage was before this happened?'

'Not good, I'm afraid. He seemed to lose interest in me after our first year together. I sometimes wonder why he ever married me at all, unless it was to have someone to escort to all the functions he attends.'

'Has he ever hurt you before?'

'Yes. A few times. I've learnt to be careful of what I say to him, especially if he's in a bad mood. He has a nasty temper. But he's never...' her voice faltered as emotion welled up inside her, blocking her throat. She swallowed and took a shaky breath before continuing. 'He's never done anything like this before. I really thought he was going to kill me.'

'He may well have done, if you hadn't had the sense to let yourself fall like you did.'

The memory of the moment came back to Erin, setting her pulses racing. 'I'm not going back. I don't want to see him again.'

'There's no need for you to see him. But have you given serious thought to what you will do?'

Erin took a deep breath. 'I've realised for some time that I wanted to leave him, because our marriage has become a sham. I've been trying to wait until I've saved a little money to support me for a while, until I can start a small business.'

Irene's brows shot up. 'My dear, your husband is a very wealthy man. You won't be penniless. Do you have a lawyer?'

Erin frowned and shook her head. 'A lawyer? No, I've never needed one.'

'Well, you need one now. You can do some research, or ask around and find one yourself, but there is someone I can recommend to you if you're interested.'

'Yes, please do.'

'I'll write it down for you.' Irene opened her purse and took out a notebook and pen. 'He handles other work as well, but he's accredited in family law, and he's helped several women I know.' She scribbled on a page, tore it out and handed it to Erin.

'Here's his name and address and phone number. You need to ring and make an appointment to see him. But you also need to think of what you're going to do in the immediate future. I'd like you to stay here another night at least, or even two or three, but you need to have somewhere to go when you leave here.'

'I can always go to a hotel for a day or two, until I find somewhere.'

'Do you have any family or friends you can go to?'

'I don't have any family. I have a good friend in Newcastle, but my only real friend down here is married to a friend of my husband's.'

'It wouldn't be wise to let him know where you are. I suggest you make an appointment with the lawyer immediately, and then go and stay with your friend in Newcastle.' Irene pushed back her chair. 'I'll leave you now but you can contact me any time you want. The bill for your stay here will go to your husband, so you can remain as long as you like.'

'He can afford it.'

'I know it won't cause him any problem to pay, but

it's some small satisfaction. Besides, it lets him know how serious his attack was, and that you've been hospitalised because of it.'

With that she left, and Erin looked at the name and address on the paper she'd given her. 'Aden Marlowe,' she read. There was an address in George Street, and a phone number. Erin retrieved her handbag from a drawer, fished out her phone, and dialled the number. When a woman's voice answered, she asked if she could make an appointment to see Mr Aden Marlowe, and it was arranged for the following morning.

CHAPTER ELEVEN

On arrival at the lawyer's office next morning the receptionist asked Erin to fill in a questionnaire with her personal and marriage details, and then asked her to take a seat. A few moments later she was ushered in to Aden Marlowe's office.

The man who came around his desk to meet her was younger than she expected. She guessed him to be in his early thirties – clean shaven, with broad shoulders, an athletic build, a strong face with eyes the colour of dark chocolate, and a determined jaw. He was dressed conservatively in a dark *Armani* suit, white shirt and dark paisley tie. Beneath the conventional exterior Erin sensed vitality and strength of purpose that inspired confidence. He would be a good man to have on your side.

'Good morning, Mrs Brightman,' he greeted her pleasantly as his hand clasped hers. 'I'm Aden Marlowe. Please take a seat.' He gestured to the chair at the front of the desk before seating himself behind it.

'Now, what can I do for you?' he asked her.

'I want a divorce, and as I've never had any reason to have a lawyer before, Dr Irene Leclerc recommended that I come to see you, to find out what to do about it.'

'I see. Well, as you may know, the only ground for divorce in this country is the irretrievable breakdown of a marriage. Do you think that applies to your marriage?'

'Yes. Definitely. I don't ever want to see my

husband again.'

'I see. That sounds very definite, so perhaps if you tell me your story I can advise you.' He leant forward slightly in his seat, and regarded her intently.

Erin wasn't quite sure where to start, so she began by telling him of the night when Giles attacked her. He listened without interrupting her.

'Was this the first time he'd physically abused you?'

'No, it's happened before, but never like this. I really believe he would have killed me if I hadn't pretended to pass out.'

'It certainly sounds that way, Mrs Brightman.'

'Please call me Erin. I'm more comfortable with that.'

He smiled, and Erin noticed how his eyes crinkled at the corners. 'Then you'd best call me Aden. If you go ahead with this we'll probably be seeing each other often, and it's more comfortable all round.'

'Right. But there's no doubt that I'm going ahead with it, Aden.'

'I hear what you're saying, but there must be a year's separation with no breaks, even for a day, before you can lodge an application for divorce.'

'A whole year?'

'Yes. And the judge must be satisfied there's no chance of reconciliation at the end of that time.'

'And how does he decide that?'

'By both parties agreeing to it. Should one party not agree, then he can order marriage counselling in the hope of reconciling the couple.'

'So there's nothing I can do now, except wait?'

'Not exactly. We can inform your husband of your intentions, and ask him not to contact you directly but to make any further contact through me. Also, it's quite common for a property settlement to be agreed during this time.'

'I don't have any property.' Erin paused, thinking. 'Except, I suppose, my car. That's in my name. And my clothes...and shoes.'

He glanced down at the paper in front of him. 'Your husband is a wealthy man. You won't leave the marriage financially insecure, Erin. You're entitled to a financial settlement.'

'Huh! Then I'll ask him for the equivalent of a reasonable wage for the years we've been married. I think I'm entitled to that for my services as his hostess all that time.'

A slight smile lifted the corners of Aden's mouth. 'I think we can do better than that for you. That is, if you decide to retain my services. Are you happy for me to act for you?'

'Yes, certainly I am.'

'Good. Then I'd like you to tell me a bit about your marriage up to the time of your husband's recent attack on you. You can trust that whatever you tell me will be in strict confidence; it will go no further than this office without your consent. And then we'll look at your present circumstances.'

CHAPTER TWELVE

Erin settled back in her chair and drew a deep breath. She gave Aden a potted history of their marriage and told him of her earlier decision to leave Giles. He listened intently, making notes on a yellow legal pad, and interrupting her occasionally to ask a question.

Finally she told him of her future plans. She even told him of how she'd gone about selling her clothes to finance the project.

His eyebrows soared. 'I can assure you that you have no need to go to such lengths for your future, Erin. I'll try to reach a financial settlement with your husband, through his lawyers, within a short time. Now, the first thing is to advise him of your intention to separate, but before I do that, I suggest you remove all your belongings from the house in Point Piper. It would be best to choose a time when he's not likely to be there, and to have someone else with you. Do you think you can manage that?'

Erin hated the thought of going back to the house again, but she knew she needed to get her things, so she nodded.

'Yes, I'll manage.'

'But you need to have someone with you,' he persisted. 'Do you have someone you can rely on?'

She frowned, and spoke hesitantly while she tried to think. 'Perhaps a friend from
Newcastle, but...'

'I have a man who does work for me who's very reliable. Steve Waterman. I can arrange for him to go with you, if you want.'

'Oh, yes please, that would be such a help. And Giles isn't likely to be home during the day, so any week day would be fine.'

'Good.' Aden nodded and picked up the phone. After speaking for a short while he asked her if today would suit her, and when she nodded she heard him arrange for her to go to Waterman's office in time to arrive at the house at approximately one o'clock. It was a time when Giles would be lunching, and almost certainly not home.

'That's all arranged,' he told her. 'He's expecting you. He'll also be protection for you should there be any problems. He'd simply whisk you away from any trouble. You can trust Steve Waterman.'

He wrote on his pad, tore it off and handed it to her. 'This is his address. He has a van and he'll help you move everything. He can also arrange a place to store things if you need it.'

'No, I have somewhere I can leave them.'

'Good. Then that's probably all we can do for today. Make an appointment for tomorrow on your way out. I'll see you then, and we'll take it from there.'

Aden stood and escorted her to the door, smiling down at her as he opened it and stood back for her to pass.

After making an appointment for the next day Erin left the office thinking he was possibly the most attractive man she'd ever met, as well as being capable and reliable.

She had to chastise herself for letting him dominate her thoughts as she caught a taxi to Edgecliff to retrieve her car. How stupid, he's probably married with a couple of kids. She was just another client to him. Besides, the last thing she needed right now was thinking about another man. She had too many decisions to make about her future. She needed to pull herself together and get on with it.

But the image of his easy smile hovered in the back of her mind.

Erin had no way of knowing that Aden sat in his chair for a long time, doodling on a legal pad as he considered his last client. She was married to one of the wealthiest men in the country, but she didn't seem to realise that she had no need to worry about her financial future. The court would certainly award her a substantial settlement – if it even went to court, which was improbable. These things were usually settled out of court. But it wasn't her legal position that had him sitting thinking about her. No. When she told him about her husband attacking her she had, understandably, been upset. Even though she tried to hide it. And he'd had an urge to put his arms around her and comfort her. Not just because she was a client in distress, but because he'd felt a strong physical attraction to her. He longed to hold her, touch her, to feel her body against his. It was a long time since he'd felt that way towards a woman, and it was dangerous. He really had to control his feelings better.

After a cup of coffee and a sandwich Erin drove to Waterman's premises in an industrial complex in Botany. Parking next to a white panel van she went inside. She introduced herself to the man who came round from behind a partition. Steve Waterman was a powerfully built man with streaks of grey through his brown hair, and steady blue eyes.

He greeted her cordially.

'So, Mrs Brightman, we need to go and collect your belongings from your former home, Aden tells me. Is that right?'

'Yes, that's right. And please call me Erin.'

'Right-i-o, Erin, so how much are we talking about here? Will you need extra cartons or boxes?'

'There'll be a few suitcases, and, yes, it might be handy to have some extra containers on   hand.'

'And where will we be taking them?'

Erin gave him the addresses of the storage facility in Chippendale, and the house in Point Piper. They arranged to drive separately and to meet at the front of the house.

They pulled up outside within a few moments of each other, and Erin motioned him to pull the van into the forecourt and park there, and then to follow her as she let herself into the house with her key.

As they entered the hall all was quiet, but as they reached the bottom of the stairs Mrs Winter appeared through one of the doors.

'Mrs Brightman,' she called.

Erin stopped on the first step and turned, resting her hand on the balustrade. In spite of herself, Erin felt a coil of tension twisting inside her. She was pleased she had Steve Waterman with her. But when she spoke her voice was cool.

'Yes Mrs Winter, I don't need to bother you. I'm here to collect my things. I'll be leaving then.'

'Mr Brightman is not in at the moment.'

'That's what I expected. I have help to carry my cases, as you can see. You may go on with whatever you were doing.'

Without a word Mrs Winter turned and went back through the door. Erin continued up the stairs, and Steve followed.

When she reached her room Erin went straight to her walk-in robe and asked Steve to reach down the suitcases sitting on the uppermost shelf. He placed three beside the bed and one on the bed. He opened it in readiness for Erin, who was already removing clothes from the rails. He gazed at the contents of the wardrobe.

'You'll never fit everything in those cases. I'll bring up some cartons for the shoes and things.'

'Thanks Steve, that'd be great.' Erin busied herself folding evening garments and putting them in the first case.

In a few moments Steve was back with a stack of cardboard cartons, and he began collecting shoes, handbags and loose items on the shelves, and putting them into the boxes.

Erin packed the next case with the clothing she decided to take with her for a short stay in a hotel until she found somewhere permanent to live. Then she placed toiletries and sundries in an overnight bag, together with her jewellery, and put both bags to one side. She quickly folded and packed each piece of clothing until the walk-in robe was bare except for some papers and a couple of books sitting on top of a chest of drawers. She slipped them into a satchel and tossed it into a case, and then started on the drawers.

As each case or box was ready Steve carried it down and placed it in the van, and returned to help with the packing.

Finally all was done, with only one case and the

overnight bag left in the room.

Erin stood in the middle of the room and looked around, then walked out through the French doors and stood on the balcony. Her gaze swept over the sparkling blue sea, and then to the garden leading down to the water, with the boat house and private jetty to one side. It hurt to leave it all behind. She would never live anywhere as beautiful again. She would miss this, as well as the love that she and Giles had shared in their first year of marriage. Sighing, she turned back inside and closed the doors behind her.

Steve stood waiting with the remaining case. After collecting her handbag from the now empty dressing table she picked up the overnight bag.

'Time to go,' she said. With one last look around she led the way out of the room and down the stairs.

As she reached the bottom of the stairs, with Steve alongside her carrying the suitcase, her heart jumped as a door opened and Giles strode into the hall.

CHAPTER THIRTEEN

Erin stood still, her body tense and her pulses hammering. Of course, she should have guessed Mrs Winter would phone him. Thank goodness she had Steve with her. His large presence by her side was comforting.

Giles crossed the space between them and stood squarely in front of her, looking down on her with narrowed eyes.

'So what's this?'

'I'm leaving you, Giles.' Erin quivered inside, but she stood her ground, and lifted her chin.

'Don't be a fool, Erin.' His gaze flicked to Steve, standing beside her, watching. 'Who's this?'

'Steve is just helping me with my bags.'

'Get rid of him.'

'No.'

'I want to talk to you Erin. I can't do it in front of him.'

Erin's lips tightened. Her anger at the memory of what he had done fuelled her determination to leave. She needed him to understand that.

She turned to Steve. 'Would you please wait just outside by the door? I'll only be a minute.'

'I'll be where I can hear you. Just call me when you're ready, Mrs Brightman.'

Giles waited until Steve was outside before continuing, his voice wheedling. 'Now then, there's no need for you to act hastily, Erin. If this is about the other night then...'

'You don't really expect me to stay after you tried

to kill me, do you?'

'Now, don't dramatise it. I'm sorry if I let my temper get the better of me for a moment, but I would never really hurt you.'

'You did a fairly good job of it, but that was just the last straw. I don't want to stay in the sham our marriage has become.'

'A sham? How can you say that? Most women would think you've got a very good marriage. Aren't I good to you? You've got everything you want, surely?' He swept his hand around. 'You live in a beautiful home. I've never stinted you as far as money's concerned. You can buy whatever you want. You have servants to look after the house. What more can you want?'

'There's no love in our marriage. I've often wondered why you married me. But I really know the answer – to have an attractive clothes horse on your arm when you want it. You've never really loved me.'

'Now Erin, don't talk like that,' he cajoled her. 'Of course I love you. You're everything to me. Look, I'm sorry if I get a bit short tempered at times, but I do have a lot of business worries, you know. A business like mine doesn't run by itself. I have important decisions to make, day in, day out. And sometimes it gets to me a bit. That's only natural, surely you can understand that?' He put his hand on her arm, and leant towards her. 'But I never forget how much I love you, how much you mean to me.' His voice became firmer. 'Now, come on, Erin, give me a kiss, and let's forget all this nonsense about leaving.'

Erin shook his hand from her arm and stepped back. How could he think she would be taken in by his sweet talk and change her mind, just like that.

'No Giles. I mean what I say. I'm leaving.'

'Now come on, you know you don't mean that. Where would you go? What would you do?' He paused. 'If you feel you want to get away for a bit, that's all right with me. Take a few days somewhere with one of your girlfriends.' He thought for a second or two. 'Or perhaps I could even take a few days off, and we'll go away together, just the two of us. Maybe have a few days in, well, somewhere like Bali, perhaps. You'd like that, wouldn't you?'

Erin took a deep breath. 'You're not listening to me Giles. Our marriage is over. I'm leaving you. Right now.'

As she tried to slip past him, he grabbed her arm again.

'No you're not. I won't let you go. I'll never let you go,' he hissed, his face dark and scowling.

'Let – me – go!' She wriggled to free her arm, her pulses pounding.

He gripped her tighter, and his fingers bit into her flesh. 'I'm the one who says when our marriage is over, not you.'

'No, you're wrong. The law will decide, not you. Now let go of me.'

'Or what will you do? Call in your gorilla from outside?'

Dropping the overnight bag she prised at his fingers, but the pressure increased.

Her anger flared. 'Yes, if you continue to hurt me like this. What headlines that will cause. 'Tycoon assaults wife, bodyguard to the rescue'. Is that what you want?' Her tone was scathing.

As Steve appeared and stood in the open doorway, Giles dropped his arm and stood back. His eyes narrowed. His mouth twisted in a contemptuous sneer. 'Don't think you'll get away with this,' he warned her. Then he turned on his heel and slammed his way out of the hall.

Erin picked up the overnight bag and walked out of the house without a backward glance. Her heart beat a wild tattoo. She tossed the bag onto the back seat of her car, and slid in behind the wheel. She sat for a few moments drawing deep breaths, willing herself to calm down, before starting up and waving to Steve that she was ready to go.

After an uneventful trip to Chippendale they unloaded the cases and boxes from the van, and added them to the already large pile in the storage space. When all were firmly stacked away Erin thanked Steve for his help. She told him she might need his services again in the future, when it was time to move it all again.

After he left she stood looking at the pile of boxes, and turned her mind to her immediate future. She tried to push Giles' threats to the back of her mind. She remembered Irene's advice that she should go to stay with Laura in Newcastle for a while, but as she'd now had a confrontation with Giles, it seemed rather pointless. Besides, she wanted to move ahead with her plans.

With the modest amount of money she had in the bank she would need to be frugal, but, although she was not really ready to start the business yet, it seemed Fate had decreed otherwise, so she must bring forward her plans. Hadn't the psychic told her Fate would guide her? Surely this was some sort of serendipity.

Now there was a good name for her store.

Serendipity. She turned it over in her mind, and decided she liked it. She smiled. Yes, *Serendipity,* that's what she'd call it.

First of all she needed to find somewhere to live. But it would take time to find an apartment to suit in busy Sydney, so as a short term option she needed to find temporary accommodation.

Erin had already decided on Chatswood as a good location for the business, being a busy shopping centre with lots of foot traffic, and well away from Point Piper, which she wanted to avoid. So that area seemed a logical choice for her to live in. She drove to Chatswood, found a small residential hotel and booked a room in her maiden name of McDonald.

Looking around the room after unpacking her case and hanging her clothes in the wardrobe, she smiled. This hotel-sized wardrobe couldn't compare with her walk-in robe at Point Piper. And this unpretentious but pleasant enough room was no match for her previous harbour view bedroom, or for the luxurious hotel rooms she'd shared with Giles on their infrequent holidays. Those days were over. It was time to move on.

CHAPTER FOURTEEN

One of the first things to do was to look for premises for *Serendipity*, and the best way to do
that was to walk around and see if there were any vacant shops. She wouldn't be able to afford the high rents in the big malls of Westfield or Chatswood Chase, but there were large areas of strip shopping with small businesses, and she hoped to find something suitable there.

In a small arcade, close to Westfield, and not far from David Jones store and Victoria Avenue, she found a shop with a 'To Lease' sign in the window, and noted the agent's details in her contacts.

Before she phoned his office, she decided to ring Bobbi. She hadn't spoken to her since Giles attacked her, but now that he knew her intentions she needed to let Bobbi know what had happened. It wouldn't be long before Laurence heard Giles' version of events and passed it on to Bobbi.

First, Erin enquired about her friend's health.

'I'm feeling good,' Bobbi assured her, 'although I'm not getting out and about too much now. And how about you? Anything much happened?'

'Well, yes, but not something I wanted to happen.' Erin went on to tell her, in as calm a manner as she could, about Giles' attack on her, and her stay in hospital. She explained she had left him, and that it was the end of their marriage.

After listening to Bobbi's expressions of shock and anger, and assuring her that she was quite all right, Erin ended in a cheerful voice. 'So now it looks as if

Fate is pushing me into starting the business sooner, rather than later.'

'Oh dear,' Bobbi lamented, 'it's too soon. I won't be able to do much to help you yet.'

'You won't be able to help me at all. Once you have a new baby your time will be fully taken up. I've realised that all along. And now, with Giles and me parting, Laurence will naturally see things from his friend's point of view, and he may well ask you not to see me.'

'Oh no, that won't happen.'

'I just want you to know I'd quite understand if Laurence takes that stand and it becomes difficult for us to spend time together. You have your baby to think of, and you mustn't do anything to jeopardise the happy state your marriage is in now. You're no longer in the unhappy marriage you were in when we made plans together.'

'But I don't want to let you down. You won't be able to manage on your own.' Bobbi's voice was full of concern.

'Of course I will. Thanks, in great part to you, I have sufficient stock to start.'

'And I have the money in the bank from selling my things. You must use that to help you get started.'

'Absolutely not,' Erin replied firmly. 'That's yours and you must keep it squirreled away for a rainy day. This has made me realise we can never be sure of anything, and that money is security for you and Baby, should you ever need it, although I hope you won't.'

'Well... I don't know...'

'I do. And that's the end of it.' Erin's voice was definite. 'Now,' she continued in a lighter tone, 'when you're feeling up to driving across town in search of coffee or lunch, perhaps we can catch up, either here in Chatswood, or in the city. I'd rather not venture over to the eastern suburbs at the moment. But only if it's not going to cause trouble with you and Laurence, and you need to see how he feels about me now.' After agreeing they would meet soon, they ended the call.

Then Erin called the real estate agent about the shop and arranged to meet him outside the premises immediately.

While she waited for him to arrive she explored the surrounding area. The arcade was quite small. It had a bank on one corner, fronting the street, and a coffee shop on the other. Behind the bank were a hairdresser and a book store, and, behind the coffee shop, a day spa. Alongside that, a toy shop. At the bottom of the arcade and across its full width was the vacant shop. It would be ideal for her purpose, with the other businesses attracting women into the arcade. Two empty display windows, one on each side of the glass entrance doors, would make attractive showcases. She peered through the doors, but the interior was too dim to see more than the first few metres.

The agent arrived a few minutes later, a tall man with a pleasant face and streaks of grey at the temples. After introducing himself as Alex Tremayne he unlocked the door. Once inside he pressed a switch, and the space filled with light.

Erin stopped inside the door. The shop was huge. The main area extended way back, and stairs led up to a mezzanine floor in the rear. She could really do something with this. Slowly she walked forward, visualising how she could make it into the exclusive boutique she imagined. The dingy cream walls needed a coat of paint, but the size and layout were amazing.

'Much bigger than it looks from the outside, as you can see,' Tremayne said, accompanying her as she made her way towards the back. 'A very nice property and an excellent location. What type of business are you planning?'

'A clothing store.'

'This would be ideal for it.'

Erin continued her inspection, with much of his sales patter going over her head as she appraised the interior. With a stylish interior design it could rival the up-market fashion houses.

At door at one side of the stairs led into a short hallway with a small room leading off – ideal for an office and a small kitchen with a sink, a bench, and a water heater. With room for a small fridge and a cupboard for essentials. Very practical. The hallway opened into a large open space, ideal for a store room. There was plenty of room. Yes, the more she saw of it, the more Erin liked it.

Returning to the main area she mounted the steps to the mezzanine. Another large area. Erin opened a door that led to a bathroom and toilet, and shuddered at the orange laminate and paintwork in here. But that could be changed. She would transform it into an elegant powder room. After inspecting it all she descended the stairs and stood in the centre of the bare expanse. Pivoting slowly around, she took in the overall layout, and tingled with excitement. Yes, she could do wonders with this. But could she afford it?

'It has possibilities,' she told the agent, 'but it would be expensive to fit out, it's such a large area.

How much is the rental?'

He named a monthly figure that would stretch Erin's budget, but was possible. She needed time to think about it, and to estimate how much it would cost to make it into the stylish premises she wanted.

'So what do you think?' Tremayne asked her.

'I'll give it some thought, and I might ask to have another look and take some measurements.'

'Just give me a call any time.' Tremayne took a card from his pocket and handed it to her.

As she took his card and said goodbye her mind was racing. She must start thinking about designs for creating *Serendipity* as a showpiece for the many beautiful garments now waiting in the storage area in Chippendale.

Her rumbling stomach reminded her she had eaten nothing since morning, so she stopped at a noodle bar for a quick Asian meal. Chatswood boasted many small eateries like this; she would enjoy living in such a cosmopolitan area if she could find an apartment here. After satisfying her hunger she went to a newsagent's to buy a sketch pad, and returned to the hotel. That evening she opened her laptop and browsed interior designs for additional ideas, and sketched different layouts for the store. When she fell into bed she dreamed about visiting the shop in the arcade, but somehow, in the dream, Alex Tremayne was replaced by Aden Marlowe.

CHAPTER FIFTEEN

Aden Marlowe's gaze appeared concerned as he sat at his desk opposite her the next morning. 'It was unfortunate your husband arrived while you were at the house yesterday, Erin, and I've already had a report from Steve about what happened. But perhaps you'd like to tell me in your own words about his attitude to you then.'

As she related the details of the visit Erin felt he really cared. 'I should have realised Mrs Winter would ring him when she saw me carrying my things out, but I didn't. And I was so glad Steve was with me. If I'd been alone I would've felt intimidated. At first Giles tried to persuade me to stay, but when he could see I mean to leave him, and told him I wanted a divorce, he became nasty.'

'Did he touch you, physically?'

'Yes. He grabbed my arm and tried to force me to stay. That was when I used Steve's presence to remind him there was a witness.'

'Was his grip enough to hurt you?'

'Yes. He gave me a couple of more bruises to add to the previous ones.'

'Visible bruises?'

'Yes.' Erin pulled up her sleeve to show the fresh bruises on her arm.

'I'd like you to go and show these to Dr Irene. I know she recorded those from his previous attack on you, but I want these recorded as well. And we have Steve as a witness to yesterday's altercation.'

'Oh yes. I asked him to wait outside but he could

hear everything, and he saw Giles gripping my arm and stopping me from leaving.'

'Good. We may never need to use this, but just in case, I want it documented. I've already taken a statement from Steve, and having Irene confirm the bruises will be additional evidence.'

'Very well, I'll see if I can see her today.'

'Good. And ask her to let me have a copy of the confirmation, please.'

'All right.' Erin nodded. 'So what happens now?'

'I've already advised your husband of your intentions to sue for divorce in due course, and that you wish all future communications from him to be through me. So now we have to wait for his response.'

'He told me he'll be the one to say when we divorce, not me, but I told him the law will decide. That's right, isn't it?'

'Yes, if an amicable agreement can't be reached, then the marriage will be deemed to have irretrievably broken down, and a divorce will be granted.'

'So now we must wait for his reaction?'

'Yes. I expect I'll receive a communication from his lawyer, and we'll take it from there.' Aden sat back in his chair and his gaze searched her face.

'Now, Erin, what about you? How are you feeling now?'

'Relieved, now I've made the move. I've actually left him, and he knows.'

'Have you had time to make any plans yet?'

'Yes. I've left my current address with Josie, your receptionist, and I'll let you know when I find an apartment.' She smiled. 'But the exciting thing is, I've found what I think is the perfect shop for my business.'

'Really? That is good news.' As Aden smiled back at her his face lit up. He looked quite boyish. 'Whereabouts?'

'In Chatswood. I'm going back later, probably tomorrow, to have another look and take some measurements. And to check the contract, I suppose, to make sure it's all right.'

'Perhaps you'd better let me take a look at that, just to see there are no hidden clauses in it to cause you problems.'

'Would you? Thank you so much. I'll bring it in before I sign anything. In fact, I'll pick up a copy now and drop it back.'

'Fine. Just leave it with Josie if I'm busy when you come. And please tell her to fit you in tomorrow, at whatever time is free that's convenient for you.'

He rose to see Erin out. When he placed his hand beneath her elbow to guide her to the door she felt the warmth of his hand through her sleeve, and her breath caught in her throat. He was charming as well as helpful. Was he as attentive as this to all his clients, or was he being particularly so to her?

As she took her leave of him she gave herself a mental shake. Perhaps when you hired a lawyer he then took care of any legal problems you might have, even if not directly concerned with the divorce. Or was he just being kind because he felt sorry for her?

Erin rang the agent and arranged to pick up the lease so she could check it, and after she read it she took it back to Aden's office.

Josie, a rather plain girl with mousy hair and a permanently worried manner, was at her desk behind the computer when Erin arrived. She stopped her work to attend to Erin.

'Aden asked me to bring this contract by for him to check. I suppose he's busy now, is he?'

Erin thought the look that flitted across Josie's face was disapproval, but it was gone in an instant. Perhaps she'd imagined it.

'Yes Mrs Brightman, I'm afraid Mr Marlowe has a client with him at the moment. But if you leave it here I'll take it in to him when he's free.'

Josie's tone emphasised their formal names. Obviously she disapproved of the familiarity of first names in client–lawyer relationships.

Erin placed the lease on the desk. 'Thank you Josie. And he said to ask you to make a time for me to see him tomorrow.'

Josie checked the appointments for the next day. 'It will have to be ten o'clock. Mr Marlowe is very busy. Will that suit you?'

'Yes, that's fine. See you tomorrow then.'

Josie nodded, and by the time Erin turned to go she had turned away and was busy on the computer again.

Erin's next stop was her doctor's rooms. Irene photographed the bruises on Erin's arms and turned her attention back to Erin.

'That was another nasty experience for you, Erin. How are you feeling?'

'I was shaken up by it at the time, but I'm okay now. I was so glad Steve was with me. I knew Giles wouldn't dare hurt me much in front of him.'

'No. It was fortunate you had the back-up.' Irene shook her head and sighed. 'You're one of the fortunate ones, Erin. Not that I mean you haven't suffered,' she added hastily, 'you have, and will go on doing so in many ways yet, emotionally if not physically. But at least you're able financially to have the support you need.' She shook her head dejectedly. 'There are many women with no financial resources, and particularly those with children to consider, who have nowhere to go when they're victims of domestic violence. They don't know what to do, where to go. We desperately need more accommodation for these women; places of safety where they can take their kids, and take time to recover, away from it all.'

'Like where I went? Or a place in the country, or something similar?'

'Yes.' Irene leant back in her chair. 'Now, I mustn't get on my hobby-horse. It's just that I see more than enough of it in my work. But you have enough to think about with your own problems. I can only advise you to have as little contact with your husband as possible, and certainly to never see him alone.'

'I'll make sure of that.'

'Good. Now, don't forget to let me have your new address when you leave the hotel, and I'll send this report to Aden Marlowe to add to the other one. Don't forget now, you can contact me any time you need,' she added.

As Erin left the doctor's rooms it was with the feeling that she was indeed fortunate to have Irene and Aden to support her.

CHAPTER SIXTEEN

When Erin returned to Aden's office at the appointed time next morning, he told her the contract was in order and, once she was sure the shop was what she wanted, she should go ahead and sign it.

'Thank you so much. I really think it's just what I want, but I'm going back later today for another look, and to take some measurements. The agent couldn't make it until after five, so I'll take the contract back to him then, and I'll have another look and take the measurements before I sign it.'

'That sounds good. So what sort of shop is it?' Aden sat back in his seat. 'Tell me all about it. This isn't me being your lawyer,' he added hurriedly, 'I'm interested, that's all. I'm quite taken with your idea.' His lips twitched. 'And the way you've gone about gathering the funds for it. Most ingenious.'

'You don't think I was too devious?'

'I think you were very clever.' He laughed. 'If you'd asked me as your lawyer I would never have advised you to take such action, but as it happened well before you became my client, or even met you, I'm commenting privately, as a friend.'

A friend! Erin's heart gave a quick lurch before she reminded herself it was just a figure of speech and meant nothing. Still, it was...nice. Nothing more.

'Did you say you're meeting the agent after five tonight?'

'Yes.'

'And you're going to take some measurements?'

'Yes.'

'Do you have a proper measuring tape? Not one of those tiny dressmaker's things but a tradesman's tape.'

'No, but I'm going to buy one.'

'It so happens I'm an amateur carpenter and DIY addict in my spare time, and I have a very good one. I don't have any appointments after five today, and you'll need someone to hold the other end of the tape, so would you like me to come along and help you take the measurements? That's if you haven't made other arrangements, of course.'

This time Erin's heart gave a definite lurch. 'No. No, not at all, and yes, I'd love some help. But...won't it be cutting into your private time?'

'That's mine to do as I like with. I'm intrigued with your ideas, and I'd enjoy seeing your shop. Before, so to speak, because I'm sure the after will be successful.'

'Then I'll look forward to your help. Thank you.'

Erin gave him the address, and arranged to meet him at the shop at five thirty. She left the office with a spring in her step. This was definitely more than just her lawyer being helpful.

Aden returned to his desk with a smile after showing Erin out. She was one gutsy little lady. Fancy her coming up with a scheme like that to finance her way into a business. Not that she needed to, because she would be awarded a generous settlement. His smile faded as he sat down. It was unwise of him to offer to help her with measuring. He shouldn't see her outside of the office; she was far too attractive and beguiling. The last thing he needed in his life was the complication of a relationship. But he was only offering a little help. It couldn't hurt to be friends with her. Well, that was where it must end.

When Erin met the agent at the shop she told him she wanted to take some measurements now, and asked if he could leave the keys with her.

'So you're definitely interested?' he asked her.

'Yes.'

'Then if you promise to have them back to me early tomorrow, I'll leave them with you.'

After Erin made an appointment to come to his office the next morning he switched on the electricity and handed her keys.

Aden arrived just as Tremayne left, and he entered the shop with her. It felt good to have him by her side.

Aden looked around as they came through the door. 'It's a good size. Plenty of room for what you want to do, I should think. Do you know exactly how you want to lay it out?'

'No, not exactly, but I do I have several ideas.'

'Then how about you show me around and then we can do some measuring? The measurements might help you with deciding.'

Erin led the way, and explained how she planned to utilise the back for storage and administration, and to use the whole of the front area for display purposes, while up on the mezzanine would be fitting rooms.

'It's a big area to fill,' Aden observed. 'I'll be interested to see what you have in mind for it. So let's measure it up, and then we know exactly what we're talking about.'

He reached into his satchel and took out his tape

measure, and Erin brought out the sketch pad and pencil. For the next couple of hours she held one end of the tape while he measured distances along the walls, and she drew it all to scale on a fresh page of the pad, noting each measurement. As they worked they discussed each area of the shop, and tossed ideas at one another. By the time they had done the whole shop Erin felt as if she had known Aden for years, and had almost forgotten he was her lawyer.

Finally Aden straightened up. 'Well, I think that just about does it.'

Erin handed him her end of the tape. As he took it their hands touched, and his fingers closed around hers for an instant. Her breath hitched in her throat. Did he feel that spark too?

She gave him a swift glance. She thought she saw a flash of response in his eyes, but it was gone in a second. Probably her imagination.

He made no comment as he replaced the tape in his satchel. He gestured at the pad in Erin's hands. 'You have a scale model of the entire area there. Now you can do some serious planning.'

Erin nodded, and concentrated on her work. 'And between us we've come up with heaps of ideas.'

'The ideas were all yours. I was just able to build on some of them.'

'Well, whatever it was, I feel full of inspiration now.'

'That's good.' He smiled down at her. 'Now, I don't know about you, but I feel like a drink and something to eat.' He looked at his watch. 'And it is dinner time. Would you care to join me for dinner?' Erin's stab of surprise turned quickly to pleasure. 'Yes, I'd like that.'

'So where shall we go? Do you like seafood?'

'Yes, very much.'

'I seem to recall there's a seafood restaurant in Chatswood Chase. Shall we try that?'

'Yes, let's. I need to start learning about Chatswood if I'm going to have a business here.'

After they locked up they headed down Victoria Parade to the restaurant, where they were shown to a table for two.

As they waited for their meal of grilled salmon and a glass of sauvignon blanc, they talked about the shop.

Erin brought out the sketches she'd made and spread them on the table. She explained some of her ideas, and told Aden how she visualised *Serendipity* as being glamorous, so that her customers could feel something of how it felt to buy designer clothes.

'I want it to be an experience for them.' The words tumbled out as her excitement grew. 'When you buy something really beautiful it's not just the garment that makes you feel good, although of course, that does too, but it's the mystique as well. Knowing that an artist has designed a beautiful garment to make you look and feel good is something special. And in the fashion houses it's all presented in a way to make you feel it's a unique experience. I remember how I felt in *Christian Dior's* boutique in Paris. It's so lavish.'

'And that's what you want to do?'

'Yes. Upstairs, I want to have alcoves down each wall for fitting rooms, and each one will be quite private, with a comfortable chair in it so a friend can accompany the customer if she wants. And we'll have mirrors placed so she can see her reflection from all angles. And it will be fitted out with silky drapes and a small chandelier in each alcove.'

'Very stylish.'

'Yes, and in lovely soft hues. Pale walls and oyster coloured drapes, I think.'

'Will you carry that theme right through?'

'Yes, but downstairs where the customers browse will be open. I'll have timber racks for garments along all the walls. I'll leave the centre of the floor open, and there will be a few dress dummies placed at strategic points displaying garments, and they can be changed from day to day.'

'It's all sounding good.'

After they finished their meal, and left the restaurant, Aden tucked her hand in his arm and walked with her back to the hotel. When he kissed her cheek as they said good night her stomach flipped. Was he just being friendly, or did it mean he found her special. She knew she found him special.

Aden left Erin with his mind in a whirl. He was entranced by everything about her. By how her face became animated as they discussed her plans for the shop, and her cheeks took on a pink glow. How she talked with her hands as well as her voice when she became excited, and how her eyes sparkled as she became animated. He was going to find it hard to keep their relationship on a purely professional level. This feeling had been simmering in the back of his mind since the first time she came into his office. He needed to watch it.

CHAPTER SEVENTEEN

As Aden swung his car off the New England Highway and headed into Armidale the next day his emotions were in turmoil. When he'd first started his regular pilgrimages up here, six years ago, he'd been full of optimism, but it had been a roller-coaster ride. His hopes had been raised time and again, only to be shattered at the next visit.

Over the last few years he'd grown to dread these visits. This time he feared it more than usual. He knew it was because of Erin. She had crept, unbidden and unwelcome, into his mind and, he feared, into his heart. He hadn't wanted it to happen – God knows he didn't need the complication of another woman in his life – but he couldn't control his feelings.

From their first meeting he'd known she was someone special. It wasn't just her looks, although she was gorgeous, but her unaffected, open and friendly manner, which was surprising in a woman who had several years of a pampered existence. And he admired her guts and determination in carrying out her audacious plan to provide for the future when she decided to leave her unhappy marriage. And her naivety in not knowing that she would receive a hefty settlement when that happened, no matter what.

As Aden came within sight of his destination he drew over to the side of the road, pulled out his mobile, and scrolled through until he found the number he wanted.

'Hi Joan,' he said, when a woman's voice answered, 'I'm only minutes away. How is Zoe today?'

'I've told her you're coming, and I've given her the extra medication the doctor recommends for your visits. She's quite calm at the moment, but you never know. We'll just have to wait and see. Cliff is here, of course.'

'Good. See you in a minute.'

Clicking off his phone Aden drove the short distance to a pair of wrought iron gates that stood open in readiness for him, and drove through. The sun shone down from a brilliant blue sky on the pleasant picture of a large, old style house with a garden of trees and lawns around it, but the bright day wasn't reflected in his mood.

He sat for a moment, trying to rid himself of the feeling of dread that gnawed his gut. With a sigh he got out, walked back and closed the gates, then mounted the three steps that led up to the verandah and front door.

As he reached the door it was opened from inside. A plump, middle-aged woman with pale hair and a worried expression was waiting for him.

'Good to see you, Aden,' she said, giving him a brief hug and a kiss on the cheek.

'You too Joan,' he replied, his voice revealing nothing of his apprehension as he returned the greeting.

'Come on in, I've got coffee and sandwiches ready.'

Joan led the way into a sunroom at the back of the house, where a small table was set with four plates and mugs, milk jug and sugar basin, and a platter of sandwiches.

A scholarly looking, grey-haired man stood by the

window. On one of the chairs at the table sat a small, thin woman in her early thirties, her face pinched and her dark hair tied back in a ponytail as she stared down at the red-checked cloth.

After greeting Cliff, Aden turned his attention to the woman.

'Hello, Zoe,' he said carefully.

'Hello.' She didn't look up. Her voice was devoid of emotion.

'Now then, take a seat, you two,' Joan said brightly, 'and I'll get the coffee.'

Aden took the seat directly opposite Zoe, with Cliff next to him. Joan poured coffee and removed the wrap from the sandwiches before taking the other vacant seat.

'Now help yourselves,' she told them, sliding the plate of sandwiches first to Aden and then to Cliff, before offering it to Zoe.

'Take one,' she told Zoe, waggling the dish at her as Zoe ignored it. 'This is lunch, you know.'

Zoe reached out, took a sandwich, and placed it on her plate.

'So how's things at the Uni,' Aden asked Cliff as they started on the meal.

'Same as ever, you know, the years roll around as usual, students come and go. But overall they're not a bad bunch this year.'

As the meal continued Aden and Cliff discussed the current year at the New England University, where Cliff was a lecturer, and where Aden had taken his law degree. Joan contributed an odd remark or two, but Zoe nibbled on her sandwich and drank her coffee in silence. Never once did she raise her eyes to look at Aden.

When they had finished eating and Joan started to clear away the lunch things Zoe suddenly came to life. She lifted her head and stared at Aden, long and hard. Then her face twisted, and she gave a shrill screech. She jumped up from her chair, sending it crashing to the floor. Rushing around the table she began to pummel Aden wildly with her fists.

Aden pushed back his chair and sprang up, raising his arms to fend off her blows.

'I know you,' Zoe screamed. 'You killed my baby. You killed my baby!' Over and over she repeated the words as she continued pounding Aden.

Aden tried to grasp her flailing fists, but she was too quick. Cliff came to his aid and grabbed Zoe around the waist, trying to pull her back. She kicked out backwards at him. She stopped punching and sucked air in great gulps, then raised her hands and ripped her nails down Aden's cheek before he was able to grasp her wrists.

'Murderer! Killer!'

Joan came to Cliff's aid, and between them they managed to drag Zoe away from Aden. They half pulled, half carried her struggling form out of the room, along the hallway into another room, and closed the door behind them.

Aden stood, white faced, his breath coming in gasps, as he took a handkerchief from his pocket and dabbed at the blood dribbling down his cheek.

A moment later Joan came out of the room, and closed the door firmly behind her.

'It's no use I'm afraid. Not today,' she said shakily. 'There's not much point in you waiting now. Cliff's the only one who can manage her when she gets like this. I'll call the doc and he'll come and give her a shot. She'll sleep till tomorrow, most likely. But thank you for persisting with her.'

Aden breathed a deep sigh. 'I'm so sorry, Joan. So sorry, and so sad.' He put his arms around Joan and kissed her gently. 'I'll keep in touch. Say goodbye to Cliff for me.'

Joan's eyes glistened with tears as she nodded.

Aden let himself out through the front door. A few moments later he was back on the New England Highway, heading towards the F3 and Sydney with a heavy heart.

CHAPTER EIGHTEEN

Erin signed the lease with a flourish. 'There now, all done.' She opened her purse, took out a cheque for the security bond and the first month's rent, and passed it across the desk with a smile.

Tremayne scrutinised the cheque with a nod. 'Good. Now I'll get the owner to sign his part, and you can have the keys and move in.'

'And when will that be?'

'I'll take it to his lawyer now, and it should be completed by this time tomorrow.'

'I was hoping to start getting quotes today for the work I want done. Can I at least have the keys now, so I can go ahead with that?'

'Seeing you've paid your deposit I suppose that's all right. But you mustn't touch anything, don't start any work, until the owner signs.'

'No, I won't.'

'As long as you understand it's not a binding contract until both parties sign.'

'I understand.'

Tremayne reached into a drawer, took out the keys and handed them to Erin.

'I'll ring you as soon as it's signed. But no work until then.'

'I'll wait for your call.' She picked up the keys and slipped them into her purse.

As she pushed back her chair and rose, Tremayne came around from his side of the desk and escorted her to the door. He promised to call her as soon as the lease was signed, and Erin stepped out into the street with a spring in her step.

She headed straight to the shop, where she spent the next hour walking around her new premises with the plan she had drawn from Aden's measurements. Her mind returned to how he'd helped her with the measurements. What had his goodnight kiss on the cheek meant? That they were friends, or more?

She could see his face clearly as she tried to concentrate on the drawings. He had unforgettable eyes the colour of dark chocolate, and they sparkled when he smiled at her. And when he smiled...

She pulled herself up sharply. This was crazy. She knew nothing about him apart from his position as her lawyer. How stupid to go weak-kneed over the first attractive man she met. With difficulty she pulled her thoughts back to the job in hand, and tried to push Aden from her mind.

As she walked around she visualised exactly where everything would go, and when she had it all firmly in her mind she called three shop-fitters firms and asked them to call and give quotes for the work.

After making appointments with them for later in the afternoon to come and view the work to be done, she decided her next step was to choose fabrics for the drapes. This would be an expensive outlay, and she needed to have an idea of prices. She headed to the large Spotlight store at Birkenhead Point, stopping on the way at a paint store to pick up colour cards for the wall paint.

For the rest of the morning she wandered among the large bolts of fabrics at Spotlight. She looked at colours, fingered the various cloths between finger and thumb, and considered the textures and weight of those she liked. She estimating the yardage she would need, and checked the prices. They didn't come cheap, and she felt a flutter of concern at her financial position as she entered costs in her notebook. Finally, from all the different silks and satins on offer, she chose the six she liked best. An obliging saleswoman cut ten centimetre length samples from each. She paid and left the shop, well pleased as she headed back to Chatswood.

She was back at her shop, poring over colour cards and fabric swatches, when her phone rang. It was Aden's secretary, ringing to ask if she could spare him a few moments, and, realising she had time before the first shop fitter's appointment, she arranged to go to his office right away.

Aden rose from his seat and came around the desk to greet Erin with a smile. After guiding her to the visitor's chair he resumed his seat and opened a file on the desk in front of him. He picked up the top paper from the folder and perused it.

'I've had a communication from Mr Brightman's lawyer,' he told her. 'He informs me that your husband in no way believes your marriage is over. He says you merely had a minor quarrel, and he's waiting for you to return to the matrimonial home.'

'In his dreams!'

'And he adds that he has stopped the credit on all your credit cards, including your Amex card, but they will, of course, be reinstated immediately upon your return.' He dropped the paper back into the file and looked across at her.

'Huh, if he thinks that's going to bring me back, he's wrong.'

'I thought you'd say that. But there's more here. He asks that you return to him, immediately, certain papers you took with you when you left. And he alludes to a pre-nuptial agreement.' He raised his brows. 'Did you sign a pre-nuptial agreement before you married?'

Erin pursed her lips as she tried to remember what she might have done in those heady days before their marriage. 'Not that I remember, but I know I signed a lot of things. Giles used to put papers in front of me and show me where to sign them. He said they were to do with the formalities for getting married.'

'And you didn't read them first?'

'Well...no.' He probably thought her a fool. 'I did sort of glance at some of them, but he was always in a hurry, and it never occurred to me to question him.'

'Did he give you a copy of any of them?'

'I'm not sure. He kept most of the important things, like our marriage certificate and our passports. I never thought anything of it. But I do have some papers he gave me that I kept in with some of my own things, like my birth certificate and my mother's death certificate. That sort of thing. They're all in a satchel, and I remember I put that in one of my cases.'

Aden tapped the desk with a pencil. It was a moment before he spoke again. 'He might have had you sign things to do with his business. Strategies for tax minimisation, that sort of thing. Which is not illegal, but he wouldn't want you to have them. I doubt you'd have a copy.' He frowned. 'I think it might be wise for me to see any papers that you didn't have before you were married. Could you bring them in to let me have a look?'

'Of course. I'll have to get the satchel from one of my cases in the storage area.'

'Could you have them by late tomorrow morning?'

'Yes.'

'Good. Then shall we say, let's see...'He checked the diary on his desk. 'Would eleven thirty suit you?'

'Yes.'

He made a note in his diary, then sat back and smiled at her. 'Now tell me, have you signed the lease?'

Erin relaxed, and smiled back. 'Yes I signed it this morning, and I'm just waiting for the agent to give me my copy once the owner has signed.'

'Excellent. Then you're going to be a busy lady from now on, getting everything under way.'

'I've already made a start. I've selected colours and fabrics, and I have some people coming to give me quotes later today for the work.'

'You're not wasting any time, I can see, but don't let the tradies touch anything until you have your copy of the lease signed and sealed.'

'No, I'll make sure of that,' Erin assured him as she rose to leave.

'Good. And I'll see you again tomorrow with the papers.'

After the last of the fitters left the shop Erin returned to her hotel room. Here she opened her laptop and started a file she labelled 'Shop Expenses'. She began to list the estimated costs to decorate the shop in the way she wanted. She worked out how much the fabric for the drapes would cost, how much to make them, and then added a fit out cost, taking the best quote she received from the shop fitters. When she added them together she stared in shock at the total.

Her thoughts jumped about like grasshoppers in a jar as she realised this was without all the accessories she'd planned – the luxury items like chandeliers, display dummies, and padded chairs – those exclusive items that would add the glamour touch. They wouldn't be cheap. And she would need money for advertising. And ongoing expenses. Rent, rates and taxes, electricity.

She breathed in sharply as she realised her money was scarcely enough to cover all these costs, let alone to live on. She slammed the lid on the laptop. She couldn't afford to stay in the hotel, she must find an apartment. Quickly.

She needed *Serendipity* to open as soon as possible. And hope it would be the success she needed.

CHAPTER NINETEEN

Erin spent a restless night tossing and turning in her bed as dollars and cents swirled through her mind like leaves in the wind. Towards morning she made a decision. If needed, she'd find a part-time job until the business started to make ends meet. She would do anything – maybe even find some waitressing at nights. Until the business grew enough to support her. The main thing was to get it up and running as quickly as possible. Having made that decision she felt calmer, and managed a few hours sleep before morning. After a quick breakfast she made a call to the real estate agent.

'I'm afraid I don't have the contract signed yet,' he told her. 'I haven't been able to reach the owner yet.'

'Oh no!' She gripped the phone tightly. 'I was hoping it would be ready by now. I need to contact the shop fitters to come and get started. I'm anxious to open as soon as possible.'

'Yes of course. I understand, and I hope to have it for you sometime today.'

'I hope so too.' She took a deep breath. 'In the meantime, I'm looking for an apartment in this area. Do you have any for rent?'

'Yes. If you care to come into the office I can take you to have a look at what's available. When would suit you?'

They agreed on mid-afternoon, and Erin ended the call. She made her way to down to her car and half an hour later she was in the storage area at Chippendale, sorting through her cases until she found the one containing the satchel that held all her papers. Opening it, she checked that the papers were inside. Yes, everything seemed to be here. In fact, there seemed to be far more than she'd realised. Certainly more than her own personal papers. Well, she would wait until she was with Aden to check them properly.

Aden greeted her pleasantly, holding the door open for her to enter, and guiding her to the visitor's chair before sitting behind his desk.

'I see you have the satchel,' he said.

'Yes, and I'm surprised to see so many papers in here.' Erin opened the satchel and took out her own papers, which were in an envelope, and placed them to one side on the desk. 'These are mine but all the rest must have something to do with the marriage. I'm surprised there are so many.'

'Then let's have a look.'

She opened a large envelope and pulled out a sheaf of papers, and read out the name at the top of the front page. 'Phoebus Mining,' she read. 'Yes, I remember this now. It was soon after we were married. Giles gave them to me. He said they were shares he'd accepted in lieu of a debt, and they were worthless at the time, but he thought I might like to have some shares in my name. He said I was to hang on to them and maybe one day they might be worth something. But he would let me know if they were, and I was never to consider selling them without him knowing.' She handed them to Aden.

Aden took them and scanned the front page before replacing the sheets in their envelope. 'Hmm, let me have a look.' He tapped the keyboard on his computer. 'Here we are. Phoebus Mining. They're not entirely worthless. In fact, the company has recently begun carrying out exploration for gold in a new location in the Northern Territory. At the moment they're worth seventy cents, but that could change if they make a significant find. Then they might be worth something substantial.'

'Huh, I doubt it. I'm sure he'd have known if that could happen. But any money would be handy. The shop is going to cost more to set up than I expected and...'

'Erin, I can probably organise some money for you. Your husband is an exceedingly wealthy man and the court...'

'No, I don't want any more of his money except what I feel I'm entitled to if I'd been working.'

'That's not very practical, Erin. Not if you're going to run a business.'

She lifted her chin. 'I've thought about it, and I've decided that if I have to, I'll find a temporary part-time job at night.'

Aden sighed. 'If you say so.'

'I do.' She reached into the satchel again and pulled out a small bundle of loose papers and a couple of envelopes. 'I don't know what these are, or how they came to be in here.' She narrowed her eyes as she scanned the top paper, and tried to recall if she had ever seen it before. 'This looks like a receipt for something.' She shuffled the papers and shook her head as she picked up an opened envelope addressed to her husband. 'How could I possibly have these?' She tried to think back. 'I can only think they were in our bedroom and somehow got into my walk-in robe and became mixed up with my things, and I picked them up in my hurry to pack everything.'

She handed the envelope to Aden, and watched as he removed the sheet of paper inside and read it.

'This is a letter to Giles,' he told her. 'A thank you letter, from someone called James.' His brow furrowed. 'I wonder who James is,' he said slowly.

'I have no idea. There are some other letters here too,' Erin said, handing them across to Aden. 'I suppose I should send them back to him. They're no use to me.'

He skimmed them and handed one to her.

'This one might be. I think you should read it.'

'My darling Giles,' she read aloud. Her eyes dropped to the signature at the bottom. 'Your ever loving Leonie.'

Fury boiled inside her. She finished the letter before crumpling it in her fist, her blood pounding.

'That bastard!' She spat the words. 'May he rot in Hell! I sometimes suspected he was carrying on with other women, but he denied it. Said I was paranoid. This proves he was taking this Leonie away with him on his so-called business trips. Where I was never able to accompany him! And it's obviously been going on for years.'

She brushed angrily at the tears that sprang to her eyes. 'It's not that I care anymore. I'm just sorry that all the while he was having a great time with this other woman I was being the faithful wife. It's not that I didn't have plenty of opportunities, because I did. And I was even tempted once or twice, but I thought it wouldn't be right. I really believed in my marriage vows. I tried to be a good wife. What a fool I was!'

'Do you want me to return these papers to him?' Aden asked quietly.

'No! Give him nothing! God, how I hate him! I hope he dies and rots in Hell.'

They sat silent for a few moments while Erin struggled to regain control of her emotions. Even through the turmoil, she was shocked at the intensity of her feelings. Closing her eyes she took deep breaths, and slowly her composure returned. The last of her illusions about their marriage was shattered. She must move on.

She fumbled in her purse for a tissue, blew her nose, swallowed, and took a deep breath. 'I'm sorry.' Her voice trembled.

'You have nothing to be sorry for.' Aden's voice was gentle.

'It's not that I still love Giles, that was gone long ago, but I...I guess on some levels I still admired him. What he is, what he's achieved. I still felt... some sort of regard for him, I suppose, in some ways. Now I feel so...betrayed. I've finally lost any illusions I had. He's left me nothing good to remember.'

'Perhaps, in a way, it might be good you've discovered this now.' Aden's voice was quiet. 'If your husband is going to fight your divorce, and I think that's shown by his response, then you're going to need plenty of strength in the next year. And if all your feelings for him are gone, it will be easier for you. '

'I can assure you I have no feelings left for him. I just want to be free from him. I don't want to be Mrs Giles Brightman for a day longer than I have to be.'

'Well now,' Aden raised an eyebrow, 'perhaps while you still have the name you should make use of it. It's worth a lot, publicity wise.' He paused. 'An announcement such as, leading socialite Erin

Brightman is set to launch a new commercial enterprise, would arouse some interest in your new venture, I'm sure.'

'Oh but I couldn't possibly...' Erin's voice trailed off as she considered the possibilities. 'Could I? Do you think...?'

'You not only could, I think you should. Look at all the socialites who take advantage of the name of the man they're married to. Think of all the models who are married to men of prominence, businessmen or sportsmen. They don't have a problem with the publicity. Why should you?'

Erin turned his words over in her mind. Ordinarily she wouldn't have considered it, she would have felt it was unfair to use Giles' name having left him, but now, after reading that letter – and if he was going to make her wait the full year to be rid of him – well, why not? She nodded. 'Yes, I imagine someone like Evie Tate would make quite a story of it.'

'Exactly. It's probably a little premature just yet, but once you have the lease signed, and you're a little further advanced with your plans, I think you should take every opportunity open to you to publicise your business. And a whisper in the ear of a journalist like her would be a first step.'

Erin's lips tightened. All that time she'd spent alone, while Giles had been enjoying himself with another woman. Yes. If Giles wanted to keep her tied to him against her will, then she would make use of his name to grab attention for *Serendipity*.

CHAPTER TWENTY

Erin arrived at the agent's office that afternoon, impatient for things to happen.

'I hope you have my copy for me now, all signed and sealed, because I have tradesmen ready to start work,' she told him.

'Well, um, no, not exactly.' Tremayne shifted his shoulders. 'I contacted the owner's lawyer only half an hour ago, and apparently he hasn't been able to get hold of him to sign it yet.'

'Why can't he contact him? Is he away somewhere? And when does he think he'll be in touch?' She was unable to keep the impatience from her voice.

'Look, I'm sorry, but I really don't know, and there's not much I can do about it.' He frowned and spread his hands with a shrug. 'I've told him it's a matter of urgency. I can't do any more.'

Erin took a deep breath. It wasn't his fault, of course.

'Now I have some nice apartments to show you,' Tremayne continued. 'Shall we go and have a look at those now? And then, when we come back, I'll call the lawyer again.'

'All right.'

'Good, then let's go. My car is just outside.'

They looked at three apartments in large, cream brick blocks of almost identical flats, none of which held any appeal for Erin. Then Tremayne stopped outside a pair of semi-attached red brick houses in a quiet side street a little way from the main Chatswood area. One side had a 'For Sale' sign on it, but Tremayne pulled up in front of the other. Each dwelling had its own separate garden and gate, and the houses were separated by a brick wall running through the front verandah beneath a gabled roof, and a low fence.

'Now, perhaps this might appeal to you more,' he said, 'a lovely Federation home. The couple who own it are living overseas. It's fully furnished except for linen, and the owners are very fussy about whom they'll let it to. No children or teenagers. No dogs. They want someone quiet who'll look after the place. I think you'd suit them just fine.'

'I see the other one is for sale,' Erin remarked as she left the car and stood looking. 'But not this one?'

'No. They're both owned by the same couple, but they only want to sell the one. They're keeping this in case they decide to come back to Australia sometime in the future.'

Erin liked the look of the little house, and when she went inside she was delighted. The front door opened into a long hallway with a timber floor, and her eyes were drawn immediately to the high ornate pressed-metal ceilings, seen only in these older homes.

Doors opened to three bedrooms down one side of the hall, while on the other side ran the dividing wall between the two houses. The hallway opened directly into a large lounge room, which had an old fashioned open fireplace with a mantel above. She could just imagine herself sitting by a real fire in the winter.

Double glass doors, open now, led from the lounge into a dining room. The rooms were furnished and decorated in a way that offered cosy comfort rather than stylishness. Of the bedrooms, the largest held a Queen-sized bed; the second had two single beds and the third, the smallest, a desk and a chair.

The kitchen and bathroom were up-to-date, and there was a separate laundry with a washing machine. At the rear was a small leafy garden, totally private, where she saw herself sitting outside after a day's work, relaxing with a glass of wine. It was just perfect. The rent was reasonable, and she didn't hesitate.

'I'll take it.'

'I thought you'd like it.' Tremayne beamed. 'It belongs to friends of mine and I promised them I'd only let it to someone reliable. There's no problem with signing this lease. I have their authority, so if you come back to the office and fix up, you can have the keys immediately and move in as soon as you like.'

Within the hour, Erin had signed the lease, paid the bond and the first month's rent, and had the keys in her purse. Returning to the hotel she advised the reception she would be leaving the next day.

It was too late now to buy linen, she would do that first thing in the morning. For now she headed to a Seven Eleven store where she bought bread and milk, some ham and cheese, and a few groceries. Then to a bottle shop to pick up a couple of bottles of white wine and, at the last moment, she added a bottle of champagne. Then she drove back to the house, parked in the carport at the side, unlocked the door and walked down the hall into the lounge room.

Standing just inside the door she let her eyes roam over the room. She was pleased with what she saw, but suddenly she felt a hollow in her chest as a wash of emotion swept through her. A lump filled her throat. Her chest ached. She took two steps into the room and stopped. She took a deep, shuddering breath. What was the matter with her?

She bit her lip. Of course, it was because she was all alone. Like when her mother died. She had no-one to share this pleasure with. That was the way it was going to be from now on. It was her choice. She was the one who had left her marriage. It was what she wanted. So why this sudden melancholy?

Swallowing the lump in her throat she walked slowly across to the fireplace and ran her fingers over the ceramic surround. Passing into the dining room she couldn't find any fault with it, and it was the same with the rest of the house. This was her home now. She liked it, and she would be happy here. So what was the matter with her? Why this emptiness inside her?

Outside, in the rest of the world, people were living and loving, laughing and crying. And most of them had someone else who cared. Someone to share their life with. Perhaps it mightn't be a happy relationship, but it was someone else in their life. There was no-one to care what became of her. It wasn't the house. It was her. It was loneliness. And a sense of failure. Hot tears threatened but she squeezed her eyes shut and breathed deeply.

She walked through the back door onto the small paved terrace outside, where she stood and looked around.

A timber table and chairs sat beneath a large frangipani tree that cast its shade to one side of the terrace. Beyond that red, pink and yellow flowering hibiscus trees, and colourful roses in full bloom, surrounded a small green lawn. Jasmine climbed over a tiny shed at the back of the garden, its aroma mingling with the scents of the roses and frangipani. The drone of bees was in the air, and the scene was one of colour and calm.

A fairy-wren perched on a limb at the bottom of the garden, the rich blue plumage on its head and throat standing out against the green leaves of a hibiscus bush. It sat with its head to one side, and seemed to be watching her. All at once it lifted its head, and from its beak came an opening trill that swelled into song.

As Erin watched, and listened, warmth entered her chest, filling the void. Slowly the sadness receded.

She walked back inside with lightened limbs. Was that surprising emotion she'd experienced something that affected everyone whose marriage failed, or was it just her? Who knows? But she must get over it.

With buoyant steps she walked through the house, out to the car, unpacked her purchases and carried them inside. When she had stowed away the groceries and put the wine in the fridge, she took a glass from a cupboard in the kitchen and poured herself a glass of wine. Taking it with her she wandered through the house, inspecting each room again, working out what she would need to buy, and where she would put her few personal items.

Yes, she would make it comfortable and attractive. And it would be all hers. A good place to begin her new life.

Erin wandered out again into the garden, and the beautiful, mild spring evening. The sun was slipping behind the trees; it's red and gold rays promising a fine day tomorrow. The garden was filled with peace and serenity. She sat at the table appreciating the sunset. She sipped her wine, and watched as the last stragglers of birds flew overhead on their way home, black against the fading sky. Contentment filled her as the light dwindled, and the night air wrapped itself around her like a gossamer cape. She was relaxed and satisfied once again.

When she finished her wine she felt reluctant to leave this little leafy oasis, so she went inside and made herself a ham sandwich, poured herself another glass of wine, and carried them back to the table. As she enjoyed her simple meal she determined to put the past behind her and to move on with her new life.

CHAPTER TWENTY ONE

The next morning Erin was up early to pack her bags, pay her hotel bill, and drive to her new house by breakfast time. She unpacked her clothes and hung them in the roomy robes in the largest bedroom, put her toiletries away in the bathroom, and opened the carton with her shoes. The woman who'd lived here before must have been a shoe-lover too, because the shoe cabinet had room to store all her favourites. The rest would go to *Serendipity* for sale. And she really mustn't buy any more. Well, she certainly couldn't afford it now. There'd be no more browsing the shoe stores for her, until the business was up and running – and making a profit.

In the kitchen she made a cup of coffee, toasted two slices of bread and spread them with butter and Vegemite, and carried them outside to sit on the terrace and eat her breakfast.

Well, here she was, in a place of her own. She'd managed to break away from Giles after years of marriage that had been a roller-coaster ride. She'd lived in luxury, known all the material pleasures of a life of wealth and privilege but without the intimacy and closeness of a loving relationship. Their marriage had been empty of warmth. She had grown up in those years. No longer was she the young woman with stars in her eyes. And finding evidence of Giles' betrayal had hardened her heart. From now on she would be wary.

But this morning she was content. The sky above shone bright blue, with a few long, wispy clouds floating lazily. The sun slanted through the leaves of the frangipani tree as a light breeze stirred it, dappling the pavers with splotches of light and dark, and the bright hibiscus flowers leant an exotic touch to the whole. Bees buzzed around the blossoms. Erin had to smile at the antics of a tiny a honey-eater as it hung upside-down from a thin stem on one of the hibiscus trees, its sharp beak probing a flower for its nectar. Her melancholy of the previous evening had disappeared.

When she finished breakfast Erin gathered the dishes and took them inside and rinsed them, then she rang Aden's office and left her new address with Josie.

A few moments later her phone rang and pleasure rippled through her as she saw Aden's name come up.

'Good morning Erin. I hear you've found an apartment.'

'Not an apartment, but something much better. A little house. And it's just amazing. It's perfect; it even has a lovely little private garden at the back. A leafy oasis. I'm so lucky to be able to have it.'

'Sounds wonderful. Perhaps I could come and see it sometime?'

Erin's heart did a little flip. But was he was just saying that to be polite? Maybe he didn't really want to come at all.

'Any time you like.'

'Are you doing anything this evening, then? A bit after five, perhaps?'

This time her heart really flipped, catching her breath.

'I'll be here. Would you like to come for a drink and a look through?'

'I would indeed. And then perhaps we could have a meal somewhere, and you can fill me in on what's happening at the shop?'

'That would be great. But rather than go out, how about we eat here? After all, I need to try out the kitchen.'

'If you're sure that's not too much trouble?'

'Not at all. You have the address, and in the meantime I'll chase up the agent, and see what's happening with the lease.'

'Hasn't it been signed yet?'

'It hadn't been by late yesterday, but I hope it has by now.'

'I hope so. Look, I have to go, I have a client waiting. I'll see you as soon after five as I can make it through the traffic. Is there somewhere I can park?'

'Yes, there's a carport at the side of the house, and I'll drive my car right through so you can park behind me.'

'Right, then. I'll see you tonight.'

When he had rung off Erin sat with the phone in her hand looking at it thoughtfully. Definitely he was sounding more like a friend than just her lawyer.

Aden sat for a moment, wondering why he'd done that. He'd only meant to enquire about the shop lease. But if he was honest with himself, he knew why. He wanted to see her again, away from his office, away from his responsibilities. But he knew it was perilous to pursue his attraction to her. He should be keeping away from her.

Erin headed to the David Jones store in Chatswood, where she spent an hour choosing linen for the beds and towels for the bathroom. Then she chose a few things for the kitchen – tea towels, placemats, oven mitts. All matching, with sprigs of red cherries and green leaves. Then she splurged on a small sound system so she could have music in the house.

Her next stop was the butcher for two steaks for tonight, then to the supermarket, where she stocked up with food and household essentials. Then it was back home, where she spent the rest of the morning making up beds and finding homes for her purchases, singing along with music from the radio as she went about the homely chores.

After a quick lunch she drove to the Chippendale storage area. She loaded her car with cases and boxes, and drove back home again. After unloading her cases at the house, she walked to the agent's office. He'd promised to ring her as soon as he had news, and he hadn't rung. She needed to find out what had happened.

Ever since Aden's call, while she'd gone about her tasks, her mind had been busy with two distractions. Her worry about the lease, and Aden's visit tonight. And their dinner date. She supposed it was a dinner date, although he'd couched it in the terms of catching up on the latest situation at the shop. She was sure he didn't ask all his clients for dinner to discuss their cases.

When Erin arrived at Tremayne's office he was on the phone, so she sat and waited, idly turning the pages of a magazine, until he ended his call. He came to greet her with a frown on his face.

This didn't look like good news. Her stomach turned nervous somersaults.

'Erin, I'm sorry, I still have nothing definite for you. This owner seems to have vanished for the time being.'

'But surely someone must know where he is? Doesn't he have a family?'

'Not as such. He has a partner, but he doesn't know where the owner is. Apparently they had a disagreement, and he left in a huff, saying not to expect him back.'

'So where does that leave me? It's been three days, and I've signed my part, and paid the money up front. I have tradesmen waiting to begin work, and boxes in my car that I want to leave at the shop. '

'I know, and I'm really sorry. If I'd known about this I would never have even shown you the place, let alone asked you to sign the lease.'

'But you did, and I've fulfilled my part, and I'm losing money while I'm waiting around, unable to start.'

'Look, I'm very sorry for what's happened, and if I hear nothing by the morning I'll try and get the lawyer to agree to you taking possession anyway. Although I can't promise.'

'So what am I to do with the boxes in my car, and the tradesmen that are waiting?'

'I can't say anything about the tradesmen, but take the boxes and leave them in the store, but don't unpack them today. And I promise I'll be in touch tomorrow morning.'

Erin had to be content with that. She could see he could do no more, so she left with his promise to be in touch first thing in the morning

When she returned home Erin ran a bath, added some of her favourite bath essence, and took a long leisurely bath; a luxury she'd been missing while at the hotel. When she stepped from the tub she dried herself with one of the new, fluffy towels, and applied body lotion all over before spraying herself with her favourite 'White Linen' perfume.

Going into her bedroom she slipped on a silky *Simone Perele* bra and bikini brief before looking at the clothes hanging in the robe. After living out of a suitcase recently, and practically living in jeans, she welcomed the thought of a change of fashion tonight. She chose a *Trelise Cooper* shift, white with an intricate black scroll design at the hem and cuffs, casual but smart, and added a pair of *Saint Laurent* black strappy sandals with a silver trim. After checking herself in the mirror she pit on a pair of long silver earrings. A dash of lipstick, and she was ready.

CHAPTER TWENY THREE

Erin had prepared the steaks and salads, a bowl of nuts, canapés, and a bottle of wine in a cooler, all ready to carry outside, well before Aden was due. When she heard a car pull into the drive she opened the door and stood waiting for him.

No suit and tie tonight, he'd changed into chinos and open-necked shirt. The relaxed image suited him.

'Welcome to my new home,' she greeted him.

Aden looked around the tiny garden as he came towards her, a wide smile on his face and a bottle bag in his hand.

'And very nice it is. I can see why you like this better than an apartment.'

As he bent his head to give her a fleeting kiss on the cheek she caught a whiff of his cologne, woody and masculine.

'I brought us a drink. I remember you like sauvignon blanc.'

'Thank you.' She took the bag and stood back for him to enter. 'I'll just put this in the fridge, and then I'll give you the guided tour.'

Aden was standing looking around the lounge when she came back.

'Very comfortable,' he approved. Moving across to the fireplace he looked at the two framed photos standing there.

'Is this you, when you were young?'

'Yes. And the other one is my mother.'

'She's not still with you, is she?'

'No, she died when I was nineteen.'

His eyes softened. 'I'm sorry.'

'That's why I left Newcastle and came to Sydney.'

'And that's when you met your husband?'

'Yes.' Erin shook away the thought. She didn't want to talk about Giles. Not tonight. 'Now come on and I'll show you the rest. Not that there's a lot to see, it's only a tiny house.'

She led the way from room to room, with Aden making appreciative comments.

When they reached the back door she opened it with a flourish. 'This is probably the main reason I decided I could be happy here,' she told him as he joined her.

As they stood in the narrow doorway she felt the heat from his body as they brushed together, and caught again a waft of his cologne.

Aden stepped out through the door and turned to her with an easy smile. 'I can see why. You have a real little oasis here.'

'That's just how I feel about it. Now, take a seat, and I'll bring out our drinks.'

When she reappeared a moment later Aden jumped up, took the tray from her, and placed it on the table. While she set out the glasses, he opened the wine. When it was poured he raised his glass with a smile.

'A toast to your new home, Erin, and to the success of your new venture.'

'Thank you.' She smiled.

As they sipped their wine Aden raised the subject of the lease on the shop. 'What's the latest news?'

Erin related her conversation with Tremayne earlier in the afternoon.

'That's a bit of a worry. If they can't find this man

soon, you'll have to make a choice. Either ask for the lease to be cancelled, and your money back, or wait around indefinitely. Do you think you can find other premises to suit you?'

'I doubt I'd find anything else as perfect.'

'Then we'd better wait a bit longer and hope he turns up. If he doesn't, and you still want to go ahead, we'd have to wait for a court ruling.'

Erin's heart sank at Aden's words. She couldn't afford to wait, but what could she do? She twisted her glass on the table top with a frown.

'Apart from the fact that I'm anxious to get going, money's going to be a problem if I have to wait,' she told him. 'No,' she raised her hand as he opened his mouth to speak. 'I know what you're going to say, and I won't ask Giles for money.'

'Very well, I accept that, but there is another avenue open to you. You could borrow against the expectations of a settlement at your divorce.'

'From a bank or something?'

'Yes.'

'But what if I didn't get a settlement?'

'Erin, that is not possible. You will receive a settlement, I promise you.'

'I suppose I just don't like the idea of borrowing money when the future's not certain, but I guess if I'm not prepared to take a chance, then I shouldn't be thinking of opening a business.'

'That's true. Let me make some enquiries for you tomorrow.' He smiled at her over the top of his glass. 'And now let's enjoy our evening. '

Erin's spirits lifted. 'Yes, let's do that. And it's probably time for me to start on some food, while you stay here and finish your wine. I haven't cooked a meal here yet, so I'm looking forward to trying out the kitchen.

'Then I'll come in and join you, if you don't mind. I'm a bit of a dab hand in the kitchen myself, you know.'

'Really?' She flicked him a smile. 'A man of many talents, I see. Well, there's not a lot to do, but I'll be glad of the company.'

While Erin heated the griddle and took out the steaks that were marinating in the fridge, Aden wandered around examining the kitchen fittings, and then went through into the dining room.

'You can set the table for me if you like,' she called out. 'You'll find everything in the buffet drawers and cupboards.'

'Okay.'

While she put the steaks on to cook, and took the salads from the fridge, she heard the sound of drawers opening and closing, and the rattle of cutlery and crockery.

A moment later Aden appeared. 'It needs one more thing,' he told her.

Erin caught a glimpse of something in his hand as he walked through the kitchen. When he returned she realised it was a vase, now full of roses.

'For the table,' he told her as he passed through.

When Erin carried the salads into the dining room a moment later she saw he had set the table with the bowl of roses in the middle.

'So, what do you think?' he asked her with a satisfied smile. 'Is it to your satisfaction?'

'Absolutely.'

'So tell me about yourself. Did you always live in Newcastle?' Aden asked after they finished their meal and were sitting outside again, lingering over coffee in the light from the candles that Erin lit as night drew in.

'Yes. It's where I grew up and went to school. I'd probably still be there, working in the office of the Newcastle branch of Atkins and Thomas, if it hadn't been for losing my mother.'

'It must have been hard for you, losing her while you were so young. Do you have any other family?'

'No. There was always just Mum and me. My father died when I was three, and they'd emigrated from Ireland a few years before, so we were all alone. How about you? Do you have any family?'

'No, I'm an only child, too.'

'And have you always lived in Sydney?'

'No. I grew up in Armidale. It's where I went to school and where I studied law.' It seemed as if a shadow crossed his face. Or was it just the candlelight?

He put down his cup and, reaching across, picked up her hand. 'But that's boring,' he continued. 'It's you I want to hear about.' He turned her hand over and for a moment she thought he was going to kiss it. But didn't. He just held it, gazing into her face, his eyes intense.

Erin could hardly breathe. She lost herself in his eyes as he watched her, the flickering candlelight making them unreadable.

'I want to get to know you, Erin.' His voice was soft. 'I want to know everything about you. What you like, what you don't like. What music you listen to. Do you like reading, or watching movies? There's so much I want to know about you.'

Her heart thumped unsteadily in her chest. 'I...I think you know most about me already.'

'Not those sorts of things, what I know on a professional level. The important things, about who you really are.'

He leant towards her, and his lips came down to meet hers. He kissed her, gently at first, and then deeper. Light headed warmth spread through her as she kissed him back.

Finally, slowly, he drew back and stood. He held out his hands to her. She took them, her pulses racing, and rose to join him.

The sound of her phone ringing brought her back to earth with a jolt.

Why hadn't she turned it off? She should ignore it.

Aden let go of her hands. 'You'd better answer it.' His voice was husky.

With her breath still coming fast Erin checked the caller.

'It's Bobbi. She never rings at night.' She pressed the button and Bobbi's distraught voice came through.

'Erin.' Bobbi sobbed. 'I'm so glad I caught you. Laurence has had a heart attack. He's in St Vincent's Hospital, and he might not make it through the night. I'm here with him, and I'm so frightened.'

Erin's blood chilled. 'Oh Bobbi, no! Is anyone else there with you?'

'No.'

'You're there all alone?' She hesitated as she looked at Aden. 'Do you want me to come to the hospital?'

'Yes, Please come. I'm so frightened,' she repeated. 'I'll be right over.'

She clicked off the phone, and gazed uncertainly at Aden.

'It's Bobbi.' She repeated their conversation. 'She needs me. I'm sorry...'

He interrupted her with a lift of his hand. 'You must go, of course.' He gave a half laugh. 'It was probably time for me to go anyhow. Before things got totally out of control.'

On the way to the hospital Erin wondered about that remark. And about what might have happened if there had been no interruption.

As Aden drove home he berated himself for letting things get out of hand like that. He had no right to come on to Erin like that. He should never have gone there in the first place, but he'd wanted so much to spend time with her. He'd thought he could keep it all on a friendly basis, but it seemed he couldn't trust himself to do that. He'd thought he would never fall in love again, but it had happened. He hadn't wanted it to happen, but it had.

As he pulled up at a stop light he thumped the steering wheel. What to do? Nothing in his life had been resolved. There was only one thing for it. If he couldn't trust himself to be alone with her he must see it didn't happen again. He must keep their relationship on a purely professional level. At least until he had the right to do more.

CHAPTER TWENTY FOUR

Erin made her way to the cardiac section and enquired at the nurse's station for Laurence Harvey.

'Are you a relative?' the nurse asked.

'No, I'm a close friend of Mrs Williams. She rang me a little while ago and asked me to come.'

'Oh yes, she said she's expecting you. Room fifteen,' she pointed down a hallway, straight along there.'

When Erin entered the room she found Bobbi sitting in a chair alongside Laurence's bed. One arm rested on her baby bump, the other covered Laurence's hand on the side of the bed. Her face was blotchy with tears, and her gaze was fixed on Laurence. He lay, motionless, with his eyes closed. An oxygen mask covered his mouth and nose. Leads attached to his body ran to the monitor at the head of his bed, and he was hooked up to a drip on the other side.

Bobbi pushed back her chair as Erin came through the door.

'Oh Erin, thank goodness you've come.'

As she stood Erin went to her and put her arms around her, wishing she could help somehow. Bobbi burst into tears.

'There, there.' Erin tried to soothe her, but Bobbi only cried harder. She rested her head on Erin's shoulder, and Erin rubbed her back, letting her cry it out.

When Bobbi finally looked up with swollen eyes Erin fished a handkerchief from her purse and handed it to her.

Bobbi mopped her eyes and swallowed, trying to compose herself. 'It's so terrible.' She blinked rapidly as she gazed at her husband, and moved away from the bed. 'Come outside for a bit,' she said in a shaky voice, 'so we can talk. There's a little room just along the passage we can use.'

Erin followed her to a small room furnished with a few chairs covered in green upholstery, and a small round table in the centre that held a few magazines.

'Tell me what happened,' Erin said as soon as they were seated.

Bobbi took a deep breath. 'It was earlier tonight. We were just sitting watching television after dinner when Laurence had a phone call. He moved out of the room, but I could hear him having a heated conversation. When he came back in he was white. I asked him what the matter was but he just shook his head, and the next moment he clutched his chest and fell on the floor.'

Erin leant across and took Bobbi's hand. 'Whatever did you do?'

'I rushed over and knelt down beside him. I thought at first he must be dead, but then I felt his pulse and I saw he was breathing. So I rang for the ambulance. I tried to give him CPR, but the paramedics were there within a few minutes, and they took over. And as soon as the ambulance arrived we came here.'

'Was he conscious?'

'No, he never regained consciousness, and he's had another heart attack since he's been here.' She pressed the handkerchief to her mouth to stifle a sob. 'They've been working on him for ages, and the doctor told me he's in a very serious condition. One of them told me I should be prepared for the worst.'

A shiver of apprehension ran through Erin. It didn't sound good for Bobbi and her unborn child.

'I wonder what the phone call was about that upset him so much. That must be what brought it on. Do you have any idea?'

'No. I couldn't hear what he was saying until towards the end when I heard him shout 'it will be the ruin of all of us'. That's all I heard. '

'Do you have any idea who he was talking to?'

Bobbi hesitated. 'Not really, although I kind of had the idea it was Giles, but I don't know for sure. I was watching a movie, and I didn't take much notice until I heard him raise his voice.'

'I guess it doesn't matter, but it sounds as if it was something to do with business.'

'Yes, I'm sure it was.' She fidgeted with the handkerchief. 'And now I'd better get back to him and see what's happening.'

Nothing had changed. Laurence still remained unconscious, and a few moments later a nurse came to check the monitor and take his blood pressure.

'How is it?' asked Bobbi.

'No change,' she replied, and after she finished writing on his chart she left them alone again.

After sitting beside the bed for some time, Erin noticed Bobbi's shoulders slump and her eyelids begin to droop. She was nearly out to it. 'You need to get some rest,' she told her firmly.

Bobbi straightened up with a jerk. 'I can't go and leave him.'

'I'm sure they'd let you know if there's any change, and you could be back here quite quickly. And you have to think of the baby. It's not good for you to become so exhausted.' Erin looked at the figure in the bed. 'Laurence wouldn't want you to stay here all night. I don't want you to go back home to your place all on your own, but I have a spare room with a bed and I want you to come home with me. We can be back here first thing in the morning.'

After consulting with the doctor, who assured her they would let her know if there was any change in Laurence's condition, Bobbi agreed to accompany Erin.

Before they left she went back to stand by her husband's bed. Gazing down at him she stroked his unresponsive hand, then leant over and smoothed the hair back from his forehead and dropped a kiss on his cheek.

'Goodbye Laurence,' she whispered with her lips close to his ear. 'I'll be back to see you in the morning.' She straightened, biting her lip. After watching him for a few seconds longer she turned and joined Erin.

The next morning Erin rose early and made coffee before she opened the door. She peeked in to see if Bobbi was awake. When she saw her lying on her back staring at the ceiling she went in and stood by the bed.

'How are you feeling this morning?' she asked.

'All right. Just dreading what the day will bring.'

'You stay there a bit longer, and I'll bring you a cup of coffee.'

She returned a minute later with two cups. She handed one to Bobbi, who was sitting up with two pillows at her back, and sat on the edge of the bed to drink her coffee.

Bobbi gulped the first few mouthfuls quickly before leaning back against the pillows with a grateful sigh. 'This is just what I need. And thanks for insisting that I came back here with you last night.'

'You haven't heard anything from the hospital?'

'I rang as soon as I woke up. There's been no change.'

'Well, at least that's not bad news.'

Bobbi shook her head. 'I don't have a good feeling about it. I fear my daughter is going to be born without a father.'

'Your daughter? So you know it's a girl?'

'Yes. Laurence wanted to know, and he was so thrilled. I thought he might have been disappointed it's not a boy, but he was over the moon.' Bobbi took a deep breath, and another gulp of coffee. 'It seems so sad, for this to happen now. He's been so looking forward to seeing his little daughter.'

'Don't give up yet, he's in good hands; he might be strong enough to pull through.'

'I hope you're right, but I fear the worst.'

At that moment Bobbi's phone rang. She listened to what was being said on the other end. 'Thank you,' was all she said as she clicked off and dropped the phone onto the bed. Tears rolled down her cheeks. 'He's gone. He just slipped away, the doctor said. He never regained consciousness.'

Erin put her arms around Bobbi, her heart aching for her friend, and held her while she sobbed, her shoulders shaking.

'It's so unfair,' Bobbi snuffled into the wad of tissues crumpled in her fist, 'just when things were going so well between us. He's been so loving and considerate to me since we found out about the baby, and he was so looking forward to becoming a father. It's just not fair.'

Remembering her own pain when her mother died, Erin knew it was best to let her friend cry it out, so she sat with her arms around her, rubbing her back from time to time, and replacing the tissues as they became soaked.

Finally Bobbi took a great shuddering breath and lifted her head. Erin dropped her arms from around her and handed her another fresh tissue, taking the sodden mass from her hand.

Bobbi wiped her swollen eyes, dabbed at her red, blotchy face, and blew her nose. 'I'm sorry.' She gulped.

'No need,' Erin told her. 'Can I get you something? More coffee? Or do you feel you could eat something?'

Bobbi shook her head miserably. 'No, nothing, thanks. I just have to try and get used to the fact that he's gone. It seems so unbelievable. Yesterday we were making plans for the future, and now....' she shook her head, and blew her nose again, 'now I don't know what the future holds.'

'I've never heard you speak about them, but did Laurence have any family?'

'No. He came here as a young man from Lithuania. I suppose he must have family back there, but he never spoke about them. He told me he arrived with a hundred dollars in his pocket. He always boasted he was a self-made man, and owed nothing to anyone.'

Bobbi paused, and chewed on her bottom lip. 'I

suppose arrangements have to be made...I don't know...I feel lost...' her voice trailed off.

'I think you need to contact his lawyer,' Erin told her. 'He'll know what to do. I imagine he'll take care of everything for you.'

'Yes, you're right, of course. Bob Simpson. I'll ring him right away.'

While Bobbi made her phone call Erin went into the kitchen and made fresh coffee, took out the toaster and cut some bread. She hoped she could coax Bobbi into eating something, so she set out plates and butter and marmalade.

The bowl of roses still stood on the table from the night before, and the sight of them made her heart flutter. If Bobbi hadn't rung when she did, what would have happened? Would she and Aden be able to take over from there sometime in the future, or was the moment lost?

She mentally shook herself. Right now Bobbi was her main concern.

Bobbi looked flustered when she rejoined her. 'Simpson was shocked,' she told her. 'Of course, he didn't know about Laurence's heart attack, or even that he was in hospital. I think he was angry with me that I didn't ring and tell him last night, but I was only thinking about what was happening to Laurence. Nothing else.'

'Of course you were,' Erin soothed her. 'As any wife would be.'

'He's very put out. Muttered something about this having terrible ramifications.'

'You shouldn't concern yourself with business matters. That's for him to sort out,' Erin told her, angry that the lawyer would upset Bobbi at this moment. 'You need to focus on yourself and your baby. That's what Laurence would want you to do.'

Bobbi took a deep breath and placed her hand on her baby bump. 'Yes, he would.'

'Did Simpson say he'd take care of the formalities, and the funeral arrangements, and whatever else needs to be done?'

'Yes. He said to leave everything to him.' She paused and frowned. 'He also suggested I should stay here with you until after the funeral.'

'I hope you will. In fact I assumed you would. You can't go back home on your own.'

'If you're sure...'

'Quite sure. Now sit down and I'll make us some toast. Even if you're not hungry you need to eat something, for the baby as well as yourself.'

Obediently Bobbi got up and put on the robe Erin handed her, and came out and sat down at the table. When the toast was ready she spread a slice with butter and marmalade, and ate the whole slice, although Erin could see she had difficulty swallowing past her grief.

'You must have been awake most of the night worrying, so why don't you go and have a lie down now, and see if you can drop off for while?' Erin suggested when Bobbi pushed her empty plate away.

'Yes, I suppose I should,' Bobbi agreed. 'Tasha is quite active this morning. Maybe if I lie down she'll decide to have a sleep instead of kicking me.'

'Tasha?' Erin asked with a smile. 'Is that what you're going to call her?'

'Yes.' Bobbi gave a weak smile. 'Natasha is what we'd picked out for her, after his mother, and when we talked about her we always called her Tasha.' Her eyes filled. She blinked and brushed her hand impatiently at the tears.

Erin's heart ached for her. She put her hand on Bobbi's arm and squeezed it gently. 'Do you want me to call your doctor for you? He might give you something to make you feel a bit more settled.'

'Not at the moment. But I will go and have a bit of a rest now, and later I'll go home and collect a few things.'

'I'll drive you when you're ready.'

As Bobbi thanked her and left the room, Erin cleared away the breakfast dishes and tidied up. She had just finished putting the plates in the dishwasher when her phone rang. Her pulses beat a little faster when she saw it was Aden calling.

'Good morning Erin.' He announced himself in a brisk voice. 'Thank you for a pleasant evening last night. I hope your friend has good news about her husband by now.'

'Unfortunately, no.' Erin related Bobbi's news.

'I'm sorry to hear that.' After a brief pause, Aden continued in an efficient voice. 'Perhaps this is not a good time but I want to let you know I've made enquiries regarding raising some finance should you need it for the business, and it won't be a problem. Have you heard anything further regarding the lease?'

'No.'

'Then we'll leave it that if you need extra money, you'll let me know. It can be arranged at short notice, so there's no need for you to worry about being short of money to complete your plans. And now I'll let you return to your friend. Please offer her my condolences.'

'Thank you, I will. And thank you for finding out

about the finance for me.'

'Just part of the service,' he replied stiffly.

As the call ended Erin held the phone in her hand, staring down at it. A cold chill settled over her. Aden obviously regretted his impulsive behaviour of the previous night. Had he merely been trying to get her into bed, and, after his plans were interrupted, decided not to press his attentions any further? Whatever the reason he had sounded, if not actually unfriendly, then certainly focused solely on business. She slipped the phone slowly into the pocket of her jeans. Well, if that was the way he wanted it, so be it. She tightened her lips.

She certainly didn't need the complication of a relationship. Her focus was to get her business up and running, and now that she knew she could raise some money if she needed it there was nothing to stop her from continuing with her planning.

CHAPTER TWENTY FIVE

Erin was sitting at the desk in the small room, that she now regarded as her office, with colour cards and swatches spread out in front of her, when a pounding on the front door brought her to her feet. She hurried up the hall.

When she opened the door she was astounded to see Giles standing there, a scowl darkening his face.

'Ha! So this is where you're holed up, is it? 'He shouldered his way in as Erin tried to shut the door in his face. 'A bit of a comedown for you after Point Piper, isn't it?'

He pushed Erin aside as she tried to stop him from striding down the hall and into the lounge. As he stood raking the room with his gaze, his lip curled. 'Huh! Cheap and nasty.' He turned to face Erin, his stance menacing.

A cold knot of fear coiled inside her, but she stood resolute as he stood glowering down at her. 'How dare you come barging into my home?' She managed to keep her voice firm. 'What are you doing here, anyway?'

'I've come to take you home where you belong.'

'Forget it! I told you, I've left you. Our marriage is over. This is my home now.'

'I'm the one who decides when our marriage is over, and I haven't decided that yet.'

'Give up. I'm not coming back. Now or ever.'

His face tightened, but his voice became conciliatory. 'Now don't be stupid, Erin. What do you want? Do you want me to swear to be faithful to you?' He spread his hands. 'I'll do that. No sweat. You know you're the only one who means anything to me. The rest is only playing games.'

'I don't want any promises from you. It would make no difference to me.'

He took the few steps between them so that he was standing full on, his face inches from hers.

Erin's palms were sweating. He was in her space, and she longed to step back, but she wouldn't give ground.

'And what's this I hear about you having some damn fool idea of starting a business?' His tone was scathing. 'You! In a business. That's a laugh.' His lip curled. 'You'd go broke in the first month.'

'Perhaps,' she snapped. 'We'll just have to wait and see, won't we?'

'Selling old rags, I hear,' he retorted contemptuously. 'Well, I'll not have my name associated with such a scummy scheme. So you'd better forget about it. If you don't you'll be sorry.'

'Are you threatening me?'

'You could call it that I suppose.' His eyes narrowed. 'Now let's cut out playing games. I want you home, and I want my papers that you took with you when you made your grand gesture of leaving. And I always get what I want, one way or another.'

'More threats, I see.'

'Call it that if you like.' Suddenly he leant forward, grabbed her wrist, spun her around, and twisted her arm up behind her.

Erin gasped as pain knifed through her shoulder.

'You'd better do as I say,' he hissed in her ear. 'Or it will be the worse for you. Is that clear?'

The pain was so severe Erin was incapable of

replying.

'Do I make myself clear?' he repeated. He jerked her arm up a little further.

A scream was forced up from some place inside her, and she was hardly aware of it as her legs buckled and her head swam.

It was loud enough to make him let go of her wrist, and seconds later the door burst open and Bobbi rushed into the room.

'What's going on?' she demanded, her voice shrill. 'Giles! What are you doing? Leave Erin alone!'

Giles stepped back, his face registering his surprise. 'Bobbi! What are you doing here? You should be home mourning for your husband.'

'Never mind that. What have you done to Erin?'

'I'm doing what any husband would do. Trying to make her forget this foolishness. To see sense and return to where she belongs. Home with me.'

'I think you have to accept that Erin doesn't want to be with you any longer, Giles.'

'That's for me to say.' His voice took on a menacing note. 'And I think you might soon have more things to think about than what's happening to Erin. Laurence has died at a very inconvenient time, for me and for others as well, and it could have repercussions for you, as well as others.'

'What do you mean?'

'You'll find out soon enough.' He swung around to face Erin again. 'And as for you, Erin, you'd better consider what I'm saying. I want you home, and I want you to forget this nonsense of starting a business. And most emphatically I want my papers you've stolen. Including my Phoebus shares, and other personal papers belonging to me.'

'I took only what belongs to me. The Phoebus shares are mine. You gave them to me, and they're in my name.'

'That was simply a business arrangement. Besides, they can't be sold without my authority. Anyway, enough of this. I expect you both to return to your own homes...' he broke off and looked from one to the other with narrowed eyes. 'That is, unless you're planning on shacking up together. Is that what this is? Maybe there's more to it than there seems.'

Bobbi stared at him, her mouth open with shock.

Even with her pain – it felt as if her shoulder was broken – Erin took the step between them, raised her good arm and slapped him across the cheek. He lifted his arm and she thought he was going to strike her back, but he let it fall again.

'That's a filthy thing to say, and you know it. Bobbi is here grieving for the husband she's lost only a few hours ago. Now get out. Get out of here, and don't ever come back. The next time I see you I want it to be in the divorce court.'

'There'll be no divorce until I say so. And don't think you're going to profit from it. I'll make sure you never get a penny from me.' He turned and strode up the hall. At the front door he stopped and turned. 'And don't forget those papers, or you'll be sorry. I want them back, and I intend to have them. One way or another.'

With that he opened the door and left. He slammed the door behind him.

As soon as he left Erin gave in to the pain and sank onto a chair, rubbing her shoulder.

Bobbi sat opposite her, her face pale. 'That bastard! He hurt you, didn't he? Before I came in. I heard you scream, that's why I came running. What did he do?'

Erin related what had happened and Bobbi sat back, shaking her head.

'Thank goodness I was in the house, or who knows what injury he might have caused you. He's dangerous, Erin. He could hurt you even worse than this. You should take out a restraining order against him.'

'I certainly don't feel as safe here as I did before. And I think I'd better go and see my doctor, my shoulder feels bad.'

Bobbi picked up her phone. 'Here,' she said, handing it to her, 'ring now and make an appointment.'

By the time Erin saw Dr Irene a couple of hours later, her wrist had turned black with bruises, but the doctor's examination confirmed nothing was broken in her shoulder.

'I'll give you a prescription for a liniment to rub into the shoulder muscles, and for pain killers to take as you need them, but I think it'll settle down in a few days.' She sat back at her desk. 'Now, what to do about your husband? I've taken the photos for your file, again, and described these injuries. And it's good you have a witness this time. You're building up quite a case against him. Your friend's suggestion to take out a restraining order is not silly, you know. Unfortunately, it's not always effective. I've seen many cases where it's been ignored, and further serious injury inflicted on the woman. Do you want me to see if I can find a place for you in a shelter for a while?'

Erin shook her head. 'No. Save that for someone who needs it more than me. I'm going to have chains put on the doors so I don't have to open them fully when someone's there.'

'Good. And you should probably have a personal alarm as well. Make sure you contact your lawyer, and let him know of this further attack. It's important that he knows about it.'

'Thank you Irene, I'll do that.'

Erin waited until she was in her car to ring Aden.

'Hello Erin, what can I do for you?' he asked in a business-like voice.

When Erin had finished telling him about the visit he was silent for a moment, and when he replied his voice was full of concern. 'It's fortunate that your friend was with you this morning. She's going to stay for a few days, isn't she?'

'Yes.'

'Good. He's not likely to try anything again while she's with you, but it's important that you have good security. I'm going to talk to Steve Waterman about it and I'll see that he fixes security chains to your doors immediately. I'll have him call you, and make a time to suit you.'

'Thank you Aden. That's good of you.'

'Not at all.' He paused for a second, before continuing in a jocular voice. 'I can't have anything happening to my favourite client, can I?'

And Erin was left wondering what exactly that meant.

CHAPTER TWENTY SIX

Steve Waterman arrived shortly after with chains for the two outer doors, and locks for the windows. It took him only a short time to fix them all securely in place, and Erin felt much safer once he had completed the job.

Erin drove Bobbi home later that day to collect what she would need for a few day's stay. As they entered the front door Bobbi's housekeeper came bustling out to meet them.

'Oh Mrs Harvey, I'm so pleased to see you. We were all so worried about poor Mr Harvey, and so shocked to hear the news. He was a wonderful man and we're all very sad.' She took a tissue from her pocket and dabbed at her eyes. 'And I want you to know that if there's anything I can do for you, or any of the staff can do, you only have to let me know.'

'Thank you, Mrs Palfrey, I know I can count on you. I'm going to stay with Mrs Brightman until after the funeral, but I'll make sure you know the funeral arrangements, and I'll keep you in touch with what's happening. I haven't had time to come to terms with it myself yet.'

'Yes, of course.' Mrs Palfrey nodded. 'Mr Simpson is here. He arrived about an hour ago, and he's in Mr Harvey's study.'

'Bob Simpson? What's he doing here?' Bobbi frowned.

'I don't know. He just came in and said he needs to go through Mr Harvey's papers, he said he needed to find some important documents. I didn't know what to do. I know that he's Mr Harvey's lawyer. I hope I did right to let him in, but I couldn't very well stop him.'

'No, of course not. I'll go and see what he's up to.' Bobbi turned to Erin. 'Come with me. We'll go and see what he's after.'

Bobbi led the way up the stairs and down a carpeted passage, and when she reached the door at the end she opened it and went in, with Erin following closely behind her.

A man stood by a filing cabinet on the opposite wall. He was in the act of removing a file from an open drawer, and he spun around as they entered. A stack of files were piled on one side of a desk nearby, and he dropped the file he was holding on to the pile.

Bob Simpson was a rotund, self-important-looking man in his fifties. He had fair hair that was going bald on top, which he tried to disguise by growing the hair longer on the side and combing it over. The coat of his suit was draped across the back of a chair and his shirt cuffs were folded back.

'What do you think you're doing...' he started to say, scowling, but he stopped short when he saw the two women.

'Bobbi,' he exclaimed. 'And Erin Brightman. What are you two doing here?'

'I was just about to ask you the same question,' Bobbi retorted.

'I'm looking for some papers I need. I know they have to be here somewhere.'

'What sort of papers are so important that you need to have them only hours after Laurence has died?'

'They're to do with a deal that Laurence was

involved in, and I need them now.'

'I know you handled Laurence's affairs, but I think it would show more respect for him if you waited until at least after the funeral to go through his things.'

Simpson's face reddened. 'This is important. I need them now.'

'Unless it's a matter of life and death, I'd like you to leave it until Laurence has been laid to rest.'

He looked as if he was going to argue with her, but after a few seconds he shrugged, adjusted his cuffs, stepped over to the chair and picked up his coat. 'Whatever you say,' he told her coldly as he slipped it on, 'but at least make sure no-one else has access to this room before me.'

'What is it that's so important?'

'Never you mind. But you'd better come to my office after the funeral. You could be in for an unpleasant surprise, I'm afraid. Laurence's business affairs haven't been going too well lately. It's most unfortunate he's passed away at this time. It could have serious repercussions.'

'What do you mean?'

'You'll find out soon enough,' he told her curtly. 'I'll have my secretary email you the funeral arrangements. Remember, don't let anyone else in here before me.' With that he nodded to them both, his lips set in a straight line. 'Good day now.'

After he left the room Bobbi's face crumpled. 'Horrible man,' she said, her voice thick. 'I've never liked him. He always sucked up to Laurence, but I always thought he was a slime.'

Erin took her hand, seeing tears close to the surface.

'Never mind about him, he's a pig. Let's get your things and go, shall we?'

'Yes.' Bobbi sniffed. 'I don't want to stay here any longer than I have to. The place is empty now without Laurence. In fact, I don't know how I'm going to ever live here again; it's so big... and...lonely. '

As they left the study she locked the door behind them and put the key in her purse. 'Now no-one else can get in.'

In Bobbi's room Erin helped her to pack sufficient clothes for a few days and carried the case down the stairs for her. On the way out Bobbi spoke a few words to the housekeeper, telling her she would keep in touch, and to ring her if she needed to, and instructing her not to let anyone else into the house. She added that she wasn't sure when she'd be back, but she would let her know.

It wasn't until they were home and sitting outside under the shade of the frangipani tree, with glasses in front of them, that Erin broached the subject on her mind.

It was late afternoon, and the sun still shone. The drone of the bees flitting among the roses, and the faint hum of distant traffic, were the only sounds to be heard, until a family of lorikeets flew in to settle in the hibiscus tree, and their gossiping disturbed the peace.

'It's very strange,' Erin said slowly, after the birds had flown on and their raucous cries grew faint. She twisted her wineglass on the table top. 'Bob Simpson used the same words Giles did. He said Laurence's passing could have serious repercussions, the same words Giles used. I wonder what they both meant.'

'I think Giles and Laurence, and probably Simpson

too, were involved with some other guys in a big deal of some kind. I overheard Laurence talking to Giles about it once.'

'Oh.' A frown wrinkled Erin's forehead. 'What sort of deal? Do you know?'

'Not really. I think it had something to do with a development of some kind, but I didn't take much notice. Laurence didn't talk to me about his business.'

'Same as Giles.' Erin's lips twisted. 'I wasn't considered intelligent enough to understand.'

'Me neither.' Bobbi gave a slight giggle, and Erin was pleased at the spark of light-heartedness from her. It seemed Bob Simpson's words had given her something else to think about as well as her grief. 'I wonder if they would've thought we weren't so dumb if they'd known what we were up to with *Serendipity*?'

Erin grinned. 'I'm sure it would have been a shock to them, and I doubt they'd have been amused, but I suspect it would've shaken them out of their complacency about us.'

'It's just as well they didn't find out. They'd have stopped us for sure.' Bobbi took a long swallow of her orange juice. 'The only bright spots in my future are Tasha and the fact that now there's nothing to stop me taking an active part in *Serendipity,* as we planned.'

'But you'll have no need to do anything now. You'll be a wealthy woman in your own right.'

'I suppose so, but that won't make any difference.' She shook her head. 'No, it's what I always wanted to do, for us to do *Serendipity* together. Besides, whatever Laurence has left I'll want to be mostly for Tasha. I know he set up a trust fund for her when we knew she was going to be a girl, but I have no idea of whatever else there will be. But whatever, I'll want us to work together.'

'I'll be very happy if that happens, but I won't hold you to anything you say now. It's too soon for you to be making any plans for the future, except to plan for Tasha's arrival.'

Bobbi rubbed her baby bump, smiling. 'Yes, it won't be long now. She's very active; I think she's anxious to be born. Maybe she can tell how much I want to hold her, and cuddle her.'

'I'm sure she can.'

Bobbi bit her lip. 'It' so unjust that Laurence won't get to hold her, but I'm trying hard not to be too depressed, because I don't think it's good for her, for me to be miserable and crying all the time.' She drew a deep breath, and blinked several times. 'I've been thinking about names,' she continued, her voice brighter. 'We'd already chosen Natasha, and that's what she'll be, but I'd like her to have Laurence's name too, but I can't call a girl Natasha Laurence, can I? So I'm thinking of Lori as a second name for her. It's not quite the same, but then she'll always know she was named after her father. What do you think?'

Erin spoke past the lump in throat as she leant over and squeezed her friend's hand. 'I think it's lovely. And Laurence would be pleased.'

Bobbi gave a quavery smile as she returned the pressure of Erin's hand. 'Thank you.'

They sat there in the deepening dusk discussing the arrangements already made for Tasha's arrival, both being determinedly bright and cheerful, and it was decided that Bobbi would again come to stay with Erin once the baby was born, even if she wanted to go home for a while beforehand.

CHAPTER TWENTY SEVEN

Walter Tremayne was an early-morning visitor the next day, waiting outside the front door with a document in his hand and a smile on his face. Erin undid the chain and invited him in, leading the way down to the lounge room.

'Well now, at long last I can give you good news. Our long-lost owner has finally returned home. Apparently he got over his spat with his partner and all's well again. He rang me last night and I went straight round to see him. He's signed the lease and here's your copy.' He handed the document to Erin. 'Now you can move in as soon as you wish.'

'Thank heavens for that. I was beginning to think I'd have to look elsewhere.'

'Well, I'm pleased you didn't have to start doing that. And I'm sure you'll make something special of it. It really is a unique space.'

'I have big plans for it.' Erin smiled as she escorted him to the door.

As she returned from showing him out Bobbi came in from the kitchen. She looked far more composed than she had last night.

'I couldn't help overhearing. Isn't that great news?'

'It certainly is. Now the lease on the shop is signed I can go ahead with the plans to get *Serendipity* up and running.'

'We can go ahead, you mean, partner. Don't leave me out. And I'm dying to see the shop.'

'So you're still sure you want to go ahead with it? Even though you won't need the money now?'

'Yes, more than ever. That's if you still want me.'

Erin realised that talking and thinking about *Serendipity* was helping Bobbi to overcome her grief, so she decided that her phone call to Aden to tell him about the lease could wait until later, while she gave her time to Bobbi.

'Yes, of course I do. In that case, let's get over to the shop and have a look.'

'It's wonderful.' Bobbi was standing at the top of the steps to the mezzanine, turning slowly around and taking in the layout. 'What a stroke of luck to find something so perfect.'

'Yes, and this is what I thought we could do with it. See what you think.' Erin took out the plans she'd drawn up from Aden's measurements and spread them out for Bobbi look at.

They spent the rest of the morning walking around the entire space, with Erin explaining her ideas, and Bobbi throwing in suggestions of her own from time to time.

Erin found herself becoming excited all over again, now that she had Bobbi to share it with, and Bobbi's face lost its strain as they tossed ideas around from one to the other.

'So what's the first move?' Bobbi asked as they sat over coffee and a sandwich at the coffee shop on the corner of the arcade a little later.

'The shop fitters. I already have prices and I've made a choice. John Stevens. He's not the cheapest but I think he's the best. I hope he can start immediately. I'll call him right away.'

Her phone call confirmed that John Stevens would

arrive the next day to commence work.

After lunch they returned to the house and Erin took out the swatches of silky fabric that she'd brought back from Spotlight, and the colour cards. They pored over the fabrics, both feeling the textures and the weights, and narrowed the choice down to three of the samples. By mid-afternoon they had settled on a pale oyster silk fabric that showed just a hint of pink as it moved, and a warm white colour for the walls.

'I thought we'd have the padded chairs covered in a patterned tapestry, and coloured scatter cushions,' Erin explained. 'And the clothes themselves will add an extra splash of colour. What do you think?'

'I think it will all look wonderful,' Bobbi enthused. 'I'm anxious for us to get started.' At that moment her phone rang. She grimaced when she saw the name of the caller. 'Bob Simpson.' She sighed as she pressed the button. She frowned as she listened to what was being said. 'Thanks, I'll see you then,' she said, and ended the call.

'The funeral is tomorrow morning, and he needs to see me urgently after it's over.'

'Would you like me to come with you?'

'Oh yes, would you?'

'Of course. I intend coming to the funeral, anyway. But I'm not sure if he'll want me present when he discusses business with you.'

'I'll tell him I want you there.'

A large crowd attended the funeral. Bobbi held Erin's hand firmly through the service and while the casket was lowered for cremation. They stood together while refreshments were being served in the room next to the chapel, and while Bobbi received condolences from Laurence's friends, many of whom she knew only slightly. When Giles came up, he bent and kissed Bobbi on the cheek.

'I'm terribly sorry, Bobbi,' he told her. 'If I can be of any help, please let me know.' He turned to Erin. 'Perhaps you should bring Bobbi back to our house now. We could help her to come to terms with her loss.'

'I'll be taking her back to my place until she's ready to return to her own home. There is no 'our house'. I thought I'd made that quite clear.'

Giles glared at her through narrowed eyes. 'I'm sure you'll get over your little huff shortly, my dear. I wouldn't want you to suffer any more, you know.' With that he turned and marched away.

'I wonder what he meant by that?' Bobbi's voice was worried.

Erin shrugged. 'I can't believe he thinks he can frighten me into returning. Forget about it for now.'

When it was all over Erin drove them back to the Chatswood house, and insisted Bobbi put her feet up on the sofa while she made coffee. She carried it in to the lounge room with a plate of biscuits.

'I think I've only now been able to accept that Laurence is finally gone,' Bobbi said as she nibbled at a biscuit. 'You know, as well as being my husband, he was almost like a father figure to me. I married him when I was very young. I was flattered by all his attention, and the presents he gave me. I was swept off my feet and infatuated with him, but once we were married he treated me like a Barbie doll, and I realised I was more like a plaything to him than a wife. It was so frustrating. He never talked to me about his business, or let me make a decision for myself. Except about my clothes, of course.'

Bobbi broke off to take several gulps of coffee before continuing. 'It was only when I became pregnant that he started to treat me like a real wife, and that was when I came to really love him. But even then he fussed over me, and pampered me, and made decisions for me. It was as if he thought I wasn't capable of doing anything for myself. And I let him do it because it pleased him. And we were truly happy then. But at the back of my mind was always the feeling that he indulged me like a favourite daughter. And I kept hoping that once Tasha was born, and he saw that I was capable of looking after a baby, his attitude would change.' She sighed. 'And now I'll never know.'

'I'm sure he was proud of you, and once Tasha was born he would've realised you were a capable mother.' Erin took her empty cup. 'And now you should try to have a little rest before we go to see Bob Simpson.'

When they arrived at Simpson's office it was obvious he wasn't pleased to see Erin, and it was only Bobbi's insistence that she remain that made him agree to speak to them both.

'What I discuss in this office is private and confidential,' he growled, 'and it's in your interest that it's not discussed with anyone else,' he told Bobbi.

'Now, firstly to the will. Laurence set up a trust fund for his expected daughter a few weeks ago. That is all finalised and can't be touched. And all his other assets he left to you, Bobbi. But I'm afraid that his finances were stretched very thin at the time of his death. In fact, he'd over-extended himself.' He leant across the desk towards them, pursing his lips. 'Of course, had he not had that heart attack, all would have been well. He would have dealt himself out of it. But as it stands now there'll only be a relatively modest sum left for you, I'm afraid.'

Bobbi frowned. 'But I don't understand. What's happened to the money?'

'He made a few decisions recently that haven't turned out too well. But mainly, he and some other business men recently formed a consortium regarding a large-scale project, and they all pledged a certain sum of money. A very large sum of money. I'm afraid that can't be reversed, even though Laurence is no longer with us, but ultimately it will benefit his estate, which goes to you. But to fulfill his part in the deal many of his securities will have to be liquidated.'

Bobbi frowned as they left his office. 'I don't trust that man. I know that he and Laurence were thick as thieves, and he wouldn't have been able to put anything over him, but I think that now I'm alone he'll be out to feather his own nest, and bugger Bobbi and the baby.'

'Perhaps you need your own lawyer, someone who has no connection to any of them, and will have your interests at heart.'

'Yes, you're right, but I don't know any lawyers. How about the one that's handling your affairs. You're happy with him, aren't you?'

'Yes, he's been very helpful. I have one of his cards here.' She opened her purse and fumbled inside, then pulled out a card and handed it to Bobbi. 'Here you are. If you decide you want to see him just ring that number and make an appointment.'

Bobbi took the card. 'Aden Marlowe,' she read. 'Yes. I'm going to ring and make an appointment. The sooner I don't have to deal with that sleaze myself, the happier I'll be.'

Pulling out her phone she made the call, and Erin heard her arrange an appointment for later that day.

CHAPTER TWENTY EIGHT

The following small item appeared on page five of the Sydney Morning Herald in a Parliamentary report.

At question time in Parliament today the member for Barraclough, Grant O'Brien, put the following question to the minister for planning, James Beck.

'Minister, can you confirm that a planning permit has been issued for a proposed development in Section 62 of Crown Land within the Council jurisdiction of Cooralinga in NSW?'

The Minister replied, 'I am unaware of this specific planning permit however I will ascertain the facts and report back.'

Bobbi decided to return to her own home for a while to do some sorting out, so Erin drove alone back to Chatswood. Leaving her car in the carport she opened the front door and walked down the hall.

As she stepped into the lounge she had a fleeting glimpse of a man's figure before she was grabbed from behind. A heavy hand clamped over her mouth, cutting off her scream. Her heart thumped with terror as an arm encircled her waist and pulled her back against a solid figure behind her. She tried to twist free, but her arms were pinned to her sides.

'Don't scream or you'll be sorry,' a voice rasped in her ear. 'You just do as you're told and we won't have to hurt you.'

She struggled against the arms holding her, her blood pounding, but the hold was too strong. She kicked out behind her and felt her heel connect.

'Ow! You bloody bitch, that hurt,' snarled the rough voice behind her. His hold slackened slightly, and she pulled hard. But before she could break free another figure, dressed in black and wearing a balaclava, appeared from the dining room. He grasped her arms roughly, his fingers digging into her arms. She was immobilised again.

'Giving you trouble, is she?'

'Yes, the bitch. We'd better tie her up.'

'Yes, we might have to. But we don't want to hurt her. Unless we have to.' His voice was menacing. 'So what do you think, lady? If we let you go, will you stand nice and quiet while we ask you some questions, or will I have to use these?' He reached into his pocket and pulled out a length of rope and a roll of duct tape. 'One squawk out of you and I'll tape up your mouth, and you wouldn't like that. So if my friend let's you go, will you stand nice and quiet?'

Erin nodded, trembling. The arms dropped away from her, and she turned to confront her assailant, only to find he too was dressed in black and wore a balaclava. She rubbed her arms where his fingers had dug in, and fear kept her still. Even through her panic Erin saw that drawers had been pulled out of cupboards and the contents scattered over the floor of the room. Were they burglars she'd disturbed, or were they looking for something?

'What do you want? I don't have anything valuable here.'

'You have something belonging to our boss, and he wants it back,' the taller man said.

'So my husband sent you?' Her pulses were still racing.

'We don't know who your husband is, and we

don't care. Our boss is a powerful man who's used to getting what he wants. And he wants some papers you've got, that belong to him.'

'I don't have anything that doesn't belong to me. And anyway, my papers aren't here.'

'She's lying,' said the other man raising his arm as if to strike her, and taking a step towards her.

Erin took a step back, lifting her arms to protect herself, but the other one raised his hand.

'No rough stuff,' he admonished.

'Huh,' he grunted, but he dropped his arm and stayed where he was.

'So where are they, then?'

'They're with my lawyer. But there was nothing that doesn't belong to me.'

His eyes narrowed behind the slits in the balaclava. 'Well, they're not in this house. I've made sure of that. Check her bag,' he instructed his companion, 'maybe she carries them with her.'

The other one picked up her bag from the floor, where it had fallen when he grabbed her, opened, it and rifled through its contents.

'Nah. Just the usual women's trash,' he snarled through his mask. He tossed the bag back on to the floor.

'The boss won't be happy, and if he finds out you've been lying to us it'll be the worse for you, believe me. He's not known for being gentle with those that cross him. We're going now, but we're going to have to tie you up first, so you can't go using that phone the minute we step out the door.'

The first assailant grabbed Erin's hands and yanked her arms behind her, holding them tight, while the other bound them together with duct tape. Then he propelled her across the room, pushed her down onto a chair, and taped her legs together.

Erin was too frightened to resist, even when he wadded up a piece of cloth and stuffed it in her mouth, then tied another piece over it to keep it in place.

'There, that won't hurt you, but it'll keep you still and quiet for long enough. And I hope we don't find you've been telling us porkies, and that we have to pay you another visit,' the tall one threatened as he headed for the door.

His accomplice finished tying the knot at the back of her head, stood back and gazed at her. Then he suddenly raised his hand and slapped her cheek. Hard. Hard enough to knock her head to one side. Pain seared through her head and brought tears to her eyes. She whimpered through the gag.

'That's for kicking me.'

'Now, now, you didn't have to do that.' The tall one smirked. 'That really wasn't very nice of you.'

They sauntered up the hall, chuckling.

The door banged.

Erin's head was ringing. Her face hurt, and the gag made her choke. Fear and pain made her nauseated, and she suddenly thought that if she vomited she could choke on the vomit. She began to panic. How was she to get free? She didn't know when Bobbi would be back. There was no-one else to come by. No-one to come and find her. She could stay here tied up like this until she died.

Her breath came faster. Her head began to swim. She tried to scream but the sound was muffled by the gag. Frantically she tugged at her hands, trying to pull them apart. But all that happened was that the tape cut into her wrists.

Her panic rose. Struggling to her feet she managed to stand, but with her ankles taped together she fell heavily sideways on to the floor. The shock of the fall seemed somehow to clear her mind of the terrifying thoughts racing through it. As she lay there, breathing heavily, she forced herself to think calmly.

Somehow she needed to free herself. Perhaps if she could reach the dining room she might find a knife and cut her hands free. She rolled over on to her back but, with her hands pulled behind her, the position was painful. She rolled back on to her side. By pulling up her knees, and pushing down with her feet, she inched her way along the floor. It was slow, and hard going, and she had to stop every few metres to rest.

When she finally reached the dining room she saw the drawers had been pulled out and the contents strewn around. Her hopes rose, for the cutlery was scattered about on the floor. She wriggled across to where a steak knife lay, and by squirming about she was able to feel around with her fingers behind her until she could grasp it by the handle. Clumsily she turned it around, and manoeuvred it until the blade was pointing upwards between her wrists, resting against the tape.

Then she used her fingers to push the knife up and down, sawing at the tape. It was slow and difficult work. Her fingers became numb with the effort and she had to stop and rest several times until feeling came back into them. At one stage she dropped the knife, and had to scrabble with her fingers to pick it up once more and start again. The point of the knife bit into her flesh. But finally the last shred of tape gave way. Her hands were free.

Rolling on to her back she sat up. Her fingers were stiff and numb, and it took a few minutes before she could uncurl them and get them to work again. She rubbed her chafed wrists, and moved her arms around for a bit to ease the pain of the stretched muscles. Then she untied the knot at the back of her head with clumsy fingers and let the gag fall away from her parched mouth and tongue. She stretched her mouth wide and sucked in deep breaths. Bending over she cut the tape at her ankles. Pulling herself up with the aid of a chair-back she managed to stand. After a moment she limped her way stiffly to the kitchen, filled a glass with water from the kitchen tap and drank it thirstily.

She washed off the blood seeping from her wrist where the knife had gouged her flesh. Tearing off a paper towel she held it firmly against the cut to staunch the blood while she hobbled to the bathroom and found a Band-Aid for it. When she checked her face in the mirror she saw a red welt across one cheek where she had been hit, and her face had puffed up under the eye.

She made her way through the kitchen and gazed helplessly at the open back door. The lock was broken. The security chain had been cut in the middle and the two sides dangled from their fittings.

Making her way outside she spent a few minutes stretching her cramped muscles. When the pain eased she sat in a chair and gazed around the garden. Her pulses slowed, but she still quaked inside. Drinking in the peace and quiet helped her to calm down, and she thought back over what had happened.

Surely Giles wouldn't go to such lengths to get the

papers. But if not Giles, then who? And which papers were so important? And why?

CHAPTER TWENTY NINE

Erin rested for a while with an ice-pack on her face, then she went from room to room. What a mess. She started to pick up things from the floor, but stopped. She should probably call the police.

Would they be able to find the men? How could she identify them? She hadn't been able to see their faces. Would they have left fingerprints? That's what the police looked for, wasn't it? She cast her mind back. Her scalp crawled as her mind replayed the horrifying episode. Two figures. She tried to see them again. Yes, they had worn gloves. Black, like the rest of their clothing. So there would be no fingerprints. What else could she remember about them? The one who'd grabbed her first was of medium height, slim. He'd exuded menace, even with his face covered. The other guy, not quite so scary, was taller and thick-set. He'd seemed older.

She needed to talk to Aden. He would know what to do. Retrieving her phone from her purse she dialled his number.

'Are you hurt?' his worried voice asked, after she told him the story.

'I'm a bit bruised and shaky but otherwise I'm okay.'

'I want you to call the police immediately and report what's happened. I'll be with you as fast as I can make it through the traffic.'

'But don't you have clients to see? I can manage...'

'Leave that to me. You just call the police. I'll see you soon.'

As soon as their call ended she phoned the police, and was told that someone would be with her as soon as possible, and to leave everything as it was.

Two police officers arrived shortly after, and, while one went from room to room checking the extent of the damage, the other took notes as she related what had happened.

'What can you tell us about these men?' he asked.

'Not much, I'm afraid. They both wore dark clothes and gloves and their faces were covered.' Erin went on to describe them as much as she could.

'How about their voices?'

'Their voices were muffled a bit by the balaclavas, but the tall one was definitely Australian, and the other one had an accent.'

'What sort of accent?'

'European, I'd say, not Asian. I can't do much better than that.'

'And you say you don't know what they were looking for?'

'No. They said I had papers belonging to their boss but I don't understand what they were talking about.'

'But you think they were referring to papers you took when you left your husband?'

'I can't think what else it could be.'

'Do you think your husband sent them?'

'I can't imagine he'd go to such extremes, but I'm not sure.'

'Do you know who else might be interested in them?'

'No, I have no idea.'

After they had all the information Erin was able to give them they left, telling her they would be in touch again.

Erin set about clearing up the mess the intruders had left. While she was picking up the cutlery from the dining room floor she heard Aden's car pull into the driveway.

She greeted him at the door, and led the way down the hall to the lounge room. Here he put his hands on her shoulders and turned her around to face him, his face tense.

'Let me look at you.'

He lifted his hand and touched her cheek, and traced a finger over the puffiness beneath her eyes. His face hardened.

'The bastards!' His voice was rough. 'They've hurt you badly.'

He reached for her hands and turned them over, examining the chafe marks on her wrists. He lifted each one in turn and kissed it.

His lips burnt into Erin's skin. Her heart hammered. She swallowed before giving a shaky laugh. 'It will all heal. I'm probably lucky they didn't do anything worse.'

'I'd like to get my hands on them.' Aden's voice was harsh, his face grim. 'But I guess the best we can hope for is that the police will catch them.' He gathered her into him arms. 'Oh Erin, Erin. I hate to see you hurt like this.'

Slow warmth seeped through Erin as she rested her head on his chest. Her pulses quickened as she caught a faint whiff of his cologne and felt the heat of his body, the strength of his muscular frame.

He lifted a hand and began to stroke her hair. 'Poor little baby,' he murmured softly. His fingers smoothed her hair, gently.

She felt his heart beating rapidly through the thin fabric of his shirt.

With a quick intake of breath his hand stilled. He dropped his arms and stepped back.

Erin felt as if she had been cut adrift, and took a faltering step towards him.

He steadied her with a hand on her shoulder. He put his other hand under her chin and tilted her head back. With a hoarse groan he pulled her to him.

Her arms crept around his neck. Her body melted into his. She wanted to stay there forever. His lips came down on hers and they kissed, slowly, lingeringly. Then his lips left hers and wandered down her throat, dropping little kisses. He lifted her hair to kiss the nape of her neck. His lips found her ear, and he nibbled gently.

Erin's pulse went wild. Heat flashed through her body.

His voice was a whisper...

'The first time you came into my office I knew you would be important to me. I love you, Erin.'

Erin's heart-strings zinged. He loved her! Before she could do more than catch her breath and murmur that she loved him too, he was kissing her again. Deeply. Passionately. As she kissed him back her heart soared, her senses swimming.

He pulled back, took her by the hand and led her to the bedroom. He stood by the bed, his gaze never leaving hers.

Watching his face, she kicked off her sandals.

His eyes were like molten toffee as he pulled her close. His fingers fumbled for the zipper at her back, and her dress pooled at her feet.

She undid the buttons on his shirt, slowly, one at a

time, her eyes never leaving his. When she was done she removed it, and dropped it to join her dress on the floor.

Easing her down on to the bed Aden undid her bra. It joined their other clothes. She wriggled free of her panties as he slipped off the rest of his clothes. His eyes never left hers.

He lay down and pulled her close. Their lips were together as they caressed each other.

And when they came together it was like nothing Erin had ever known.

He took his time, slowly, lovingly, seeking to pleasure her, murmuring words of love. When they finally moved as one, in perfect harmony, he didn't try to hurry her. Higher and higher she soared, until she tipped over the precipice, calling his name.

He cried out, and then they were both lying tangled together. And Erin had never known such bliss as they relaxed in each other's arms.

It was much later, the sun gone and the moon in its place, when Aden pressed his lips to her hair and drew away. He rested on his elbow and looked down at her.

'I hate to leave you, but I must go, my love,' he told her. He bent his head to kiss her, long and lingeringly. 'We need to talk, but not right now. There's something I must do first.'

'Mmm,' Erin murmured sleepily.

He pulled up the sheet to cover her before leaving the bed. She watched him dress, not wanting him to go, but unwilling to press him to stay.

He sat on the edge of the bed and leant over to

give her another kiss. 'I'll see you soon. Go back to sleep.'

Moments later Erin heard his car drive away. She pulled up the bedclothes and settled back. His leaving left a little hole in her happiness but she consoled herself with the thought that she would see him again soon, and she drifted back into the mists of sweet contentment.

CHAPTER THIRTY

The next morning Erin woke early. She couldn't keep the smile from her face as she slipped from the bed and moved across to the window. Stretching, she looked out on this perfect day where the sun shone in a dome of azure sky and a few wisps of cloud floated lazily. Erin was in love, truly, deeply in love. And Aden loved her in return. What more could she want? Just knowing it filled her with joy. Whatever else happened in her life she could face it calmly, knowing Aden loved her.

After showering she inspected her face in the mirror. The ice pack had done a good job and the swelling had begun to subside, but she was certainly going to have a black eye. That couldn't be avoided, but, after she finished dressing and applied makeup, she decided it didn't look too bad.

She hummed to herself as she prepared coffee and toast for breakfast, unable to keep her mind from Aden and her wonder that he felt the same about her as she did about him.

When her phone rang a little later she picked it up eagerly, hoping it was Aden calling, but Bobbi's name appeared.

'Hello Bobbi, how are you this morning?' She managed to keep the disappointment from her voice.

'I'm fine,' Bobbi replied. 'I've been doing a lot of thinking, and I have an idea I want to discuss with you. Is it convenient for me to come over?'

'Yes, of course. What's the idea? Something to do with the shop?'

'No, although I'd like to see how they're going with that. Perhaps we can pop over later and have a look-see?'

'Of course. Have you had breakfast yet?'

'Yes. I was up early.'

'Then I'll have coffee ready when you arrive.'

'Great. See you soon.'

As she put down her phone Erin reflected that, whatever Bobbi's idea was, she certainly sounded much brighter this morning. She hoped it meant she was working through her grief.

When Bobbi arrived a little later Erin sensed an air of quiet excitement about her, but when she saw the bruise on Erin's face she demanded to know what had caused it. Erin went through the whole story, making as light of it as she could. And saying only that Aden had come to check that she was all right.

Bobbi was shocked, and immediately decided Giles must be behind the attack. Finally Erin satisfied Bobbi that she hadn't received any lasting harm and that the police were on the job of looking for the intruders.

'Now tell me about your idea,' she said

Bobbi's face lit up. 'Well, I've had what I think is a great idea and I want to know what you think of it. The house next door is for sale, right?'

'Yes.'

'And it's the same as this one?'

'I believe so.'

'Well, I'm considering buying it.' She said this with a triumphant air, like a magician pulling a rabbit from a hat.

'You're joking!'

'No.' Bobbi grinned.

'Well! If you wanted to surprise me you certainly have. You mean you'd leave your lovely home for this?'

'Yes. According to Bob Simpson it looks as if there's a strong possibility that the big house will be too expensive for me to keep. Besides, now that Laurence is gone I don't want to stay there on my own. And as you're living in this one, it would be perfect for us to live next door to each other. And if your landlords decide they want their house back, you could always move into my spare room, and live with me and Tasha.'

'That's a big decision to make. Perhaps you shouldn't make it so soon.'

Bobbi drew a deep breath. 'Tasha will be arriving soon, and I want to be settled by the time she comes. And as we'll be working together, it makes sense for us to live close to each other. Like you I have no family, so I'd like to think you'll be near when I bring my baby home.'

Erin felt a surge of affection for her friend. Their aloneness had been the bond that made them friends in the first place, and over the years they'd become as close as sisters. She threw her arms around Bobbi and hugged her, as well as she could without crushing her precious baby bump.

'Then if that's how you feel, it will be ideal.'

'Then let's ring the agent right away. We don't want someone else to get in first.'

While they waited for Tremayne to arrive Bobbi rang Bob Simpson to explain what she had decided. When she finished her phone call she turned to Erin.

'He says there won't be any problem. He seemed mighty pleased when he knew I wanted to sell the big house and buy something smaller. Very sensible, he told me, and I could just imagine him rubbing his hairy hands together with glee. I suppose it means more money for the estate, and for Tasha's trust. At any rate, he said to tell the agent to contact him and he'll take care of everything.'

'So now you have to see inside the other house and make sure it's what you want.'

'Yes, and if it's as good as this, then it could soon be my new home.'

The agent was all smiles when he arrived a little later. He opened the front door to the house with a flourish.

'This is a real beauty,' he told Bobbi as he ushered them inside. 'It's all been freshly painted throughout, as you can see, and the kitchen was renovated only a year ago. You can move in here without having to spend a cent. I'm surprised someone hasn't already snapped it up.'

As they moved through the house, inspecting each room as they went, they discovered that it was a mirror-image of Erin's place. Even the terrace and the garden at the back were similar, with the added bonus of a garage with a door that opened into the house, instead of a carport.

After checking out the kitchen cupboards and appliances, and the storage in the bedrooms, Bobbi pronounced herself delighted.

'If I decide to buy, I want to be settled before my baby's due,' she told Tremayne. 'How soon could I move in?'

'It takes a few weeks for settlement, but once contracts are exchanged and the deposit paid, I'll negotiate with the owners and try to arrange for you to take possession earlier.'

'I'll only buy if they agree to that.'

'I'm sure I can arrange it,' he assured her.

By the end of the morning Bobbi had put her signature on a contract to buy the house, arranged to put her house up for sale, and made arrangements for Aden to go with Tremayne to see Simpson about the financial arrangements, pending probate of Laurence's will.

All through Bobbi's excitement of the morning thoughts of Aden kept hovering in the back of Erin's mind. He'd said he would see her again soon, but she knew he led busy days, filled with clients to see and matters to sort out, so she curtailed her impatience see him again, consoling herself with the thought that he would ring her and make arrangements for them to be together again when he could.

After lunch Erin and Bobbi decided to visit the shop to see how the work was progressing. They paused inside the door and looked around. A radio blared out the latest hit tunes, and workmen seemed to be everywhere.

There had been changes. The old floor covering was now a soft, cushiony vinyl that subtly simulated marble, and the pale walls and floor made the space seem even larger. On the ground floor, in front of them, two workers were struggling to manoeuvre a large timber rack into a space along one wall.

Upstairs, on the mezzanine floor, two workmen were erecting the shells of the alcoves for the fitting rooms.

As Erin and Bobbi stood inside the door the music stopped, and one of the men put down his end of the rack and came to meet them.

'Afternoon, ladies,' he greeted them. 'I'm Bob, the foreman here, and I'm guessing one of you is Mrs Brightman, right?'

'Yes, I am.' Erin turned to Bobbi. 'And this is my partner, Bobbi Harvey.

'Pleased to meet you both. Come to see how things are going, have you?'

'Yes. We've just popped in for a quick look.'

'You chose a good time. The chandeliers you ordered have just arrived.' Bob gestured towards a trestle stand. 'You'd probably like to see them.'

He led them to where several boxes stood side by side on a makeshift bench, one large and the rest smaller. Extracting a crystal chandelier from each he placed them carefully side by side. Their glittering drops winked in the light from the open door.

'What do you think, Bobbi?' Erin asked. 'The large one is for down here, and the smaller ones are for the alcoves upstairs.'

'I think they're beautiful, and it's all going to look wonderful. I can't wait to see it all finished.'

'It'll look wonderful, don't you worry,' Bob told them as he replaced the chandeliers in their boxes.

'Now, unless there's anything else I can help you with...' he raised his brows as he looked from Erin to Bobbi, who both shook their heads. 'Then I'll leave you to continue your inspection and I'll get on with my work.'

Bobbi's enthusiasm rubbed off on Erin. She buzzed with pleasure as she showed her around, and explained all the details of her plans. It was all coming together as she'd envisioned it – the pale walls and floor worked well with the light coloured timber of the pine fittings – and she was delighted that Bobbi approved her ideas so wholeheartedly.

Bobbi's phone rang as they were ready to leave. 'Tremayne,' Bobbi mouthed at her as she answered the call. As she listened a smile spread over her face. When she clicked off the phone she turned to Erin and hugged her.

'What a day this has been. That was the agent to say the vendors have agreed to me moving in right away. As soon as I can arrange to have the furniture that I want from the big house brought over I can move in. Then we'll be neighbours as well as partners.'

'That's wonderful news.' Erin was happy at the thought of them being so close, and relieved that her friend seemed to have shaken off the terrible melancholy that had overwhelmed her.

It seemed as if Bobbi was ready to move ahead with her life and able to feel happy again as she awaited the arrival of her baby. Life seemed to be picking up for both of them.

CHAPTER THIRTY ONE

The following item appeared on page five of the Sydney Morning Herald in a Parliamentary report.

At question time in Parliament today the minister for planning, James Beck replied to a

question previously put by the member for Barraclough, Grant O'Brien.

He confirmed that a planning permit has been issued for a proposed development in

Section 62 of Crown Land within the Council jurisdiction of Cooralinga in NSW.

The member for Barraclough then asked if a full environmental study had been undertaken before the permit was issued. The minister for planning replied that it had.

Aden hadn't rung to tell Joan he was coming. He'd started out as soon as he left Erin, and he didn't want to wake the household too early. As he headed up the highway towards Armidale his emotions were mixed. First and foremost in his mind was the fact he was in love. He'd never expected it to happen again. Indeed, he'd fought against it, had erected a wall around his heart and told himself he must let his head rule his heart, because he didn't need more complications in his life. He cursed himself now for being so weak.

But the sight of Erin, bruised and hurt after her ordeal, had swept away his defences. He'd taken her in his arms to comfort her. That had been his first mistake. The feel of her body in his arms aroused the most primitive feelings in him. Physical feelings stronger than any he'd experienced before. But also a gut-wrenching feeling of wanting to protect her, to take care of her, to make everything in the world right for her.

His second mistake, and the one he chastised himself for most of all, was that he'd blurted out that he loved her. He had no right to say that when he wasn't able to offer her anything definite for their future. But the memory of her response, that she loved him too, and their love-making, so passionate, so full of caring, filled him with joy and wonder. There was no way he could let her go now.

So he was on his way to set in motion the process that would free him from his restraints. And that brought with it a strong sense of guilt.

When Joan opened the door to him she stepped back and looked behind her nervously.

'Aden. What are you doing here? Why didn't you let me know you were coming?'

'I'm sorry Joan, I left early and I didn't want to disturb you, and when I was on my way up I decided it's time for me to see Zoe without the extra medication.'

'You might be sorry. She's not been too well lately.'

Aden's stomach churned as the old feelings of anxiety and hopelessness came rushing back. He took a deep breath and thought of Erin. He must remain resolute.

'I'd better come in. There's something I need to tell you.'

'All right. She's in her room. We might have a few

minutes peace.'

He followed Joan down the passage into the sun room, where she gestured to him to take a seat.

The house was quiet.

Aden cleared his throat, but before he could speak Joan put out her hand and touched his arm.

'Perhaps before we talk I should warn you that she's been worse lately. She spends hours on end just sitting staring at nothing, much more than she used to, and other times rocking the doll she calls her baby – for hours on end.'

'Anything else?' Aden winced.

'Yes. All the old stuff is worse. She's having delusions more often and she hears voices. It's God, telling her she has to avenge the baby's death, she says.'

Aden closed his eyes briefly as knots of tension coiled in his stomach.

'I'm so sorry Joan.'

'It's not your fault. I've never blamed you, Aden, you know that. No-one could have predicted she'd go like this.' She leant back in her chair and folded her hands in her lap, regarding him keenly. 'Now, what is it you want to tell me?'

'I've met someone. Someone I care deeply about.'

'Ah.' Joan sighed. 'It was bound to happen. You've been very patient; no-one could have done more.'

'I've always blamed myself, you know.'

'Yes, I know, and it's not necessary. Zoe knew the score right from the start.'

'No use re-hashing it all. The point is, I'm not going to be able to lend the support I've always tried to.'

'You're entitled to your freedom. You've been very

supportive over the years.'

I wanted to tell you myself, in person. Will Cliff be home soon? I'd like to see him too.'

'Yes, he won't be much longer.' Joan stood up. 'I'll put the kettle on and we'll have a cuppa while we wait.'

As Joan poured the tea Zoe erupted into the room. With hair in disarray and drab brown clothing she looked like a startled sparrow. A doll dangled at her side.

She stopped abruptly when she saw Aden. She let out a loud shriek and cowered back against the wall.

'Get away from me,' she cried, swinging the doll frantically in front of her.

'Zoe.' Aden's pulses raced as he called her name and rose from his chair. 'It's all right, don't be frightened. I won't hurt you.'

'You killed her.' She waved the doll at him. 'You killed my baby and now you want to kill me. I know all about it. God told me. He said you were coming to kill me.'

'No, Zoe, no. I won't hurt you.'

Zoe flung the doll at him on her race across the floor to the kitchen drawers. She yanked open a drawer with such force the drawer came off its runners and clattered to the floor. Its contents spewed out. She reached down and picked up a peeling knife and lunged at Aden. She slashed wildly at him with the knife, screaming obscenities.

Joan sprang forward and grabbed her around the waist. It threw her off balance. Aden attempted to grab the arm wielding the knife. Zoe half turned towards Joan, but Aden managed to catch her arm. He twisted her wrist. She cried out and dropped the knife. Aden kicked it away, his heart thudding, and grabbed her other arm. Zoe kicked and fought as she tried to free her arms, shrieking at the top of her voice.

Cliff suddenly appeared. He took in the scene at a glance and moved to help Aden. While Aden held Zoe's arms, Cliff bent down and caught her around the knees. Between the two of them they carried the struggling woman to her bedroom and laid her on the bed. Cliff held her down and began speaking to her in a soothing voice. Aden stepped back out of her line of vision.

The sight of Cliff seemed to calm her, and she stopped struggling. She looked up at him with wild eyes.

'He tried to kill me, Daddy,' she sobbed. 'He killed my baby and now he wants to kill me.'

'There, there, lovey, it's all right. I'm here now and nobody's going to hurt you.' He looked over his shoulder at Joan, hovering in the doorway, and nodded. Then he turned back to Zoe. 'Everything's all right now, there's no-one here who's going to hurt you. Would you like me to read you a story?'

Her sobbing stopped and she wiped her eyes. 'Yes please Daddy.'

'All right. Now here's Mummy with a nice drink for you. Drink this up and then we'll have a story.'

Cliff raised Zoe's head and put the glass to her lips. She drank the contents and sank back on her pillow.

'Now, what story would you like?' Cliff asked as Joan took the glass and tiptoed out of the room. closed the door behind her.

'That's a strong sedative, she'll be asleep in a few

minutes,' she told Aden, who had been hovering outside the door.

They headed back to the sunroom. 'I'll call the doc now and tell him what's happened. I'm afraid we've passed the time of being able to care for her at home; sad as it makes us. The doc has suggested a very nice place, secure and not too far away. She'll be able to have constant care and perhaps, with time, she might be well enough to come home again.'

'She's lucky to have such caring parents.' Aden's heart was heavy with sorrow. 'I only wish I could have been the husband she wanted.

'Don't feel guilty. Her weakness had to be there in the first place, and what happened tipped her over the top. There's no blame for anyone. And it's time for you to get on with your life. There's nothing more you can do.'

'I hate leaving you to bear the brunt of it all.'

'Once you have children you have them for the rest of your life. You don't stop loving them when something goes wrong, and you always do the best you can for them.'

'I know. I just wish it had ended differently.'

Joan nodded. 'Now I'd best make that phone call.'

After she had finished her call, Joan turned to Aden. 'The doc is going ahead with the arrangements but he would like you to be here, as you're still legally married. But Zoe can't be admitted until tomorrow. He'll be bringing an ambulance for her then, and there's no need for her to see you, even if she wakes up, which is unlikely. Will you stay over?'

This wasn't what Aden wanted, but he felt he had no choice. 'Of course,' he agreed.

Erin was in his mind and he walked outside to call

her. His battery was flat, and he'd forgotten to bring the charger. Damn and blast!

He went into the house and used the landline to call his office. He asked Josie to reschedule his appointments. 'Oh, and if Mrs Brightman calls, please tell her I'll contact her as soon as I'm back,' he added.

When he disconnected he stood holding the phone for a moment. Should he call Erin now? He longed to talk to her, but Joan was nearby, and he wanted to be private when he first spoke to her after their night together. He sighed and replaced the phone in its cradle.

CHAPTER THIRTY TWO

Erin checked her phone yet again. Why hadn't he called? He was probably flat out with clients during the day, but she had expected a call last night. By the afternoon she began to worry that something had happened to him. She called his mobile and it went to voicemail. She left a message, just to say she'd called.

After she put the phone away she gnawed on her lower lip. What if something had happened to him? Suppose he'd had an accident? Her stomach lurched at the thought. There was no reason why anyone would notify her. She picked up her phone again and rang his office.

Josie answered her call. 'No, I'm sorry, Mrs Brightman, Mr Marlowe is away at the moment.'

'Away?' Aden hadn't mentioned anything about going away.

'Yes, he left yesterday for Armidale. To be with his wife, you know, and I'm not sure how long he'll be gone. I suppose he'll stay for the weekend, but I'm not sure. He'll want to spend as much time with her as he can. They can't be together as much as he'd like.'

Erin felt as if she'd been punched in the stomach. She struggled to breathe. 'His wife,' she repeated stupidly.

'Yes, that's right. Zoe. She doesn't like the city so she stays up there most of the time. It's hard on Mr Marlowe. I know he misses her terribly.'

Erin swallowed as she felt her world crumbling around her. She forced words out. 'Of course.' She paused, almost frightened to utter the words, but she had to know. 'And family too, I suppose. Do they have children?'

'No, not yet, but I do believe not too long in the future...' her voice trailed off. 'But there, I mustn't discuss their business,' she continued briskly. 'Now, let me see if he's left any message. I don't think there's one here for you...'

'Don't bother.'

Erin disconnected the call. Her legs refused to hold her and she collapsed onto a chair. The blood ran ice cold through her body. Aden was married.

She remembered her own observation when she'd fist felt attracted to him, that he was probably married. Well, she'd been right. It would have been different if he'd told her – after all, she was, technically, still married.

But what hurt so much was that he'd gone straight from her bed to his wife's. It seemed that her previous thoughts about him had been right; he'd only ever wanted to get her into bed. Sex was all he was interested in. He didn't really care for her. He'd only told her he loved her to make sure she'd fall into his arms. And into bed with him. And she had believed him – believed the words of love he'd whispered to her. Fool that she was! Her heart twisted in her chest.

Putting her head in her hands she gave way to her emotions and let the tears come. Great sobs forced their way from deep within, and racked her body.

Bobbi found her like this a little later.

'Whatever's the matter?' Bobbi asked in an anxious voice.

'I've been such a fool.' Erin hiccupped between

sniffles as she tried to stem her tears.

'Why? What have you done?'

'I've fallen for the oldest trick there is, the one men have been playing forever.'

'Uh-oh. This is about the gorgeous Aden, isn't it?

Erin nodded, and dropped her head into her hands again.

'Come on now,' Bobbi cajoled her, sitting next to her and putting an arm around her shoulders. 'Tell Auntie Bobbi all about it. What's he done?'

Erin lifted her face, choking back the tears. 'Made a fool of me, that's what.'

'Ah. Am I to infer from that, that he's had his wicked way with you, so to speak, and it hasn't worked out?'

Erin nodded and blew her nose with the tissue Bobbi handed her.

'He's married, and he never told me. And he told me he loved me, and the worst thing is I believed him. And it was only to get me into bed with him.' She bit her lip as the pain surged again. 'And then he left me and went straight up to her – from my bed to hers. Straight away.'

'So right after getting into your pants he went and spent time with her?'

'Yes.'

'I never would have thought that'd be his style.' Bobbi shook her head. 'It just shows you can never tell. And you really care for him, don't you?

Erin nodded, trying to hold back the tears.

Bobbi rubbed her back. 'How did you find all this out?'

'I phoned his office and his secretary told me. At least she told me he'd gone to spend time with his wife up in Armidale, and she didn't know when he'd be back.'

Bobbi's mouth twisted. 'So you haven't heard from him since you...spent time together?'

'No.' Erin felt a sudden rush of anger, so strong it swamped all her other feelings. 'Perhaps I won't now – now he's got what he wanted. But if and when I do, I'll let him know I never want to see him again.'

'That could be a bit difficult, seeing he's handling your divorce.'

'Well then, any contact we have in future will be strictly business.'

'I'll make sure my dealings with him are strictly business too. I'd say I'll ring him and tell him not to bother with my business, but...

'That's not necessary. He's a good lawyer.'

'So what are you going to do?'

'I'm going to forget all about him, and focus on getting *Serendipity* up and running. There's still so much to do.' Erin blew her nose again and stood up, trying to bury the anguish deep inside her. She ran her fingers through her hair. 'I must look a mess. Give me a few minutes while I make myself presentable.'

In the bathroom she splashed her blotchy face with water until the redness lessened, applied some make-up, and brushed her hair. When she looked into the mirror she decided no-one would be able to tell by looking at her that she'd just had her heart broken. And she would never let them know. From now on she would forget about love and concentrate on business.

'That feels better,' she told Bobbi with forced brightness when she came returned. 'Now tell me what the latest is with you. Have you chosen the furniture you want to bring with you to the house?'

'Yes, I have, and the removalist's van will bring it all early tomorrow morning. I just came to let you know I'll be moving in tomorrow, and to bring over some small boxes of bits and pieces now.'

'Do you have them in the car?'

'Yes.'

'Then I'll come and give you a hand to carry them in.'

'If you're sure you feel like it.;

'I'm quite sure,' Erin told her determinedly. 'I'm going to put this behind me and get on with my life.' But all her brave words were not enough to thaw the chunk of ice that sat in her chest where her heart was supposed to be.

Bobbi had gone and Erin was in her study trying to concentrate on a to-do list, and to work out a possible opening date for *Serendipity*, when she heard a car pull into the drive. Going to the window she looked out, and when she saw Aden a tumult of emotions swirled inside her – anger, sorrow, grief – all churning together, making her feel sick. Her heart pounded as she marched up to the front door and flung it open. She stood waiting as Aden walked towards her, a smile lighting his face.

'Erin, my love...' he began.

His words died as Erin spun on her heel without a word, and strode stiff-legged down the hall. He followed her without speaking.

'Erin, what is it?' He frowned as she turned to face him. He saw the accusation in her eyes. 'What's the matter?'

'You. You're the matter.' Her voice was bitter. 'Why didn't you tell me you're married?'

With a look of shock on his face he reached a hand out towards her.

'I never set out to deceive you...'

She slapped his hand away. 'Don't touch me! Don't ever touch me again!' Her voice rose, but she didn't care if she sounded like a shrew. He deserved her anger.

A hot flush burned her cheeks. 'You're a liar, by omission you're a liar. You could've told me you have a wife, but no, you wanted to have us both, didn't you? You couldn't wait to go to her after you'd slept with me, could you? Straight from my bed to hers.'

'That's not the way it was.'

Aden took a step towards her, but she stepped back, hands raised to fend him off.

'Are you denying you've been to Armidale to be with your wife?'

'I have been to Armidale, yes, but it's not what you think. Please let me explain.'

So he couldn't deny it. The blood pounded in Erin's temples. Her anger exploded.

'What is there to explain? Josie already explained it to me. She told me how much you miss your wife, how you try to spend time with her. But perhaps you find it convenient to have an absentee wife. It must make things easier for you.' Her lips twisted. 'Tell me, did you think I was naive and gullible enough to believe your sweet talk? Or do you make a habit of sleeping with all your female clients?'

Aden's face paled beneath its tan. 'Erin, I can understand you being upset, but I can't believe you'd think that of me.'

'Oh, I can think it. I can believe anything about you now.'

His body stiffened. 'Then I guess there's no point in trying to say anything more now. Perhaps when you've had more time...'

She bit off his words. 'There's no point in trying to say anything more at any time, because any relationship between us is over. From now on please conduct any further business by letter or email. The less I have to see you, the better. And now you'd better go.'

Without a word Aden turned and left the room. She heard his car drive away.

Erin's heart lay like a lump in her chest. Trying to stifle the pain, she moved from room to room, straightening a cushion here, moving an ornament there. When she came to the dining room she saw the empty rose bowl still sitting in the middle of the table.

With a howl she picked it up and hurled it against the wall. It shattered, and the pieces scattered across the floor. She kicked viciously at a chunk that landed close to her foot. She stood looking at the mess for a few seconds before flopping down onto one of the chairs and resting her forehead on her arms on the table. The tears she'd held back came then great heaving sobs that welled up from her shattered heart as grief overwhelmed her.

CHAPTER THIRTY THREE

The following day Bobbi's move into the house next door went without a hitch. When the removalists had emptied their van and driven away Erin went in to help her friend sort things out. She was pleased to have something positive to do after a night spent tossing and turning as she re-lived Aden's betrayal. She had glimpsed a happy future, only to have it snatched away.

Physical activity helped to ease her heartache, although it remained just below the surface, ready to take over at any moment when she wasn't busy. She threw herself into the task of helping Bobbi unpack boxes and stow things away.

Their talk soon turned to their plans for *Serendipity*.

'As soon as we have a firm date for when we'll be ready for business, we must plan an opening,' Bobbi said. 'Have you given it any thought?

'Yes, I have. How about we hold a fashion parade?'

'Good idea. And maybe a cocktail party before?'

'Excellent. A cocktail party followed by a fashion parade.'

'And we need to think of ways to publicise it, don't we? I suppose ads in the local newspapers?'

'Yes, and Aden...,' her mouth twisted as she uttered his name, 'suggested we make use of our husbands' names in promotion.'

'How could we do that?'

'By letting someone like Evie Tate know what we're doing.'

'You mean by bumping into her accidentally or something?'

'Something like that, yes.'

Bobbi paused in the act of transferring shoes from a case into a cabinet. 'Well,' she said slowly, 'we know she lunches out most days she always says it's one of her best ways of finding out what's going on and her favourites are Catalina's, Aria or Quay. I wonder where she's going to be today,' she mused.

'How could we find out?'

'Leave it to me.'

Bobbi picked up her phone and punched in some numbers. She ended the brief call with a shake of her head. She tried again, and this time she gave Erin a thumbs-up, and when she finished she put the phone away with a satisfied grin.

'It's not what you know, it's who you know. We're lunching at Aria today, and it just happens Evie Tate is too, and our table is right next to hers.'

'How did you arrange that?'

'The head waiter's a friend. Now hurry up, we're booked in an hour's time.'

The table next to them was empty when they arrived at Aria, and this gave them time to set the stage to, hopefully, pique Evie Tate's interest. After they gave their order to the waiter Erin took out a notepad and pen. Bobbi dived into her bag and pulled out a calculator.

When Evie Tate arrived a short time later they were seemingly absorbed in quiet conversation, with Bobbi's fingers flying over the calculator, and Erin scribbling down figures.

Evie leant over and greeted them after taking her seat, and they paused in their charade to return her greeting.

'Well, now, Erin Brightman and Bobbi Harvey,' Evie continued. 'How nice to be seated next to you two ladies. I haven't seen either of you recently. I was so sorry to hear about poor, dear Laurence, Bobbi. My heart aches for you, darling, so terrible at any time but especially so now.' She indicated Bobbi's baby bump. 'But I am pleased to see you looking well, and feeling able to come out into company again. I always think it's such a mistake to lock yourself away with your grief.'

'Thank you, Evie,' Bobbi replied.

Evie's sharp gaze swept their table. 'And what's happening here? To see you two totting up figures is a surprise.'

Erin draped her hand across her page of figures.

'Oh, it's just something we're working on.'

Evie's brow's rose. 'You two working?' She paused, and then smiled. 'Of course. For one of your charities. Which is the lucky one to have you two?'

'Um, well, no.' Bobbi squirmed in her seat. 'It's not for a charity.'

'Really?' Her eyes narrowed. 'You two are up to something, aren't you?'

'Oh, it's nothing really,' Erin interjected. 'We're just sort of working on something. An idea we've had, that's all.'

'How interesting.' Evie's eyes gleamed. 'What sort of an idea?

Bobbi looked away and fluttered her hands. 'Well, a sort of a business...'

Erin cut off her words. 'Bobbi,' she said in a

warning voice, 'you know we're not ready to say anything yet.'

Evie's gaze flashed from one to the other. 'So it is a business. What sort of business?'

'Evie wouldn't say anything if we didn't want her to,' Bobbi said, twisting her fingers together.

'Of course not.' Evie hurried to agree. 'Not if you want it kept quiet at the moment. Just give me a hint now, and I won't say a word to reveal your secret.'

Erin pursed her lips. 'Well,' she said hesitantly. 'It's to do with fashion.'

'Fashion! Well, you both know plenty about that. There are not too many more fashionable women around than you two.' Her eyes flashed. 'Are you going into designing?'

'No, no, nothing as ambitious as that.' Bobbi shook her head. 'More on the retail side.'

'Ahah. A boutique. You're going to open a boutique, aren't you?'

'It's a whole new concept, and we're really not at the stage of talking about it yet,' Erin insisted.

'You can trust me,' Evie purred. 'But make sure you let me know when you're ready to talk about it.'

'You'll receive an invitation to the opening,' Erin promised.

Evie leant back with a smile. 'I wouldn't miss it for the world. I suppose Giles will be there to support you,' she added.

Erin was saved having to answer by the arrival of Evie's luncheon companion, a young actress recently signed for a supporting role in a television series. She arrived with a flurry of excuses for being late. After the two air-kissed and the newcomer took her seat, Evie devoted her attention to the actress. But she threw occasional surreptitious glances their way.

Erin and Bobbi huddled over their papers and went on talking in low voices until the waiter arrived with their meals, when they put away their props and concentrated on enjoying their lunch.

Erin was well pleased with the encounter. She felt they'd captured Evie's attention, and hoped for a mention in her column.

CHAPTER THIRTY FOUR

Erin spent another restless night. In spite of Aden's betrayal she couldn't help reliving their night together, and longing for him to be there alongside her. When morning finally came she stood under the shower, wishing the hot water could wash away her pain. After drying her hair she checked her face in the mirror. At least the bruising had faded and makeup could cover it easily now.

She slipped into jeans and a tee before retrieving the Sydney Morning Herald from the front garden. She carried it outside to read while she enjoyed her first cup of coffee for the day. She turned to Evie's column and the following snippet brought a smile to her face.

'It is being whispered around town that Erin Brightman and the recently bereaved Bobbi Harvey, who were seen lunching together at Aria yesterday, have their heads together planning a new fashion venture. Few details are known yet, but a little bird tells me we can look forward to a new concept in fashion boutiques sometime in the near future.'

As Erin turned back to continue reading the paper she discovered Evie Tate's announcement was not the only item to mention the name of Brightman in the news that morning.

A row erupted in the House yesterday when the minister for planning, James Beck, was accused of having accepted a bribe. It is alleged that during the period when the proposed development in Section 62 of Crown Land within the Council jurisdiction of Cooralinga in NSW was under review, the minister had been the recipient of a gift from Mr Giles Brightman, one of the members of the consortium that was applying for the permit for the development. James Beck denied that a swimming pool and landscaping work carried out at his home by 'Best Pools,' a company owned by Mr Brightman, had been a gift from the consortium who were applying for the planning permission, but that it had been paid for 'in the normal way, by my accountants'. Mr Brightman was unavailable for comment.

Erin finished reading the article and put the paper down. Had Laurence had been part of the consortium as well as Giles? Was Bob Simpson involved as well? If so, what had the three of them had been up to?

At that moment her phone rang. It was John Stevens. He told her he was calling from the shop. 'You'd better come around as soon as you can,' he told her. 'There's been a break-in and some damage done. I've reported it to the police, but you need to see it yourself.'

Stevens was waiting for them when Erin and Bobbi arrived at the shop a little later. 'We were held up waiting for a delivery yesterday,' he told them, 'and when we learnt it wouldn't be here until today we knocked off mid morning and went to another job. So sometime between about ten o'clock yesterday and this morning vandals broke in and did this.' He swept his arm around towards the walls.

In the centre of the longest wall a large message had been painted in red.

It said, 'GIVE UP'.

Red and black graffiti disfigured the rest of the wall.

'Giles!' Erin gasped. 'It has to be him.'

'Looks like it,' Bobbi agreed. 'Can you think of anyone else who would do this?'

'No.' Erin stared in dismay at the damage. 'After all, not many people even know about our plans.'

'No, let's think who does.' Bobbi ticked them off on her fingers. 'There's Giles, and Bob Simpson, and Tremayne, the agent. And Aden Marlowe. That's four. And of course now there's Evie Tate, although she doesn't know the details.'

'No, it comes back to Giles, doesn't it? Who else would want to stop us?'

'There's more damage,' Stevens told her. 'Come and have a look.'

He led the way to the storage area at the back. The boxes of garments left there were ripped open and the clothes scattered around the area. A broken window, leading to a back lane, showed where the intruders had smashed their way in.

'Does it look as if anything's been taken?' Stevens asked.

'Well, at first glance I'd say no,' Erin said. 'But it's hard to tell. The boxes all contained clothes, and they look as if they're still all here.'

'Perhaps they hoped to find something else?'

'I wonder if this could've been done by the same people that broke into your house, and beat you up,' Bobbi interjected.

'Oh! So this isn't the first trouble you've had?'

'I had a break-in at my home recently.'

'I think you'd better arrange some security.' Stevens frowned. 'It looks as if you're being targeted.'

Erin chewed her bottom lip as she realised the sense in his words. 'Yes, I'll do that. But right now I'll clean up this mess out here. And what can you do about the walls?'

'I can get some stuff to clean off the graffiti. Then it'll mean repainting the walls, I'm afraid.' He paused. 'Or, alternatively, we could wallpaper over it.'

'Wallpaper?' Would that mean you wouldn't have to clean off the graffiti?'

'No, we'd still clean off the worst, but paper would cover better. I have some samples in the van if you'd like to see them.'

'Yes, let's see.'

When he brought the samples Erin and Bobbi leafed through them. Coming to a gold flocked paper they stopped, and looked at each other.

'This is beautiful,' Erin breathed. 'It would look wonderful on that main wall.'

'Absolutely,' Bobbi enthused.

'Then let's go with it.' She turned to Stevens. 'Can you get on with it straight away?'

'Yes.'

'How long do you think it's going to take?'

'I'll go and collect the graffiti cleaner now and we can do that today. It shouldn't set us back more than a couple of days.'

'Good.' Erin turned to Bobbi as he left. 'Are you up to helping me for a while?'

'Of course I am.'

Bobbi picked up a red silk jacket and checked the label. '*Valentine*,' she read. She held it up and inspected it carefully. 'It's not damaged. It just needs pressing.

Erin held up a black *Trelise Cooper* skirt. 'This has had the zipper partly ripped out, and the seam torn.'

Bobbi reached out for it. 'Let me have a look.' She

took the skirt from Erin and examined it. 'I think I can repair this so you'll never know.'

'Really?'

'Yep, piece o' cake. I'm quite a dab hand with a sewing machine.'

'Can you sew? Properly, I mean?'

Bobbi nodded with a smile, obviously delighted to surprise her friend.

'Sure. I did a course in dressmaking years ago, when I was in my teens. I made all my own clothes before I met Laurence. '

'Well, you are a dark horse. All the time we've known each other you never mentioned it.'

'It never came up, did it? A couple of fashionistas like us would never consider sewing anything, would they?' She giggled.

'Well no.' Erin smiled. 'I must say I'm impressed. I've never been able to do much more than sew on a button or, at a pinch, take up a hem.'

'Well, things are different now.' Bobbi paused, a reflective look on her face. 'And it might come in handy once we open. There are bound to be people who want alterations done to something they buy, something taken in or let out, or hems altered. I can do all that.'

'That's wonderful. You are clever, and it'll certainly be an asset.'

'Well, for now, we'll just put aside anything that's been damaged and see if it can be repaired rather than tossed out. So let's get on with it.'

They set to and found that, although some of the clothes had been ripped, and the heels broken off a couple of pairs of shoes, much of the stock was merely crumpled and creased, and could be rejuvenated with pressing.

They sorted the clothing into three piles. Anything beyond redemption in one pile to go out, things that were damaged in another for Bobbi to check and see if they could be repaired, and lastly items that only needed pressing.

When they finished Erin looked around.

'We're going to need somewhere for pressing, not only just now, but when the shop is up and running. We can easily fit a bench in here. I'll ask Stevens if he can put one in before he finishes. We'll need an ironing board and iron, too. Some of the things from storage will need a touch-up.' She paused thoughtfully. 'It's time to make a firm list about the things we need to do. We're going to need dozens of coat hangers, for one thing. And several portable clothes racks for hanging things out here.'

'And if we're going to have an opening with food and cocktails, we're going to need caterers,' Bobbi added.

'I already have a to-do list. But I can see I'm going to have to add to it. First of all, we need to set an opening date.' She looked at Bobbi's baby bump, and smiled. 'And we're going to have to work around the date when Tasha is due. And remember that you mustn't overdo it between now and then.'

'I'm fit as a fiddle. I don't need to be mollycoddled.'

'There are lots of things you can do that aren't too strenuous. How about organising the catering? You've had plenty of experience at that.'

'We both have, but, yes, I'll do that.'

'So when is Tasha expected?'

'In three weeks.'

'Then it must be a few weeks after that. Let's aim for having everything organised by when she's a month old, shall we? Do you think that would be all right for you?'

'Yes.'

CHAPTER THIRTY FIVE

Aden sat at his desk in his shirt sleeves, with his coat draped over the chair behind him. He stared at the papers spread out before him without seeing them. A tricky litigation case was coming up and he needed to clear his mind and work out the best strategy. But he couldn't concentrate.

Dropping his pen, he pushed back his chair and crossed to the window. He ran a hand through his hair as he watched the traffic streaming by in George Street below. He was weary with thoughts that ran endlessly through his head. It was no use. He couldn't get Erin out of his mind. Every time he thought of her, and how he'd bungled their relationship, steel bands tightened around his heart.

Just when he'd thought his life was taking a turn for the better, it had all crashed around him. And he had no-one to blame but himself. Himself. And Josie. His mouth tightened as he thought about Josie. There had been quite a scene when he'd arrived back at his office.

Josie greeted him as if nothing had happened, while he was bursting with anger and ready to take his frustration out on her. He demanded to know why she had discussed his private life with a client, and had given out misinformation about something she knew nothing about.

Josie started to cry. 'I could see what was happening, and that woman's no good for you. A social butterfly like her, she could never make you happy.'

'What do you know about me?' he raged, 'and what I need.'

'You need someone reliable,' she told him through her tears. 'Someone trustworthy and dependable. Someone like me. But you never even look at me. You treat me like a piece of the furniture. And I could see her worming her way into your life.'

Josie looked up at him with a tear-streaked face as he gaped at her, shock rendering him speechless.

'I could see what was happening,' she repeated through her misery. 'You were falling under her spell. I just wanted to save you from her.'

When Aden recovered from the shock of her revelation he controlled his anger enough to tell her she no longer worked for him. He wrote her a cheque for a month's wages, and told her to clear her desk immediately.

He should have told Erin the truth about Zoe right from the start. It wasn't because he wanted to keep it hidden, but it seemed somehow disloyal to discuss Zoe's problems with anyone but those close to her.

At first it hadn't been an issue. And later, after he'd lost his self control and told her he loved her, he was ecstatic to hear her own words of love. He'd known then that he wanted to spend the rest of his life with her. But he'd made the mistake of deciding it was only right to tell Cliff and Joan what was happening. After telling them, he'd be free to tell Erin everything.

As he drove down the highway to Sydney after leaving Armidale his dreams were all about life with

Erin. And it wasn't about the sex, wonderful though that had been. His body responded as he remembered her passionate response to his caresses, making him shift in his seat. No, it was about love. About spending the rest of their lives together. He visualised a little house with a garden, and children. Erin would have beautiful babies, and she'd make a wonderful mother. After all these years of worry, and hope, and loneliness, he had a future to look forward to. He could put the past behind him now and look forward.

Aden had driven the rest of the way with a lightness of heart he hadn't felt for the last six years, only to find Erin had been misinformed, and had drawn all the wrong conclusions. And his world came crashing down.

Turning away from the window, Aden resumed his seat and picked up his pen with a sigh. He must try to concentrate. He set his jaw firmly. Erin had told him she didn't want to see him again, but she'd also told him she loved him. He resolved not let her go easily. He would try to win her back. But he would have to take it slowly, and hope she would give him another chance eventually.

CHAPTER THIRTY SIX

Things were moving along. Erin and Bobbi had decided on a provisional date for the opening. Bobbi had met with the caterers and decided on the menu. The walls in the shop had been cleaned and re-painted, and the wallpaper hung on the main wall. What had seemed a disaster when it happened had ended up being a bonus, for the papered wall lent elegance to the space that paint could never have achieved.

'So instead of harming us, Giles' effort at sabotage turned out to be good for us.' Bobbi giggled. 'Wouldn't he be pissed off if he knew?'

All of the tradesmen's jobs were now complete and the workmen gone. Hanging the drapes was the last big task on order. Erin and Bobbi stood watching as the curtain-hangers went about their task. At last their plans were coming to fruition.

If only Aden was with her to share the excitement. Erin bit back the wave of desolation that rose inside her every time his face swam into her memory. Forget him. He was a cheat and a liar. She was well rid of him. But her heart refused to listen to what her head told her.

It took all her willpower to focus on the curtains.

'They look wonderful,' Bobbi enthused, as the last curtain was put in place.

Erin drew a deep breath. 'They do, don't they? After all our planning, it's finally all coming together.

Serendipity is about to become a reality. Although there's still plenty to be done.'

'Yes, and we can start bringing our stock over now.'

'I don't want you to think about any of that.' Erin patted the baby bump. 'It's too strenuous for you at this stage.' She suddenly pulled her hand away as if she had been stung. 'I felt her! I felt Tasha move.'

'Oh yes, she's been very active lately. I think she enjoys kicking me.'

'Can I have a feel?'

'Be my guest.'

Bobbi watched with a smile as Erin placed a tentative hand on her stomach. Right on cue, the baby kicked beneath her hand.

'Oh my God. She's moving. I can feel her. I can feel your baby.'

'You should have to put up with it.' Bobbi laughed. 'It's not what you want in the middle of the night, when you're trying to get some sleep. She doesn't give me much rest.'

'Are you sure you feel all right? You shouldn't be here. You should be home with your feet up.

'I feel fine. I'm full of energy, as a matter of fact. I feel as if I want to do something. If you won't let me help with bringing over the stock let's go and look at chairs. We still have to select those.'

'We can do that, if you're sure you're up to it.'

'I'm sure.'

Half an hour later, in a furniture shop in Willoughby, they were checking displays. As they browsed Erin came to a pair of reproduction tub chairs, upholstered in a silky fabric patterned with a delicate floral design. They had finely carved legs and frame of walnut coloured timber. They would look wonderful in the alcoves.

She called Bobbi over for her opinion.

'They're perfect,' Bobbi agreed.

'Then let's see if they have enough for one in each alcove.'

'I'll just sit here and wait while you fix it up,' Bobbi told her. She took a seat on a straight backed carver nearby.

Erin found a saleswoman arranging a display in the next section. She assured her they had more of the chairs in stock, and Erin placed an order for them to be delivered the next day. By the time she walked back Bobbi looked distinctly uncomfortable, sitting rigidly in the chair with her hands gripping the armrests.

'This is probably enough shopping for today,' she told Erin. 'I think we'd better head for home.'

'What is it? Are you sick?'

'No, not sick, but I think Tasha's getting ready to enter the world. Very soon.'

Erin's breath caught in her throat. 'Have you got pains?'

'Yes, but don't panic. They've just started, and there's hours to go yet. Let's just get home.'

Erin took a deep breath, willing herself to stay calm, and held out her arm. 'Come on then, take my arm and we'll go to the car. If you think you can walk that far.'

'Of course I can.' Bobbi gave a shaky laugh. 'It's stopped now.' Nevertheless she took Erin's arm, and when they reached the car she slid into the passenger's seat with a sigh.

Erin took her seat behind the wheel, backed out of

the parking spot, and turned the car towards Chatswood.

She shot Bobbi quick, anxious glances on the way. 'Are you sure you're all right to go home? Do you think we should go straight to the hospital instead?'

'No. I rang the doctor while you were busy with the saleswoman, and the pains aren't coming quick enough yet. We'll go home and collect my bag. It's already packed and waiting. When they're coming regularly and closer together it'll be time to go. But you don't have to come; I'll be quite all right to go in a taxi.'

Erin threw her a scornful look. 'You think I'd let you go alone? Think again, girl. I've felt Tasha kicking inside you, and I'm going to be there when she enters the world.'

Bobbi managed a grin. 'You realise you'll have to be her godmother if you do that, don't you?'

'You're on. Just hang in there, and let me know when you get the next pain.'

The drive home seemed interminable, but finally she pulled out of the traffic and into their street, and parked outside Bobbi's house.

Erin hurried to the passenger's side to help Bobbi from the car. She took the keys from her and opened the door. Bobbi pointed out the hospital bag, waiting ready near the door, and Erin picked it up and carried it out to the car.

Then she made them both a cup of camomile tea with a dollop of honey, and they settled down to wait. When the pains became worse, and faster, a phone call to the hospital advised Bobbi to come in right away. She finished the call and looked at Erin with wide eyes, her phone clutched so tightly in her hand that the knuckles were white.

'I'm scared.' Her voice wobbled. 'People can die when they're having babies and I've just had a terrible thought. What if I die and Tasha's left all alone in the world? What would happen to her, with no mother or father to care for her?'

Erin looked at her friend's eyes, full of anxiety, and realised how badly she must be missing Laurence at this time. She hurried to Bobbi's side and put her arms around her.

'You're not going to die,' she told her firmly, 'but to put your mind at rest, if anything should happen to you, I'll take Tasha and I'll bring her up, and love her.'

'Would you do that? Do you promise?'

'Yes, I promise.' Erin hugged her. 'Now come on, let's get going. We don't want her to arrive while we're on the way to the hospital.'

Erin helped Bobbi into the car and adjusted her seat belt, then hurried back to lock the front door before hopping in herself, and pointing the car in the direction of the Prince of Wales hospital in Randwick
.

Bobbi had two more contractions on the way to the hospital, the second one painful enough to make her cry out in spite of biting on the handkerchief she shoved between her teeth. Erin drove as fast as the she could within the speed limit, and breathed a sigh of relief when they finally turned into Barker Street and headed into the car park below the hospital.

From here they took the lift, and as soon as they stepped out onto the maternity floor Bobbi was whisked away by the pleasant-faced nurse's aide waiting for them.

Erin was asked to wait in the visitor's room. As

she sat there she knew that she envied Bobbi. If only Aden hadn't turned out to be a fraud she might have been able to look forward to this in the future. If only his words of love had been true. But now any hopes she'd held were dashed. She would have to be content with being a godmother.

Her thoughts were cut short by the nurse's aide coming to collect her and take her into one of the birthing rooms where Bobbi, clad in a hospital gown, lay on a bed with a nurse checking her blood pressure. Erin sat at the other side of the bed, and when the nurse left she took Bobbi's hand.

'How are you feeling?' she asked.

'Better, now I'm here. I feel secure knowing the doctor is here, and all this.' She took in the medical equipment in the room with a sweep of her hand.

'Yes, it gives you confidence. Are you comfortable?'

As Bobbi was about to answer another pain gripped her and her body strained. Perspiration shone on her face, and when the pain passed she panted from the exertion.

Erin held her hand tighter, biting her lip.

'You don't have to stay,' Bobbi told Erin when she was calm again. 'It's not very pleasant for you.'

Erin swallowed. 'I told you I'm staying to see my god-daughter come into the world, and that's what I'm doing.'

'Thank you.'

Erin held her friend's hand, and wiped her face with a damp cloth when she needed it. In between contractions Bobbi rested, gathering her strength for the next bout of pain. But at last, when Erin thought Bobbi couldn't stand much more, the doctor arrived.

Finally, with encouragement from the doctor and nurses, and instructions to PUSH, and again, PUSH, Bobbi uttered a long, piercing cry. A few seconds later, as Bobbi lay back gasping, a baby's cry filled the room.

'There now, you've got a lovely baby girl. Well done,' the doctor told Bobbi.

Bobbi raised her head and pushed herself up to look at the little bloodied bundle that was her daughter. A nurse slipped a pillow beneath her head, and the doctor placed the baby on Bobbi's chest. Her face shone as she gazed at her daughter. Red faced and screaming, with her hair plastered to her scalp, she looked beautiful.

The wonder of it all choked Erin's throat.

Soon after, she left them together. She drove home through the deserted streets and fell into bed. After a few hours sleep she hurried to shower and dress, and made her way back to the hospital. Bobbi was sitting up nursing Tasha, glowing with health and happiness. Mother and baby were doing fine.

CHAPTER THIRTY SEVEN

Erin moved one of the newly delivered chairs a little more to the right. That was better. Standing back, her critical gaze roamed the shop. She walked slowly around, checking and appraising everything. Yes, it looked good. It had turned out much as she'd envisaged it when she drew the scale model and let her creative mind run free.

Her heart clenched as she remembered how Aden helped with the measuring, and the pleasant evening they'd spent together when they were just getting to know each other. She bit down on her lip. No. She mustn't think of him – the hurt was still too raw. She needed to forget. But, hard though she tried, he came sneaking into her thoughts. Resolutely she picked up the list she'd written of all the things she still had to arrange for the opening of *Serendipity*. She needed to push him from her mind. And her heart.

She concentrated on her list. There was still a lot to do. Going through it she prioritised items in order of importance.

First was the stock from the storage depot. Then the hangers to put it on. And the dummies for display.

Opening her laptop she found a local supplier who stocked dummies, coat hangers, ironing board, press and iron. She ordered a box of beech wood hangers, ten female dummies, plus iron and board.

That shortened the list.

The next item was sign writing for the exterior. She rang the agent to see if he could recommend someone. Tremayne was happy to give her the contact details for the sign writer who did their work. After making a time to meet him at the shop, she crossed that off the list and moved to the next item. Advertising. A splashy ad in the local paper would be a good idea, but it was too soon for that.

She decided to start bringing the boxes from storage. By the end of the afternoon she'd made two trips, each time with her car full. It would be best to unpack and sort this lot before bringing any more. She needed to appraise everything to check if they needed pressing. No point in doing that until she had hangers to put them on.

This was enough work for today. Time to visit Bobbi and the baby.

When she walked into Bobbi's room at the hospital Erin was happy to see her out of bed, clad in dressing gown and slippers, and sitting in a chair by the window, reading. Tasha was asleep in a baby cradle alongside her.

Bobbi looked up as Erin entered the room, and her face lit up. She placed the book on a small table alongside, her and stood up. 'Hi,' she greeted Erin, coming to meet her.

'Hello, little mother.' Erin enveloped her in a hug. 'How are you feeling?'

'Marvellous.'

'And you look marvellous too.' Erin smiled. 'And how's my god-daughter?'

'Come and see for yourself.'

The baby lay sleeping peacefully with her head turned slightly to one side. Long, black eyelashes rested on her cheeks, and the lips of her rosebud mouth were closed. One pink arm lay outside the rug, flung up beside her face, the tiny fingers curled, and the miniature fingernails almost transparent.

Erin's heart lurched. She reached out a tentative hand, but stopped short of touching the baby. 'No, I mustn't wake her,' she whispered, stepping back and turning to Bobbi. 'She is so, so beautiful.'

Bobbi beamed. 'She is, isn't she? And I think she's going to be a good baby. She spends most of her time sleeping.'

'I hope she wakes up before I go, I'm dying to give her a cuddle.'

'She'll be awake in about half an hour. She'll be ready for a feed then. She's regular as clockwork, every three hours, and she'll let me know all about it. Now, come and sit down.'

As soon as they were seated Erin turned to her. 'Now, I want to know all about her. Have the doctors checked her all over? Is everything all right?'

'Yes, it's the first thing I asked this morning, and the answer is yes, she has no health problems. She weighed three point one kilos when she was born, and she has no physical defects.' Bobbi laughed. 'And I checked myself and she has all her fingers and toes, and everything seems to be in the right place.' She paused, and a pensive look crossed her face. 'I'm very happy, but it's so sad Laurence isn't here to see her.'

Erin felt her pain, and leant across to press her hand. 'I'm sure that wherever he is now, he's looking down and he's watching over you both.' Her voice was positive.

Bobbi's eyes were bright with unshed tears. 'Do you really think so? I'm never really sure if I believe in the after-life or not.'

'I'm sure there is, somewhere, somehow, and I'm sure he's seeing you both, and feeling proud of you.' Erin took a deep breath and patted Bobbi's hand. 'And I know he wouldn't want you to be unhappy.'

Bobbi swallowed. She dashed a hand across her eyes, and blinked a couple of times. 'No, you're right.' She gave a little sniff. 'He'd want me to be happy.' She blinked again and gave a shaky laugh. 'Besides, I mustn't get upset, it's not good for the baby. Apparently our moods affect them.' She leant back in her chair. 'Now tell me what's happening at the shop. What have you been doing?'

Erin told her about the order she had placed, and about starting to bring the stock in. Bobbi was especially excited about the dummies, and they discussed where to place them, and what clothes to clad them in for the opening. The time sped by as they talked.

'I'm coming home tomorrow,' Bobbi told her, 'and I'm anxious to be part of it all.'

'I think you're not going to have much time left over from looking after Tasha.'

'I'll make at least some time. I still want to be an active partner in *Serendipity*.'

Tasha stretched in her cradle and opened her eyes. She stared unblinkingly at the two faces peering into her crib, then opened her mouth and yawned.

'Now's the time if you want to hold her.' Bobbi rose from her chair. 'She'll soon decide she wants to be fed and then she'll yell her head off.' She picked Tasha up and placed her in Erin's waiting arms.

Erin cradled the baby and inhaled her wonderful, sweet, baby smell. She looked down into her face. The little eyes seemed to be watching her, and her heart tumbled with love. She touched the tiny palm of Tasha's hand with a finger, and the baby fingers closed tightly around it, surprising her with the strength of their grip.

Erin's heart ached with the yearning inside her. How she wanted a baby of her own. But this was a yearning unlikely to be satisfied. The thought left a hollow, empty feeling inside her. She put the thought aside, and concentrated on Tasha.

'Her eyes are blue, like yours, but her hair's dark, so it's hard to say whether she's going to have your colouring or not. I've heard that all babies are born with dark hair, so I suppose it's too soon to tell.'

'I think so.'

At that moment Tasha began to squirm. She opened her mouth and uttered a loud cry.

'Uh-oh, feed time. I'd better take her.'

Reluctantly Erin handed Tasha to Bobbi and watched as she opened her top and positioned Tasha to take her nipple. The baby grasped it in her mouth and began to suckle energetically. Bobbi settled back in her chair with a smile.

'I can't wait to bring her home, and I'm glad we're going to be so close to you now. You'll be able to see her whenever you want.'

Erin was glad too, and before she left she pushed aside Bobbi's protests that she could get a taxi to come home, and made arrangements to pick them up the next day.

CHAPTER THIRTY EIGHT

Erin was in the middle of opening boxes and sorting clothing and shoes a few days later when she was surprised to receive a phone call from Aden's office, asking if she would be available for an appointment at eleven o'clock the following day. After Erin agreed, the voice on the other end continued.

'Mr Marlowe asked me to inform you that he's arranged to see Mrs Harvey at the same time, as the discussion will affect both of you.'

'Is that you, Josie?' Erin asked hesitantly.

'No,' the woman's voice replied. 'Josie no longer works here. I'm Mr Marlowe's new secretary, Mrs Crawford.'

'Oh. I see. Did Mr Marlowe say what this is all about?'

'No, I'm afraid not. He just asked me to make an appointment at a time when you could both come, and Mrs Harvey has already confirmed tomorrow.'

'I see. Well, thank you, I'll be there.'

Mystified, Erin disconnected the call, and immediately rang Bobbi, who was at home with Tasha.

'No, I have no idea what it's about,' she told Erin in reply to her query.

'Well, it's all a bit of a mystery, but I suppose we'll find out tomorrow.'

The next morning they arrived at Aden's office a little before the appointed time. Mrs Crawford greeted them pleasantly. A middle aged woman with bobbed silver-grey hair and smiling eyes, she left her seat behind the desk and came around to coo over Tasha, who was sound asleep in her carry-basket.

'What a darling. You can leave her here with me while you have your meeting, if you want,' she offered. 'I've had three of my own, so she'll be quite safe with me.'

The door to his office opened and Aden appeared. Erin's heart skipped a beat.

He looked thinner, and his usual smile was missing, but he was as handsome as ever.

'Good morning Mrs Brightman, Mrs Harvey.' Aden inclined his head to both of them, his face impassive. 'Please come in.'

He held the door open and stood aside for them to enter. Bobbi gave a quick nod of thanks to the secretary as she followed Erin.

Aden closed the door behind them and ushered them to their seats, then took his own seat behind the desk.

Erin forced herself to appear composed, but her pulses skittered as she waited for Aden to open the conversation.

He cleared his throat before speaking. 'I'm sure you're both wondering why I've asked you to come here together, but it's to discuss something that could affect you both, through association with your husbands.'

His voice was calm and his manner professional, but he picked up a pencil and twisted it in his fingers before continuing, as if gathering his thoughts.

Aden wasn't as calm as he wanted to appear.

He dropped the pencil on the desk. 'Recently a

planning permit was issued for a development on what was Crown land in a heavily timbered area fronting a long beach, on the mid north coast of New South Wales. This is an area of considerable environmental significance, and it's caused questions to be asked in Parliament, as to why development should be allowed in such a sensitive location.'

'How does this affect us?' Bobbi asked.

'The permit was issued to a consortium that was formed, apparently, specifically for this purpose. The members of the consortium are listed as...' he glanced down at a sheet of paper in front of him. 'Mr Giles Brightman, Mr Laurence Harvey and Mr Robert Simpson.'

Erin raised her brows. 'And...?'

'There have been allegations of bribes from the consortium having been accepted by the planning minister, allegations that have not yet been conclusively proved. If that happened, the application would be subjected to scrutiny by independent officials, and the permit might be cancelled. If this should happen, all parties involved could be subjected to an accusation of corruption. A very serious charge.'

'What our husbands might have done really doesn't affect us much now,' Erin said. 'As you know, I've left Giles, and intend to apply for a divorce as soon as I'm able. And Laurence has passed away.'

'I am aware of that, but there would be a fair amount of scandal if the parties of the consortium are charged with conspiracy, along with any MP's involved. Would you be able to cope with that?'

Erin and Bobbi looked at each other.

'How about you?' Erin asked.

'Okay with me.'

'And me.' Erin nodded.

'If you're both sure then I'll continue.' Aden sat back and regarded them both with a grave expression. It was a minute before he spoke again.

'I've had to do some soul searching of my own over this. I've seen an item that I realise is damning evidence relating to this matter. However, it is in a paper that belongs to a client of mine, a client that I would be reluctant to involve in anything disreputable.' He looked directly at Erin. 'The privilege of client confidentiality between legal representative and client means that I could possibly withhold this piece of evidence.'

'But you don't want to do that, do you?' Bobbi asked.

'No. I believe we should be able to trust our politicians to act in an honest way. And if they don't, then they should be brought to justice.'

'So what is this piece of evidence?' Erin asked, convinced by his manner that it had to do with her.

'You might remember that when you brought some documents here there was a letter to your husband amongst them that had somehow become mixed up with your papers. A thank you letter, signed only 'James'.'

'Yes, I remember.'

'I've since managed to obtain a copy of James Beck's handwriting, and there's no doubt that he was the writer of that letter.'

'Meaning that Giles had bribed him?'

'Yes, on behalf of the consortium. I'm afraid it leaves no doubt about it.'

'And you still have that letter?'

'Yes, it's with all your documents.'

'So if it's produced, it will prove the consortium bribed the MP involved?'

'Yes.'

'Then I think you must produce it.'

'I wouldn't do it without your consent, and your name won't be linked with it in any way. The letter will simply appear and no-one will know where it came from.'

'Go ahead and do it.' Erin turned to Bobbi. 'Do you agree with me?'

'Yes, of course. Though I'm sorry Laurence was involved in something as shady as this.'

'Then you handle it in the way you see best,' Erin told Aden.

'Thank you. I'm pleased you both look at it in this way.' He turned to Bobbi. 'And on a more pleasant topic, I must congratulate you on the birth of your baby daughter. I hope you were comfortably settled in your new home well in time?'

'Yes, I was, and thank you for helping to push it through so quickly.'

'It's all part of the service. I'm glad it's all gone so well. And now I suppose you're both pushing ahead with your plans for the shop.' His lips curved. 'I saw that Evie Tate gave your project a mention in her column recently. That was good publicity.'

'It was a good suggestion on your part,' Erin told him.

He shrugged, picking up the pencil and twisting it again. 'Just a lucky thought.' He dropped the pencil and pushed back his chair. 'And now I must let you ladies go. Thank you both for coming in, and for your help. Once this letter comes to light I doubt you'll have any more trouble with break-ins, Erin.'

As he shook hands, first with Bobbi and then with her, he held Erin's hand a fraction longer than necessary. His touch scorched her hand. His face looked bleak, and just for a second she wondered if, perhaps...but no, she couldn't forget his betrayal. She withdrew her hand hurriedly.

'Erin...,' he started to say, but she pushed past him with her head in the air, and he stepped back and closed the door behind them.

Aden sat at his desk and dropped his head in his hands. He had a hollow inside him where his heart should be. It was agony to rein in his emotions, when all he'd wanted was to scoop her in his arms and crush her to him, and tell her how much he loved her – tell her he couldn't face a future without her.

He wanted to say how much he regretted his foolishness in not being honest with her right from the start, but it was no good. Erin despised him now. She wouldn't want to hear anything from him. So he'd done as she obviously wished, and kept it all on a professional level. Perhaps when more time passed...

He sat there for a long while, then stood and walked to the window. He stared down into George Street, trying to bring his thoughts back to the task at hand.

Finally he went to his safe and removed the letter from where he had put it for safety. He read it through again, and then made a call to his friend Dougal, a journalist with the ABC known for his reasoned and factual reporting.

'I have something I think will interest you,' he told him, and arranged to meet him in the old Lord

Nelson pub later that evening.

Later that week, under a headline splashed across its front page, 'MINISTER RESIGNS AMID CLAIMS OF BRIBERY', the Sydney Morning Herald proclaimed the news regarding the previous day's proceedings in the House of Parliament.

There was more drama in the House today surrounding the bribery allegations in the granting of a permit for the proposed development of Section 62 of Crown Land within the Council jurisdiction of Cooralinga in NSW.

It has been alleged that a swimming pool and landscaping work carried out at James Beck's home by 'Best Pools,' a company owned by Mr Giles Brightman, had been a gift from the consortium who were applying for the planning permission. This has been rigorously denied by James Beck.

The drama continued today when the member for Barraclough, Grant O'Brien, produced a hand written note from Beck thanking Mr Brightman for the work.

When faced with this evidence, and unable to substantiate his claim that he had paid for the work, James Beck denied the charge but said that under the circumstances he had no option but to resign his post as planning minister.

Amidst catcalls from the Opposition Mr O'Brien called for a corruption enquiry into the matter.

Mr Brightman was unavailable for comment.

CHAPTER THIRTY NINE

The next week was busy for Erin and Bobbi as they worked to have everything ready for the opening. Bobbi, with Tasha in her basket, joined Erin daily to help with the job of unpacking the stock from the boxes that Erin brought each morning from storage.

Tasha, true to Bobbi's prediction, was a good baby who slept much of the time from one feed to the next, and Erin was glad to have her with them at the shop. It gave her plenty of opportunities to pick Tasha up for a cuddle, but, rather than curing it, that seemed only to intensify her longing for a baby of her own.

As they opened each box they found that most of the garments, which had been carefully folded for packing, still needed a touch-up with the iron before they were put on hangers – a job that seemed never-ending. Added to which the shoes and accessories had to be arranged on shelves or, for the more eye-catching pieces, in a glass topped counter.

Erin called a halt to their efforts one morning.

'Time for our coffee break,' she told Bobbi. 'I'll go and get the coffee. You sit down while I'm gone. Take the weight off your feet and read the newspaper until I get back.'

As Erin returned, Bobbi looked up from the paper.

'Well, here's a surprise.'

'What is it?'

'Here, take a look at this.' She handed the paper to Erin, pointing to a picture in the social pages.

Erin looked at the picture, and felt a jolt of surprise. There was Giles, dressed in his dinner jacket, holding the arm of a tall, statuesque brunette who wore a black, low-cut gown that revealed a great deal of her cleavage. The caption below the photo read, *'Giles Brightman was seen escorting Carlene Powell to the Black and White Ball'*.

'It hasn't taken him long to find consolation,' Bobbi remarked drily.

'Huh. No different to when I was with him. Only now he doesn't need to try and hide it.'

'Perhaps he'll forget about you now, and leave you alone.'

'I can but hope.'

'Wait a bit. There's more in Evie Tate's column.' She took the paper from Erin. 'Listen to this. 'While Erin Brightman and Bobbi Harvey are reported to be busy organising the opening of their new joint venture, *Serendipity*, due to launch shortly, Giles Brightman has been seen escorting the lovely legal eagle Carlene Powell around the night spots. Carlene has recently been admitted to the bar and is one of the brightest new stars in Sydney's current legal firmament.' Bobbi put the paper down and raised her eyebrows. 'What do you make of that?'

'I think it's very interesting in light of the fact that it's been confirmed there's going to be an enquiry into corruption over the bribery allegations. I would say he's making sure he has some good legal advice nearby.' Erin's lip curled. 'It would be his style to make up to someone like that for his own benefit.'

'Perhaps now he won't contest the divorce.'

'Perhaps.'

'And he must be worried about the enquiry.'

'Yes.'

The next day Erin received a call from Mrs Crawford to make an appointment for her to come in to see Aden, and she arranged it for the following day.

As she drove in to the city, she wondered if she should change lawyers. It was hard seeing Aden again. The reminder of his betrayal didn't stop her from remembering their time together, and wishing it had been real love, instead of merely sex. Trying to keep her emotions under control in his presence wasn't easy, but she was determined not to let him see she still cared about him.

Aden looked tired. The dark circles under his eyes highlighted the fatigued look on his face. He cleared his throat and picked up a sheet of paper.

'I've had a letter from your husband's lawyers. It seems as if he's changed his tune and is now ready to agree to a property settlement.'

Whatever Erin had been expecting, it was not this.

'Well, that is a surprise. But as I've told you before, I don't want anything more...'

Aden held up his hand. 'Please Erin, hear me out before you jump in to make decisions.'

She breathed in sharply, but sat back and waited for him to continue.

'I remember asking you at your first visit if you'd signed a pre-nuptial agreement. You said, not that you could recollect.'

'That's right.'

'So you obviously don't remember, but it appears

you did.'

'Oh, really? Well, no, I don't remember it, but he often brought me papers and asked me to sign them.'

'And you did? Without reading them?'

'I trusted him.' Her mouth twisted. 'It seems to be a failing of mine, to trust people when I shouldn't.'

A shadow crossed Aden's face but he continued. 'The letter I've received says he's now prepared to settle under the terms of that agreement.'

'I see. And what are the terms?'

'An outright sum of five million dollars. And nothing else.'

Erin's jaw dropped. 'Five million dollars!'

'Yes.'

Erin's heart raced. It was a huge sum of money, but she'd said all along that all she wanted from him was an amount equal to what her wages would have been. She despised him, and she didn't want to take his money.

She shook her head. 'No, I can make my own way. And, indirectly, he's paid me through the use of his Amex card. It bought my stock. The money won't hurt him, I know. But it's my small revenge, to know that I've been able to make him pay for my future without him knowing. He'd be mortified if he knew.'

'Perhaps so, but think about it before you do something you might regret. It's a lot of money to refuse. It could have many uses. And I must point out that the court would award you much more, considering your husband's wealth.

Erin took a deep breath, willing her mind to stop racing. She must look at this rationally. It was a lot of money, more than she could ever hope to make. And suddenly it came to her. She remembered Dr Irene's words. 'There are more women seeking refuge than there are boltholes for them.'

Wouldn't it be poetic justice to use a wife-beater's money to create more shelters for battered wives? Perhaps she could buy a place where women could go for shelter. Maybe one with enough land to have a pony for the children. A place where they could find safety. Yes, she would use Giles' money for that.

She smiled. 'Yes, I'll take it. You can write and tell them I accept the offer.'

'I'm pleased you've made that decision. What's made you change your mind?'

'I'm going to see Irene Leclerc, and we're going to buy a property to offer shelter to women who've been victims of domestic violence. We should be able to find something good for five million dollars.'

Irene positively bubbled over with enthusiasm when Erin told her what she proposed to do with the money. After she got over her shock at Erin's offer, and listened to her ideas, she hadn't been able to contain her excitement. She hugged her so hard Erin thought her bones would break.

'I know just the place,' Irene said. 'It's a big, roomy old house called Arundel, not too far from the city, but far enough away to be safe. It has a modern kitchen and all the amenities. It has previously been run as a tourist venture, so it's fully furnished. There are several small rooms built adjacent to it, motel style. It has five acres of land with it. Room for chickens and vegetables, and even for a pony. It would be just perfect.'

'Can we go and see it?'

'Of course. Now, let's see.' She checked her appointment book. 'I can get away this afternoon. Will that suit you?'

'Yes. I'll contact the agent and arrange it.'

The morning had been overcast but the sun came out from behind the clouds as Erin and Irene headed off to inspect Arundel. It was in a semi-rural area about two hour's drive from the city.

When they arrived they found a large stone house, solid looking and well-designed, surrounded by gently-rolling, green paddocks.

A sweeping drive through the front garden led them to the front entrance to the house, which had a verandah across the front and down both sides.

'Perfect for mothers and children on rainy days,' Irene approved as they mounted the short set of steps to the front door.

The caretaker was expecting them. He admitted them into a large entrance hall with high ceilings, and timber panelled doors leading to rooms on both sides.

'Take your time, ladies, have a good look around, and ask me if you have any questions,' he told them.

After thanking him they entered the front room on their right.

'Oh, this is lovely.' Erin beamed as they came into a huge sitting room. It was furnished with plump chairs and sofas covered in floral linen tapestry in a cheerful yellow pattern, a bookcase stacked with books, and a large open fireplace.

'Even a piano,' Irene exclaimed, as she lifted the lid on a piano-stool with a lift-up seat. 'And a stack of sheet music.'

On the opposite side of the hall was a huge dining room, and, beyond that, well-equipped kitchen and pantries. A cosy study, four bedrooms, two with en-suite bathrooms, a large bathroom with a spa bath, and a laundry, completed the main house.

At the back a new wing had been built, forming an L-shape with the main building. It contained ten rooms fitted out as motel rooms, each with its own small en-suite bathroom.

A swimming pool with timber deck surrounds, properly fenced for security, occupied the area formed by the house and the new wing.

Further away from the house stood a group of outbuildings.

'These could be used as kennels and such, so we can accommodate dogs and other animals as well. That's very important when families break up,' Irene explained to Erin, 'they can't bear to lose their pets.'

They walked all over the grounds, exclaiming over the fruit trees growing near the house, and a hen house complete with chooks, and with a large poultry run.

'Fresh eggs.'

'And the paddock is plenty large enough for a horse, and we could even have a few sheep,' Erin added. 'They'd keep the grass down.'

'And they'd be good for the children.'

After their walk they made another examination of everything in the house.

'What do you think?' Irene asked, as they stood again in the sitting room.

'I can't fault it. It seems to have everything – plenty of room, a bright, cheerful atmosphere, and wonderful outdoors space.'

'I agree. Do you think we need to look any further?'

'No. I think Arundel is perfect.'

Aden greeted Erin and Irene, and stood back to let them pass as they entered his office. Erin caught the faint scent of his cologne as she passed him. Heat rose in her cheeks as the memory of his hands on her body sprang unbidden to her mind. Sinking down into her seat she bent her head and fumbled in her bag, hoping to give her face time to cool. Had he noticed?

If so, he gave no sign as he perused the copy of the contract to purchase the property. After reading it through to the end, Aden nodded and looked up, his face impassive. 'This seems to be all in order,' he assured them. 'It seems a reasonable price for a property like this, but it is a lot of money. Are you sure you don't want to look at some others before you make a final decision?'

They both shook their heads.

'No, it's just perfect,' Erin said.

'And I've been keeping an eye on properties for some time, and I'm sure there's nothing better for our purpose than this,' Irene added.

'Have you thought about how you're going to structure this?'Aden asked them.

Irene looked at Erin. 'It's Erin's money, so that's up to her.

'I thought I could give Irene the money, and she would buy it.'

'I suggest it'd be better if you create a Trust, with you both as the Trustees.'

'If you think that's the best way to go, then that's what we'll do,' Erin told him. 'As long as Irene can do what she wants regarding using it a shelter for the women who need it.'

'That can be arranged.'

'Will you be able to handle it all for us?'

'Certainly, if that's what you wish.'

Whatever his personal shortcomings, Erin had faith in his legal abilities, so she had no hesitation in replying. 'Yes, you go ahead and organise it all.'

Aden nodded. 'Very well.' He paused. 'After paying all the other costs associated with the purchase there will be little left over for you, Erin, and...'

'I don't want anything. After all the fees are paid, the rest will go into an investment fund for the Trust to help provide running costs.'

Aden's brow furrowed. 'I think you should take time to consider all this.'

'I've made up my mind. I don't need to consider it any longer.'

'So those are your instructions?'

'Yes.'

'Then I'll contact the agent immediately and get things under way. I'll prepare the Trust documents, and then the property will be purchased in that name. I'll let you both know when the papers are ready to be signed.'

Erin pushed back her chair. 'Thank you. We'll look forward to hearing from you.'

CHAPTER FORTY

Bobbi heaved a sigh of relief as she left Simpson's office, carrying Tasha in her basket. She should have insisted that he deal with Aden, but Simpson had been insistent that she come herself, and she had agreed. In future she would be firm and insist he deal with her lawyer. She stopped by Reception to say goodbye to the girl at the desk. After a few words she turned to go. A tall, young woman with striking looks rose from her desk nearby, and came over to her.

'Hello Mrs Harvey. Can I have a look at the baby,' she asked.

'Of course you can, but she's asleep at the moment, so you can't see much of her. You're Suzi, aren't you?'

'Yes, that's right.' Suzi smiled as she bent over the baby. 'Isn't she beautiful? Perhaps I'll be able to see her sometime when she's awake, I don't want to disturb her now.' She straightened up. 'I'm just going for my lunch break. Can I carry her to the car for you?'

'No, it's all right, Suzi. She's not heavy, but thanks anyway.'

As Bobbi moved towards the door, Suzi moved ahead of her, opened the door, and stood waiting for her to go through.

'I'll walk down with you then. That's if you don't mind.'

'No, of course not.'

Suzi pulled the door closed behind them, and they headed towards the elevator.

'Actually, I really want to talk to you.' Suzi's dark eyes were pleading, and her voice wavered. Her words came tumbling out. 'I'm sorry, but I don't know who else to go to, and Mr Harvey was always so nice to us all when he came here, and you too, and I'm desperate. And now you've got a baby too, so I'm sure you'll understand.'

Bobbi could tell Suzi was distressed. She stopped walking and turned to her with a frown. 'Suzi, relax! Whatever it is, I'm happy for you to talk to me about it, and if you're in some sort of trouble then I'll help you if I can. Has Mr Simpson been hassling you?'

'No, no, it's nothing to do with him.'

'Let's go to my car. We can sit there while you tell me what's bothering you.'

Suzi shot her a grateful look. 'Thank you Mrs Harvey.'

'There's nothing to thank me for yet, and please call me Bobbi. You make me feel old with Mrs Harvey all the time.'

Suzi bobbed her head and gave a wan smile as they stepped into the elevator. They didn't talk again while they walked through the car park to Bobbi's car, where Bobbi strapped Tasha in, and they sat in the front seats.

Bobbi turned to Suzi. 'Now, tell me what's got you so worried.'

'It's my sister, Annie. She's in terrible trouble and we don't who to go to.'

'Surely your parents…'

'No, that's just it…'Suzi took a deep breath. 'That's part of the problem. We can't go to anyone in the family. You see, Annie's married and she's just had a baby – a girl – and her husband wants to have the baby circumcised, and Annie doesn't know how to stop him. So she's run away from him. But we don't know what to do.'

Bobbi's blood chilled as she heard Suzi's words. 'But that's…that's monstrous…it's barbaric. Surely that doesn't happen these days. Not here in Australia.'

'Oh yes, it happens. Not much, but it still happens.'

'But it's against the law. Her husband could be prosecuted for it, perhaps sent to gaol.'

'Oh, yes, he could be.' Suzi spoke bitterly. 'But not till it's all over. And that's too late for the baby, isn't it?'

Stunned by the enormity of Suzi's story, Bobbi gazed at Tasha sleeping peacefully. How could anyone contemplate committing such an atrocity on a helpless infant like her? Her mind whirled as she wondered what to do to help.

'Where is Annie now?'

'She's at my place. But it won't take them long to find her there. She doesn't have anywhere else to go. When I left this morning I told her not to answer the door, and to take the baby into the bathroom so she couldn't be heard, if anyone knocked. My place is only tiny, just a bed-sitter.'

'Where is it?'

'In Turramurra.'

'Then we'd better go and get them; they can't stay there.' Bobbi started the car. 'They can come home with me until we figure out what to do.

'Oh! Thank you, thank you, how can I ever thank you enough.'

As she backed out of the car park Bobbi saw tears running down Suzi's cheeks, and she leant across and patted her hand.

'It'll be all right. We'll work something out. We're not going to let it happen, you needn't worry about that.'

Suzi drew a shuddering breath and wiped her eyes, and sat silent as Bobbi manoeuvred her way through the traffic.

'I can see you're shocked,' Suzi continued after a few moments, 'so I should probably give you a bit of background, so you can understand how it can happen. That's if you want to hear?'

'Yes.'

'I came here with my parents when I was four, and Annie was born two years later.' Suzi hesitated. 'I think my parents found it hard to adapt to Australia. They still respect the culture of the old country, whereas Annie and I are every bit Australian. It made it hard at times, and I think we were often a disappointment to them.'

'I've heard that's often the way.'

'Yes, unfortunately. At any rate, when I was seventeen my parents told me they'd arranged a marriage for me. A suitable match with the son of a friend in the old country. When I turned eighteen he would come here and we'd be married. I told them there was no way I was going to marry someone I didn't know, that I was going to do it the Australian way, and choose a husband for myself.'

'Good for you.'

'Maybe, but they still went ahead with the arrangements anyway, so a few days before I turned eighteen I left home. I had a job, and found somewhere to live, and once I was eighteen they couldn't do a thing about it.'

'It must have been hard, to leave your family like that.'

'Not really. I missed Annie, but we still see each other, although she has to hide it from our parents.'

'How long has she been married?'

'Just over a year.'

'And was that an arranged marriage?'

'Yes. I told her not to go ahead with it, to leave like I did. But they watched her like a hawk until he arrived, and she wasn't strong enough to defy them, so she went through with the wedding.'

'Was she happy once she was married?'

'No. Her husband's a pig. He started to beat her right from the start.'

'Didn't she tell her parents?'

'They wouldn't interfere.'

'I can hardly believe this, it's incredible.' Bobbi's hands tightened on the wheel. 'How could they not try to help her, their own daughter?'

'That's the way it is. The husband is the master of the house and no one else will intervene.'

'Not even if he mistreats her?'

'No.'

Bobbi took a deep breath, filled with rage that this could happen. They continued in silence until Suzi began directing her as they reached Turramurra. They came to a stop outside a large brick apartment block.

After parking the car and lifting Tasha's basket out, Bobbi followed Suzi into the building and up the stairs to the second floor.

CHAPTER FORTY ONE

When Suzi reached her door she called out to her sister. 'It's okay Annie, it's only me.' She knocked loudly before inserting her key in the lock.

As Bobbi followed her inside Suzi closed the door behind them and locked it. A door opened down the passage, and a frightened face peeped out. The next moment it opened wide and a petite young woman clutching a baby stepped through. Her gaze darted around as she took a tentative step towards them. She looked fearfully at Bobbi.

Suzi hastened to reassure her. 'It's all right. This is Mrs. Harvey. She's helping us.'

'We'll find some way to help, Annie. We won't let this monstrous thing happen, believe me.'

'What can you do?' Annie's voice was a frightened whisper. 'My husband is determined to have his way in this.'

'I'm sure he can be stopped. This barbaric ritual is against the law here, but first of all we must make sure he can't find you. So I want you to come home with me until we work out what to do. You'll both be safe there.' She turned to Suzi. 'I'll drop you off at work on the way. In case he comes looking for you, you need to act as if you haven't seen Annie'.

'I can't tell you how grateful...'Suzi began.

'Never mind that. Come on, let's get going. Do you have a bag, Annie?'

'Yes.' She nodded towards a carry bag on the table.

In a couple of strides Suzi snatched it up, and hurried to the door. She unlocked it, looked around outside, then nodded.

'Let's go.'

Within minutes they were safely in the car and heading back into town.

On the way Bobbi gave Suzi her address and arranged for her to come there after she finished work. She stopped the car a block away from Simpson's office. With a wave Suzi was gone.

Annie cowered in the back seat alongside Tasha's basket, hugging her baby.

'Try not to be afraid, Annie,' Bobbi called back over her shoulder. 'You'll be quite safe at home with me; there's no way your husband will ever find you there. I've never had any contact with him, so he doesn't know I exist.'

'He's very resourceful. I'm afraid he might find out.'

'No, there's no way he could, I'm just one of Bob Simpson's clients. So stop worrying.'

'Thank you.' Annie gave a deep sigh, and settled back in her seat.

When they reached home Bobbi drove the car into the garage. She ushered Annie and the baby straight into the house, and locked the door behind them.

'You see, we're safely locked in here. You're quite safe.'

Bobbi put Tasha's basket down and came across to Annie, who stood gazing around with worried eyes. She gently moved the rug aside and looked at the sleeping baby in her arms.

'What a darling. What's her name?'

'My husband registered her with a traditional name, but I call her Emma. We're Australian, Suzi and me.' Her voice became firmer. 'And Emma is going to be, too. I must escape from him, so I can find a way to keep her safe. I want to bring her up as an Australian.'

'She's born in Australia, this is the country of her birth, so she is Australian,' Bobbi assured her.

'George is a cruel man. He cares nothing for me, and he threatens to take us back to the old country.'

'We can make sure that doesn't happen. But first we must get you and Emma settled in, you'll use the spare room, and fortunately I have a spare carry-basket that you can use for Emma.'

'I don't know how to thank you.' Annie's voice was thick with emotion.

'You don't have to thank me. We women must stick together.'

She picked up Annie's bag and led the way to the room, then left Annie attending to her baby.

In the middle of the afternoon a loud knock came at the front door.

Annie, her eyes wide with fear, jumped up from the table where they had been sitting over coffee.

'It's him! It's George! I knew he'd find me.'

'Wait in your room,' Bobbi told her.

She walked up the passage and opened the door. On the other side stood a thin-faced man with slicked-back black hair, angry eyes and black eyebrows like question marks that gave him a satanic look. She felt a flash of fear, and was glad the security door was locked.

'I've come to take my wife home,' he hissed through thin lips.

'I beg your pardon.' Bobbi lifted her chin. 'Who are you and what are you talking about?'

'I'm talking about my wife. I know she's here.'

'I have no idea what you mean. Your wife, whoever she is, is not here. You obviously have the wrong address.'

The man's eyes narrowed. 'Don't tell me that. I know she's here. Her sister was seen getting into your car. I know she brought her here, and I want her. Right now.' He yanked at the handle of the security door handle, and turned it. When it didn't budge he uttered an angry oath. 'If you don't let me in to take her back where she belongs it'll be the worse for you.'

'How dare you come here threatening me?' Although her heart hammered, Bobbi drew herself up and stared haughtily at him. She pulled the phone from her pocket. 'If you're not gone in thirty seconds I'll call the police.' With that she closed the door. Moving to the window in the front room she stood back where she couldn't be seen, and watched as he stood by the door for a minute. Then he turned and stalked back to a car parked outside in the street. When he reached it he turned and looked back at the house. He pulled out his phone and talked on it for a few seconds, then got into the car, slammed the door and drove off with a squeal of tyres.

Bobbi hurried down the hall. 'It's all right. He's gone. You can come out now,' she called through the door.

Annie emerged, ashen-faced. 'I knew he'd find me.'

'He's only guessing you're here. He says someone saw Suzi get into my car. He obviously found out where I live and came here on the off-chance, hoping to bluff his way in.'

'He'll be back. He won't give up until he finds me, and has my poor baby cut.' Her voice shook.

'He won't find you, because we're going to move you. We'll wait until it's dark, and then you're going next door to my friend's house, until we find how to stop him legally.' She put her arm around the trembling girl. 'You must be strong, Annie. For Emma's sake. You're all she's got to protect her. But you're not on your own now; you have friends to help you.' She squeezed Annie's shoulder. 'Come on now. Sit down and finish your coffee while I make a phone call.'

Annie took a deep breath and squared her shoulders. Her eyes were huge in her face as she resumed her seat, but her voice was firm as she answered. 'Thank you.'

Bobbi nodded and dialled Erin's number. 'I have a young woman and a baby here with me who need some help,' she told her, and went on to tell Erin briefly what had happened. When she ended the call she told Annie it was all arranged. They would move tonight.

Bobbi suggested to Annie that she ring Suzi, and tell her not to come visiting, but to go home as if she knew nothing. That should throw her husband off the scent.

Bobbi waited until it was fully dark, then she switched off the lights at the front of the house. She walked outside, pulling the door to behind her. It seemed that Heaven was on their side. The moon was behind the clouds, and the only light came from the street-lights. All was quiet. No-one was about. She wandered out to the front gate and looked to the left and right. The street was empty, the only sign of life being from a pale flicker of light in the house opposite and the faint sound of their television. She hurried back to the house and opened the door.

'Quick, let's go.'

Annie came out carrying the baby, and Bobbi picked up her bag and closed the door behind them. They stepped to the front of the verandah and turned to the dividing fence. Erin was standing in the shadows on her side of the fence. She reached over and took the baby from Annie, who clambered over the fence. Bobbi handed her the bag and passed Tasha over in her basket, then she climbed over. Within seconds they were inside Erin's house, with the door locked securely behind them.

Erin switched on the light and led the way down the hall to the living room, where she handed the baby back to Annie. They stood for a moment, facing the doorway, listening. But there was no sound from outside.

After a moment of silence, Bobbi drew a deep breath.

'Well, that went okay. I think we're safe.'

'Yes,' Erin agreed. 'You're safe now, Annie.'

Annie hugged her baby, her eyes glistening. 'You're both so kind, how can I ever repay...'

'Don't worry about that,' Erin told her. 'Let's all sit down and relax. But first I'll show you where to put the baby down in the spare room. Then I'm going to get some tea and I want to hear the whole story.'

When Annie finished her account, Erin sat back thoughtfully. 'There are two things we have to do. The first is to find a safe place for you. You're safe here for now, but Bobbi and I have to go to the shop during the day, and I don't want you left here on your own. You need somewhere else until we know what your legal situation is.' She sighed. 'If only Arundel was settled, you could go there, but it's not, and until it is you need somewhere else, where your husband can't find you. The second thing is to see a lawyer, to see what the legal situation is.'

'Aden Marlowe, I think,' suggested Bobbi.

'Yes. And Dr Irene might have somewhere safe she can suggest.'

Annie twisted her hands in her lap. 'I...I don't have much money. Only a few dollars. I know Suzi will want to help me but I think all this will cost a lot and...'

'Forget about the money,' Bobbi said. 'However much you need I'll pay.'

Annie bit her lip. 'But I don't know...'

'Money's not a problem for me,' Bobbi told her decisively. 'If it makes you feel better you can pay me back when you have a job. Now let's concentrate on what's important.'

'Yes. First thing in the morning I'll make the phone calls,' Erin said. 'In the meantime, we should all try and get a good night's rest.

CHAPTER FORTY TWO

The next morning Erin phoned Aden's office and made an appointment for Annie to come and see him later that afternoon. Then she rang Irene's surgery, hoping to go there first thing. When she learnt that the doctor was operating that morning, and was unavailable until late that afternoon, she had to make an appointment for later in the day.

Annie had finished feeding the baby and now sat crooning softly to her as she held her.

Erin turned to her with a slight frown.

'I don't want to leave you here alone, but Bobbi and I need to go to the shop. I think you should come with us. I'll ring Bobbi and suggest she goes first, just as a precaution in case your husband should be watching, and then we'll follow a little later.'

When it was time for them to leave Erin bundled Annie into a coat with a stand-up collar, and gave her a pair of large sunglasses to wear.

'It's not much of a disguise, but at a quick glance you'll look a bit different.'

She walked out to the letter box and checked it, then gazed casually up and down the street.

When she was sure no-one was watching she called to Annie.

Annie's gaze flicked from side to side as she hurried to the car, strapped the baby basket in, and hopped in alongside it.

Erin put her bag in the boot.

'Keep you head down as much as you can,' Erin advised her as they pulled out of the drive for the short trip to the shop.

Annie huddled down into her seat as much as she could.

As they came into the shop Annie removed the glasses and coat and placed them on a chair, then turned and gazed around with awe-struck eyes.

'It's so beautiful,' she breathed. Her eyes travelled the length of the downstairs area and up to the ceiling, dominated by the chandelier. She walked across to stand alongside the wall with the gold-flocked wallpaper, and gently touched it with the tip of a finger.

'It's like a palace.'

She moved into the central area and walked around the racks of clothes, inspecting the garments hanging there, and testing the feel of the fabrics between her fingers.

She walked back to join Erin and Bobbi.

'Everything is so beautiful. And you own all of this? Both of you?'

'Yes, we're partners,' Bobbi told her. 'We've been working hard to have everything ready for our opening.'

'I would love to work in a place as beautiful as this. With all these beautiful clothes. It must be such pleasure to come here every day to work.'

'You seem to have a great interest in clothes,' Erin said. 'In fact, I've noticed the unusual top you're wearing today. It's lovely.'

Annie's face lit up. 'Do you like this?' she plucked at the top. 'It's my own design.'

Erin raised her brows at the words. 'So you design

clothes?'

'Just for myself.' She smiled shyly. 'I like to draw clothes, you see, I imagine what I'd wear if I was going to a big ball, or somewhere special. Just for fun, you know. Oh, and I have made some for Suzi too.'

'So you make them as well.'

'Yes, I make all my own clothes. I did a dressmaking course, at night after work, so I'd know how to sew properly.'

'The fabric in your top is a very unusual print. Where did you get it?'

'It's from my parents' old country. My aunt sent it to me.' Annie's voice became animated. 'They have some wonderful ethnic fabrics there. Different. Some of them are hand printed, so you can make it into a really unique garment.'

'Have you ever thought about going into business for yourself?'

'You mean making things for other people?'

'Yes.'

'Oh no. I couldn't do that. I'm not nearly good enough.'

'I think you might be.'

'I wouldn't know how to go about it.' Annie shook her head. 'You have to be clever to do those sort of things.' She gestured around. 'Like you and Bobbi here. I wouldn't have a clue.'

'Well, I think it's something we could talk about later.' She looked at Bobbi. 'Don't you think?'

'Absolutely.' Bobbi nodded. 'Beside which, we're going to need another pair of hands once we get *Serendipity* up and running.'

'Yes Annie, we'll talk about this later. But first of all we have to get you and Emma safe from your dangerous husband. And we'll have help with that later today."

'In the meantime,' Bobbi added, 'we must get on with our work here.'

'I'd love to help, if you'll let me.'

'We'd be glad of help. Let's get the babies settled, and I'll show you what needs doing.'

Annie was an apt pupil. She soon picked up what had to be done, and the three of them worked together until one of the babies woke and started to cry, and the other soon joined in.

It was feed time, and the mothers settled companionably together to feed their babies.

Erin felt a lump in her throat as she watched them. How she envied them. Would this ever happen for her?

When the time came for Annie to go to her first appointment Erin drove her into the city. She sat in the reception area to wait while Annie went in to consult with Aden. Her mind see-sawed between worry about Annie, and memories of her time with Aden. She riffled heedlessly through the pages of a magazine.

When Aden opened his door for Annie to leave his parting words died on his lips as he saw Erin. His head jerked up, and he cleared his throat. She thought he was going to speak to her, and her pulses quickened. But he nodded a quick greeting and withdrew into his office. She swallowed as she put the magazine aside.

'So how did it go?' she asked Annie.

'We're going to apply to the court for a restraining

order, which means George will be legally unable to come near me or Emma. But I told Aden I'm sure that won't stop him. I told him I want a divorce, but that is going to take a long time, and he advised me to stay hidden until I can work out what to do.'

'That's sound advice, and that's why we're going to see my doctor. I'm hoping she might be able to suggest somewhere safe for you.'

Annie's hands clutched the handles of the basket tightly. 'You and Bobbi are being so kind to me, but I don't know what I'm going to do. How am I ever going to get free from George? How can I stop him from doing this terrible thing to Emma? I'm so scared he'll find a way to take her away from me.'

'Try not to worry too much until we see Dr Irene.'

Irene tapped a pencil on the table in front of her as she looked at the two women seated opposite her.

'This is particularly worrying. It always is when children are involved, of course, but even more so when it could affect her life – her womanhood – so much. We need to find a safe place for you to stay until we know the outcome of your lawyer's application to the court.'

Annie hugged her baby to her chest. 'I must keep my husband away from Emma. I must!' Her face contorted. 'He won't rest until he does this terrible thing to her.' Tears welled in her eyes. 'The law won't be able to keep him away, even if I have a divorce. He'll never let me go. Never! He'll kill me first.'

Erin's heart turned over at the sight of Annie's distress. If only she could help. Even as she searched her mind to see if there was a way she could send

Annie and the baby away – to another city, perhaps – Irene spoke again.

'The threat of a long spell in gaol can work wonders in forcing a man to see that he can't get away scot free from the consequences of his actions. Our immediate concern is to find somewhere safe for you now.

Annie brushed a hand across her face. 'I'm sorry. It's just that I'm so frightened.' She drew a deep breath. 'I'm weak. I should have listened to Suzi and refused to marry him. But I didn't realise he's such an evil man. He seemed pleasant enough when I met him, and it's very hard to go against my parents, against the family.'

Irene nodded. 'I understand that. I've seen it before. But for now, we need to get you right away from Sydney, if possible. He'll continue searching, so while you're in the city there's a chance he might be able to find you. I have a friend in the country who has helped me on one or two occasions. I'm going to phone her and see if she can have you to stay until we can find somewhere more permanent.'

Erin leant across and gave Annie's hand a squeeze as they waited while Irene made the phone call. After a short conversation, in which she briefly outlined Annie's situation, Irene replaced the phone and turned to them with a nod.

'That's all arranged. You're going to stay in the country, well away from here, where your husband will never find you.'

'Oh!' Annie gasped. 'Oh, how wonderful. How can I ever...'

Irene cut off her thanks, looked at her watch, and turned to Erin. 'I still have a few more patients to see, so can Annie go back to the shop with you now?'

'Yes, of course.'

'Good. I think that's best. I'll arrange for a car to pick you up from there, Annie. By tonight you'll be safely ensconced on a farm in a remote part of the state.' She gave a grim smile. 'And we'll leave Aden Marlowe to see what can be done about your husband.'

While you've been away I've been thinking,' Bobbi said after she had heard the outcome of their visit.

'What about?' asked Erin.

'About you, Annie.' She tipped her head towards Annie, who was sitting with them over a cup of coffee. 'And the clothes you design and make. Do you have any more of them in your bag?'

'Yes.'

'Can we have a look at them?'

'Of course. They're in my bag.'

When she opened the bag she removed a skirt and a top, and held them up for both to see. They were made from a light cotton fabric, and their bright colours seemed almost iridescent. The full, swirly skirt was layered, and patterned with abstract swirls in pink, yellow and green, while the simply cut, fitted top echoed the pink in solid colour.

'I made these,' she told them.

Bobbi took the skirt and inspected the inside. 'Layered seams, I see.'

'Oh yes, I like to finish things properly.'

Bobbi handed it to Erin, who examined it critically, inside and out, then laid it on the table and paired it with the top.

'These are very well made, and beautiful.'

Annie pulled another item from the bag.

'This is more conventional, but it's one of my favourites. I couldn't leave it behind when I left.'

It was a black frock in a silky fabric, with finely detailed stitching shaping that followed body lines. Elegantly simple, with the scooped neck and armholes outlined in seed pearls, it looked as if it could have come from a fine couture house.

Erin checked it inside and out and looked at Bobbi, who stood watching with a little smile playing around her lips.

'Are you thinking what I'm thinking?' Erin asked.

'That Annie should be making these to sell? Absolutely.'

Annie's eyes widened. 'Do you really think they're good enough for other people?'

'They are every bit good enough. I think you have a lot of talent,' Erin told her, 'and if it's possible we'd like you to come and work here with us when your troubles are settled. That's if you're sure you'd like to?'

'Oh yes, I'm absolutely sure.'

Bobbi threw her arms around her. 'Welcome to the *Serendipity* team.'

Annie returned the hug, her face alight, before breaking away. 'But we mustn't forget George,' she said, all traces of jubilation gone.

The car called for Annie before it was time for Erin and Bobbi to leave, and Erin was pleased to see Steve Waterman driving. Annie would be safe with him.

When Bobbi arrived home she found the lock on her back door had been forced. Nothing had been taken, but she knew someone had been inside the house. A cupboard door had been left ajar, and a drawer in the spare room half opened.

She rang the police. When the duty officer heard nothing had been taken, and there was no damage, he promised to have a patrol car visit her street during their night patrol to keep an eye on her house. He suggested she call a lock-smith to replace the lock and install an alarm system immediately. The job was done that evening, but Bobbi still spent a restless night, feeling sure the intruder had been Annie's husband.

CHAPTER FORTY THREE

The following day Bobbi told Erin about the broken lock, and they both believed it had been Annie's husband who had broken in to her house, hoping to find Annie and the baby, or signs they had been there. They discussed Annie and her problems while they worked.

'It's hard to believe that in this day and age such a barbaric practice is still carried out,' Erin said.

'I found it hard to believe when Suzi told me. But now that I've seen what her husband is like, I believe he's capable of it.' Bobbi shuddered. 'He frightened me. Poor Annie.'

'And poor Emma. But at least they're safely hidden away now. Irene rang me early this morning to tell me all went well. They're now somewhere on a farm, well away from him. And hopefully he's now satisfied that you know nothing about them.'

By the time they finished work they both decided they were too tired to cook, so Erin stopped on the way home to pick up a takeaway from their favourite Chinese cafe. They ate at Erin's dining table, and by the time they finished their meal and tidied up, the evening was drawing in. They discarded their plan to sit out in the garden, and went instead into the sitting room, carrying a sleeping Tasha with them in her basket.

Erin seated herself on the sofa and Bobbi sprawled in one of the easy chairs.

As they discussed the mound of jobs still ahead of them Tasha opened her eyes and began to cry, squirming and waving an arm in the air.

Bobbi looked at her watch. 'Yes, you're getting hungry, I know.' Standing, she bent over the basket. 'And I suppose you've got a wet bum too, have you?' She leant over and picked Tasha up. 'Yes. Come on, we'll go into Auntie Erin's spare room and change you.'

Picking up a nappy from the bottom of the basket she carried the baby into the spare room. 'As I thought,' she told Erin when she returned a few moments later. 'She was wet and uncomfortable.'

'Is there time for me to have a cuddle before her feed?' Erin asked.

'Sure.'

Bobbi placed the baby in her lap, and Erin smiled down into the little face. 'I think she's starting to recognise me,' she told Bobbi. 'Look at how she's studying my face.'

'Well, she should know you by now. She sees almost as much of you as she does of me. The main difference is that I'm the feed basket.' Bobbi laughed.

At that moment there was a knock at the front door.

'I'll go,' Bobbi said.

'Make sure to keep the security door locked.'

Erin heard the tap-tap of Bobbi's heels up the hall, and then the murmur of voices as she opened first the front door, and then the security door.

She strained to hear who was talking, wondering who their visitor was, hoping it wasn't bad news about Annie. But it was impossible to tell.

Bobbi tap-tapped back down the hall, and Erin

looked expectantly at the door as Bobbi stood aside to let the visitor past. Her body stiffened when she saw Aden. Her heart almost stopped, then it picked up its beat. Faster.

Why had he come, here? Drawing a deep breath she opened her mouth to speak, but was stilled when she saw his face pale as he stood inside the door gazing at her, his jaw clenched.

Slowly he crossed the room and stood looking down at Erin and the baby. His eyes were dark pools of misery. He stood there for what seemed like minutes, just staring. Slowly his face cleared.

He reached out and ran his fingers lightly across Tasha's tiny form. 'She's beautiful.' His eyes searched Erin's. 'You're beautiful.' He lifted his hand, and his fingers stroked Erin's cheek.

His touch burned her, and shock radiated through her body.

Love shone in his face. It lit up his eyes, and softened his features. It took her breath away, and brought a lump to her throat. In that moment she knew he loved her.

When he spoke his voice was so low she had to strain to hear.

'You're meant to be a mother, Erin. You should have babies of your own, you're made for it. For a short time I hoped we'd have a family together. But that was when you thought you loved me, and I messed that up, didn't I?'

Bobbi had been standing by, looking from one to the other. Now she crossed the room and whisked the baby from Erin's arms. Erin relinquished her as she struggled to find words. She swallowed at the ball of nerves that seemed to be blocking her throat.

'I...if you love me, why did you deceive me?'

'I never meant to deceive you, but I should have told you right from the beginning, instead of waiting. You would have understood. I've regretted my stupidity every day.'

Erin's mind whirled. Could he possibly have a valid reason for spending time with his wife? She took a deep breath.

'Perhaps you'd better tell me now. I need to understand why.'

'It's a long story.' His voice was uncertain.

'I want to hear it.'

'Are you sure?'

'Yes.'

Aden sank down next to her. He rubbed his hand across his face and took a deep breath. 'Zoe and I were married eight years ago, but for the last six years we've lived apart, with her up in Armidale and me down here in Sydney.'

'But you still go up there to visit her?'

'Yes, I've been doing it ever since we parted. But it hasn't been a proper marriage.'

'What, then?'

'I'll have to explain a few things for you to understand.'

'I'm listening.'

'Zoe and I knew each other since we were kids. We went to the same school, same Uni. We started going out together and eventually everyone assumed we'd get married, and I suppose I went along with it. I was very fond of Zoe, I still am for that matter, and I wish things had turned out differently for us.'

'So what happened?'

'We got engaged on her eighteenth birthday, but

we planned not to marry until we finished our degrees. After we married we would move to Sydney, and I'd buy into a practice. And that's what happened. It all went well for the first year. Then Zoe became pregnant.' He took another deep breath. 'I was over the moon. I always wanted us to have children, and she seemed happy enough. But then she started having fancies.'

'What kind of fancies?'

'As you know, Sydney has always had more than its share of crime, but she became paranoid about it being unsafe. She said Sydney wouldn't be safe for the baby. She wanted us to move back to Armidale. I told her I couldn't possibly just up and leave the practice. It was our future security, and I'd worked hard to build it up. So I compromised by having us spend every weekend in Armidale, staying with her parents. It all went okay up to the last month of her pregnancy. Then she started having delusions that someone wanted to kill her. So one day she left and drove up to Armidale.'

'Did she tell you she was going?'

'No. I didn't know where she was until her mother, Joan, rang to tell me she was there, in a terrible state, and the doctor recommended she stay until after the birth.'

'So you agreed?'

'Of course. And we all thought she'd be right once the baby was born.'

'And was she?'

Aden took a deep breath. 'She might have been, but the baby was stillborn.'

Erin pressed a hand to her mouth. 'Oh, no!' Tears pricked her eyes. She reached for Aden's hand, unable to utter a word. He grasped it tightly in his own.

'It was a girl.' His voice thickened. 'She had black hair.' He brushed his free hand across his eyes.

Erin put her arms around him, and held him tight. His shoulders shook.

They stayed like that until Aden gently disentangled himself, and sat back, taking her hand in his own again.

'Sorry. I don't mean to be so weak. It's just...talking about it...brings it all back. I don't usually talk about it. But you have a right to know.'

'You must have both been devastated.'

'Yes. But, you see, Zoe blamed me for the baby's death.'

'How could she blame you?'

'She said it was because I forced her to stay in Sydney, when everyone knew how evil Sydney was, and it was the evil that killed the baby.' He swallowed. 'I know a lot of women suffer from post natal depression, but she developed a psychosis, and she hated me. She called me a murderer. She tried to stab me when she first came home from hospital.'

'Oh my God! What did you do?'

'I managed to get the knife away from her, but her doctor warned me she was in a dangerous state of mind. She was hospitalised for a couple of months, and then Joan told me she thought it best for her to stay in Armidale until she got over this paranoid hatred of me. So that's what happened. She's been there ever since. I've been going to visit her regularly, hoping against hope she would recover.'

'And has she, ever?'

'There have been times when she seemed to respond to treatment, but even then she was wary of me, even if she didn't attack me physically. Which she did often. But the improvement never lasted long. And this last year her condition has worsened.'

'And you've been visiting her all these years, hoping she'd recover?'

'Yes.'

Erin's throat tightened. 'You must love her very much.'

'I did love her when we married, though it was never a grand passion. And if we hadn't lost the baby we'd most probably still be together today. But it's been out of a sense of duty that I've persisted all this time, certainly for the last few years. I didn't feel I could abandon her.' He tightened his grip on Erin's hand. 'And I've never had reason to want to leave her. Not until I met you, and fell in love.'

Erin's heart leapt. When he turned and drew her to him she melted against him.

His lips sought hers and they kissed, a long, tender, lingering kiss that filled her with warmth.

When they pulled apart he sagged against the back of the sofa. He was emotionally wrung out. Now was not the time to start a conversation about their future. She would have to wait and see where this would lead them. Enough for now to know he loved her. His words had not been lies. A surge of tenderness filled her. She reached up and touched his cheek.

He caught her hand in his own and held it. 'Will you...can you... forgive me...?'

She put her fingers to his lips. 'We don't need to go into that. It's over now. I think we need to come back to the present, and give ourselves time to just enjoy being together. Right now I think we need something very ordinary to bring us back to today.

Would you like a cup of coffee?'

'Yes, that's probably a good idea.'

When Erin came back with the coffee a few moments later Aden was still on the sofa, leaning back with his eyes closed. He sat up as she came into the room.

She handed him a cup and sat beside him.

'I've just remembered I haven't asked you why you called to see me this evening. I suspect you didn't call in just to say hello. Is it something about Annie?'

'No, we have a restraining order against her husband, and that's all I can do for at the moment. It was to get your signature on the Trust document that I need to have ready tomorrow. As well as something else I need to discuss with you about the purchase. But now is not the time for such a discussion. Do you think you can come into the office in the morning?'

'I can manage that.'

'Good.'

They sat there, drinking coffee and talking about business, about Annie and her problems, and about Bobbi.

When they finished the drinks Aden stood and pulled Erin to her feet. He gathered her to him, and her arms twined around his neck. Their kiss was long and sweet.

She walked to the door with him and watched him drive away. She would see him again tomorrow.

CHAPTER FORTY FOUR

When Erin arrived at his office next morning Aden was waiting for her, and he ushered her straight into his office. When he closed the door behind them he took her in his arms and looked deep into her eyes.

'I love you,' he said.

'I love you too.' She smiled.

He smoothed a tendril of hair back from her face and kissed her, long and lingeringly. When he released his hold on her he guided her to the visitor's chair.

'Now to business,' he told her, as she regained her breath. 'If you pay the asking price for the property, five million dollars will be just enough to cover the purchase price, the stamp duty, and fees associated with it. There'll be absolutely nothing left over, for you, or for running costs for Arundel. How are you situated financially? Do you have enough money to cover all your expenses for the shop?'

Erin hesitated. 'We certainly need the opening to be successful, and for us to start selling. Bobbi has arranged thirty days payment for the catering, so a lot depends on our initial sales, and we don't need any more setbacks, or unexpected expenses. As it is, we should scrape through. But I am concerned at not having any funds for running costs for the Centre. Irene expects some women will be able to pay their way, but not all of them.'

Aden frowned. 'There will be significant costs involved with running a property like that, as well as caring for those who need shelter.'

'Irene has started fund raising, but I'm sure that

she's going to need more than she'll be able to raise quickly, if ever.'

'I suggest we have the agent make the vendors an offer on the property, one that will leave some cash over for expenses.'

'If they'll accept it, that would be wonderful.'

'Do you want me to go ahead and contact the agent, and instruct him to make the offer?'

'Yes. Will you calculate the amounts we need, and make the offer accordingly?'

'Yes, I'll do that right away, and then we'll just have to wait and see what happens.'

'Thank you.'

'Think nothing of it. It's all part of the service.' His eyes twinkled. 'However, there is a certain payment that I expect.'

'Oh, what is it?'

He stood up and came around to her side of the desk. 'You'll need to stand up to pay.'

She smiled as she rose and stood by the chair. 'Like this?' she asked.

'More like this.' He put out his hand, and when she took it he pulled her closer. Her head tilted back so she could look up into his face. 'This is the payment?'

His hands came up to frame her face. 'That's just the deposit. This is payment.' His mouth came down on hers, soft and firm.

Her heart beat throughout her body.

Abruptly he released her and stepped back, breathing heavily. 'This really won't do,' he told her. 'In future our business discussions must be held in the presence of a third party, or I'll never get any work done.'

'Then perhaps we should have our future meetings

to report developments at my place.'

'What an excellent idea.'

'And in the meantime, I must go to the shop and get on with the preparations for our opening.'

With a chaste kiss on the cheek Aden led her to the door and opened it for her.

'Then I'll see you at the next appointment,' he said in a formal voice as she walked through to the outer office.

Yes,' Erin replied, equally as formal.

As Aden closed his door she stopped and exchanged a few words with Mrs Crawford, hoping her face didn't look as flushed as it felt.

When Erin arrived at the shop Bobbi greeted her with a smile.

'I couldn't help but notice Aden's car was there for a long time last night. Did you have a good talk?'

'Yes, we did.' Even to Bobbi, Erin couldn't repeat the story of Aden's marriage that he had told her. It was his story and private.

Bobbi's shrewd eyes appraised her. 'And is everything all right?'

Erin caught the hint of anxiety in her voice. She was anxious for her.

'Everything is just perfect,' she told her with a smile.'

'So have you two made up?

'Yes.'

'So he's not the womaniser you thought?'

'No, definitely not.'

'Good.' Bobbi grinned. 'I do like a happy ending.' She hugged Erin. 'And now we'd better get on with our preparations.'

'Yes, we need to make sure everything is ready for the opening.'

'Well, the good news is that Evie Tate rang me again this morning. Apparently she's quite intrigued by our venture, and she's going to make mention of it again in her column. And she told me she was speaking to a friend of hers who's an agent for shoe distributors, and he's going to call on us with a proposition.'

'How interesting. I wonder what he has in mind.'

'I guess we'll find out when he arrives.'

The next day they had a visitor who introduced himself as Evie's friend.

'Jim Stacey,' he told them when he breezed through the door pulling a large wheeled case behind him. 'Evie thought you might be interested in doing a deal on the samples I have left over at the end of each season.'

They stood by while he opened the case.

'Wow, it's like Aladdin's cave.' Bobbi gasped when they saw the array of shoes inside.

'They're samples, like I said,' he told them, 'and mostly small sizes, but there's a big range. I act for all the big designers.'

Erin picked up a sandal and examined it. '*Balenciaga.*' She dropped it and picked up another, and another. '*Prada*, and *Valentino.*'

'And *Lanvin*, and *Christian Louboutin*,' Bobbi added, eagerly examining the contents of the case.

'So what do you think?' Stacey asked. 'Are you interested in them?' He gazed around at the elegant surroundings – gold flocked wallpaper, crystal chandelier, stylish fittings. 'This is a very chic establishment. This footwear will be an asset to you. I can just see a trendy display set up on your shelves.'

'Yes, I think we're interested, don't you Bobbi?'

'Yes.'

'Then it comes down to finances. How much are you asking?'

He named a figure, and, mindful of their financial situation, Erin shook her head. 'Not at the moment, I'm afraid. Perhaps once we're established and have a cash flow.'

Stacey pursed his lips. 'I can't give them away, but I'm willing to talk turkey. What about I give you a twenty percent opening order discount, and sixty days to pay? How would that be?'

'Yes, I think that would suit us. Don't you, Bobbi?'

'Yes, that would suit us fine.'

'Then it's a deal. We'll just fix up the paperwork and I'll leave these with you.' He looked around again. 'I'm very impressed. When do you open?'

Erin told him the date. 'We're having a launch,' she told him. 'Would you like to come?'

'I certainly would, and I know a few others who would like to come too, if you'll have the room.'

'Just tell us how many, and we'll send you invitations,' Bobbi told him.

When he left after completing the paperwork, Stacey shook hands with enthusiasm, and promised to spread the word about *Serendipity*.

CHAPTER FORTY FIVE

As she went about her tasks Erin was overflowing with happiness as she thought of Aden. But she was worried about Arundel. What would she do if the offer wasn't accepted? Irene would be disheartened if they had to look elsewhere. And she wouldn't be able to help the women who needed help right now, including Annie. Her present stay at the farm was only temporary, and she needed help desperately.

That afternoon she received the unwelcome news she'd been dreading. The owners had refused their offer. They wanted the full asking price. If she paid that, there would be no money left over for running expenses. No, they couldn't go ahead with the purchase.

Irene tried to put on a brave front when Erin rang to tell her the news, but Erin heard the disappointment in her voice.

When she arrived home Erin parked her car as usual in the carport and walked to the front gate to check her mailbox. There was a letter for her with a return address that she didn't recognise. It looked like a circular of some kind, or perhaps another request for a donation. At that moment her phone rang. It was Aden. She stuffed the letter in her bag.

'I've just rung to see if you're getting over your disappointment,' Aden told her. 'We'll make it a special priority to find another property just as good. Neither of us has time to go looking during the week, but every weekend we'll go searching. There has to be something else just as good out there, and we'll find it.'

'It could take us months, perhaps even years, to find anything as perfect. And all the while there are all these women in danger, including Annie, who need shelter.' She paused. 'I know what it's like. I've been there, but I was fortunate enough to be able to afford to go to a hideaway. Many women can't afford that, and that's why this is so important.'

'Right now, you must concentrate on the opening of *Serendipity*. That has to be your number one priority right now. You can worry about the finances after that.'

'Yes, I know.' Erin tried to sound happy, but as the call ended disappointment weighed heavily on her.

The next day Erin was so busy she had no time to fret, but, as she and Bobbi went about putting the finishing touches to everything, her pleasure in seeing it all come together so beautifully was marred by the cloud that hovered in the background. She tried to push the problem from her mind as she put the finishing touches to the special window display she was creating for the shoes. A well-displayed window enticed browsers into the store, so she had decided on a display of designer shoes in the smaller of the two windows, after all, what woman doesn't love shoes and a few stylish garments in the other.

She had almost finished the display when she ran out of the oyster coloured fabric she was using as a backdrop. She had another piece in her bag, so she left the window and went back inside to get it. As she opened the bag she saw the letter she had shoved in there the night before. She'd quite forgotten it. She took it out and opened it. It contained several sheets of printed matter, and she saw it was from Phoebus Mining, announcing the date of their Annual General Meeting.

Of course, the gold mining shares. She'd never received one of these notices before. Probably Giles would have always received them and never passed them on. Aden must have notified the company of her new address when he'd first taken her on as a client.

Well, she wasn't much interested in attending their meeting; she had too many other pressing things to be concerned about. But...wait a moment. Aden said they weren't worthless, but...what was it he'd said? Of course! He'd said the company had started exploration and that one day they might be worth something. Maybe something substantial.

She smoothed the sheets of paper and began to read the letter. Her heart jumped as she read. *The exploration site yielded significant traces of gold, and further exploration has discovered an extensive seam of gold, and mining has commenced. We advise all shareholders to hold on to their shares as the price is expected to rise, and paying of dividends will commence forthwith.'*

Dividends will commence forthwith? What did that mean? When? And how much? With a quickened pulse Erin checked the other sheets. They gave details of the exploration, relating to depths of drilling and something about cores, using technical terms that she couldn't understand.

Erin went to her desk and opened her laptop. She

Googled in Phoebus Mining. Yes, there it was. The shares were now listed at twenty dollars each. And she had fifty thousand of them.

Trembling with excitement she rang Aden.

'Now I can sell the shares,' she told him when she'd explained the contents of the letter, 'and that way the Trust can have the money for running expenses.'

'There's no need to sell the shares. They'll increase in value as the mining proceeds. No, you need to hang on to them. But what you can do is give the dividends to the Trust, and that, combined with any donations Irene obtains, should be enough to keep Arundel operating.'

'You mean I'll still own the shares?'

'Certainly, they'll be your safeguard for the future.' He paused. 'Now, shall I instruct the agent to go ahead and prepare the contract for the purchase?'

'Yes, absolutely! And I'll ring Irene and tell her the good news.'

'We'll need your signature on the shares. I know you're busy with all your preparations so I'll bring them to you. I'm sorry I can't make it tonight, but I have an important case coming up and I'll be working late every night. Will you be working in the shop on Saturday?'

'Yes.'

'Then I'll see you there on Saturday.'

CHAPTER FORTY SIX

Steve Waterman's van pulled up outside the shop on Saturday morning. He jumped out, slammed the door behind him and ran towards the door. He looked at bursting point, panting, and with his face flushed and perspiring.

'Erin! There's been an accident.'

Aden! It had to be Aden. Erin's blood chilled.

'What's happened?' Her voice shook.

'It's Aden. He's been stabbed. He's in hospital.'

'Stabbed?' She grasped the door frame and held on tight as her legs threatened to give way. 'Stabbed?' she repeated. 'How could he be stabbed?'

'An intruder in the office. Aden walked in on him and he stabbed him.'

'How badly...is he badly hurt? Will he be all right?'

'He's in surgery now.'

'I must go to the hospital. I have to see him.'

Bobbi grabbed her hand. Yes, go, go. I'll see to everything here.'

'He's still in intensive care, he hasn't woken up yet,' the nurse told them as she led them to the recovery room.

Aden lay in isolation. With his eyes closed, and so still and white, he looked lifeless. He was hooked up to a drip in his arm and various tubes and wires that led to a beeping monitor above the head of his bed.

Erin's stomach clenched, a knot of fear coiling inside her. Please don't let him die. Please.

'How is he?'

'He's holding his own.'

Erin touched his cheek. She rested her hand there for a moment before leaning to kiss his forehead. He gave no response.

'He doesn't know you're here. He hasn't come round from the anesthetic yet. He might be a while. We're keeping a close watch on him, but you can stay if you want.'

'Yes, I want to be with him when he wakes up.'

'That's all right. I'll be popping in often to check on him.'

As the nurse left Steve pulled up a chair. 'Here, sit down,' he told Erin.

She sat as close to Aden as she could, her body tense as she took his hand. It lay in hers, limp and unresponsive. She sucked in a mouthful of air. What did 'holding his own' mean? It must mean they thought there was a chance he might not pull through. Despair twisted her heart. How could she bear to lose him, now she'd just regained the assurance of his love?

But how had this happened? Why had he been attacked? She turned to Steve.

'Why would anyone want to stab him? How did it happen?'

'It was earlier this morning. As you know, Aden isn't usually in the office on Saturday, but he'd arranged for me to come in to pick up details of some work he wanted me to do for an important case that's coming up. When I walked into the reception his door was ajar, and I heard voices in his office. And then I heard the sound of a scuffle, and Aden shouting.'

'A scuffle?'

'Yes. I rushed in just in time to see Aden and some fellow grappling, and then the other guy pulled a knife from his pocket and stabbed Aden in the stomach. I rushed at him and knocked the knife out of his hand, and I managed to wrestle him to the ground. Then I sat on him. I was lucky I'd taken him by surprise. He was a tough nut. But I was very worried about Aden.'

Erin could hardly breathe. 'What was he doing?'

'He'd collapsed on the floor, and he was holding his stomach. I could see blood coming through his fingers and I knew he was in a bad way. This other guy was fighting to get out from under me, and I needed to phone triple-oh urgently, so I did the only thing I could think of. I stood up and yanked him to his feet and punched his jaw as hard as I could. He dropped, out like a light. I phoned then, and told them to send an ambulance and the police.'

'Thank heavens you came in when you did. Otherwise...'Erin gulped at the thought of what might have been.

'Yeah, well, Aden was out to it by then and he was bleeding pretty badly. I didn't have anything at hand to try and stop it, so I pulled off my jacket and held it over his stomach. But blood was still leaking through. I was terrified for him, I can tell you.' Steve shook his head, as if to dispel the memory. 'Thank God the paramedics and the police arrived in minutes, both at the same time. As soon as the medicos attended to Aden's wound they took him out on the stretcher, and I told the police what I've just told you.'

Erin looked at Aden, lying there so still and pale, with only the beep of the monitor to indicate he was alive and breathing. Was she going to lose him? She clenched her fists until the nails dug into her palms.

'The reason I came straight away to get you was because he wanted you,' Steve continued. 'As they carried him out he opened his eyes and he said, 'Erin'. He could hardly get the word out, but he repeated it, 'Erin... I must tell her...' and then he faded again, and never said anything more. He wanted to tell you something, but I don't know what.'

'I wonder what it was? What was so important?'

'Maybe when he wakes up he might remember.'

'Maybe. It's not important right now.'

She turned her attention back to Aden. Would it help him if he knew she was with him? Would he last long enough to realise she was here? She felt so helpless. If only she could do something, anything, to keep him alive. But there was nothing she could do except wait. And pray that he survived.

A little later Erin suggested Steve should go home. There was nothing he could do here, and she promised to let him know if there was any change in Aden's condition.

She was unaware of time passing as she sat holding Aden's hand, trying to send him messages of strength. And love.

The nurse came into the room at regular intervals to check Aden's vital signs, and when Erin asked her how he was doing her reply was always the same.

'He's holding his own.'

The next time the door opened it was to admit a doctor. After he examined Aden and checked the clipboard that hung at the foot of the bed, he turned to Erin.

'I'm Dr Barlow, and I performed Mr Marlowe's surgery. I believe you and Mr Marlowe are close friends?'

'Yes.'

'And you want to know the extent of his injuries, and his present condition?'

'Yes.' Erin's heart thumped.

I'll be truthful with you. In simple terms, the stab wound he received punctured a blood vessel in the abdomen, and he lost a lot of blood. This causes the body to go into shock and, in some cases, it can even cause organ failure. We've replaced as much blood as we can, but there was a lot of damage caused to his body.' He paused. 'I had hoped to see him wake from surgery before this. I'm afraid I can't give you a definite prognosis, but we're doing all we can, and I hope to see him rally soon.'

A chill of fear ran through her. 'And if he doesn't rally soon?'

'The longer he goes without any response, the more critical his condition becomes.'

'That's all you can tell me?'

'At this stage, yes, I'm afraid so.'

'Thank you. I'll stay here and hope he wakes up soon.'

His eyes were full of concern. 'Would you like some coffee?'

'Yes. Thank you. That would be good.'

'I'll have some sent up for you.' With a nod he left.

Erin took Aden's hand again.

There was nothing in the world outside this room. Its beeping monitor. And Aden...his breathing light as thistledown.

CHAPTER FORTY SEVEN

The light outside the window was fading. Aden lay still, unresponsive to Erin's presence. She let go of his hand and stood up, stretching her tired muscles. It seemed as if she had been in this chair forever. She walked over to the monitor. The beeping line seemed to be regular. Surely this was a good sign? She looked at the other instruments, with their flickering dials. She didn't know how to read them.

If only he would wake up, or even stir to show he had life left in him. His hold on life seemed so fragile. Was he slipping away from her? Cold dread filled Erin. How could life do this to her taunt her with the promise of happiness, only to snatch it away? Could Fate be so cruel?

Her throat closed around the lump lodged there. She leant over and kissed his cheek. Her eyes ached with unshed tears as she tried to focus on sending him wake-up messages. Could his mind pick up on them?

Taking several deep breaths she squeezed her eyes shut, trying to hold back the tears threatening to erupt. Her chest pained with the effort of suppressing her worst nightmare. She needed to remain calm. She would be no use to him if she fell to pieces.

She walked to the window. There was nothing to see but a red brick wall opposite. A sight as depressing as her feelings.

She turned as the door opened again.

This time it was Bobbi who came in. She stooped inside the door to place Tasha's basket on the floor, and looked across at Aden's motionless figure. Then she flew across the room with her arms outstretched. Erin went to meet her and as they hugged Erin's self control gave way. She broke down, heaving great sobs as Bobbi held her close.

Finally Erin pulled away and fumbled for her tissue.

'Sorry,' she muttered.

'Nothing to be sorry for.' Bobbi turned to look at Aden. 'How is he?'

'Not good. They say his condition is serious.'

'Can't they tell you anything more?'

'No. I think they're just waiting for him to wake up. Or something. They come in regularly to check on him, but they always say the same he's holding his own.'

Bobbi pulled up another chair and joined Erin in her vigil by the bedside. Erin repeated what Steve had told her of the attack.

They sat there, watching over Aden and speaking in hushed voices. But there wasn't much to say. They were just waiting. Hoping.

The nurse came in to check on Aden again, and the sound of their voices woke Tasha. She began to cry, beating the air with her little fists.

Bobbi looked at her watch. 'It's almost time for her feed, but I hate to leave you.'

'It's all right. I'm okay.' Erin squeezed Bobbi's hand.

'Are you sure?'

'Yes. I'll ring and tell you if there's a change. Thank you so much for coming.'

'You call me if you need me.'

'I will.'

When she left Erin resumed her vigil by the bed.

Much later two men, dressed in suits and ties, entered the room with a purposeful air.

'Mrs Brightman?' queried the tallest as he approached.

'Yes.'

'I'm Detective Wells and this is Detective Maracini. We're investigating the attack on Mr Marlowe this morning. We've been talking to Steve Waterman, and he told us we'd find you here.' He walked across and stood by the bed, looking down at Aden. 'This is a terrible thing. We understand Mr Marlowe is in a serious condition, and we're trying to find out as much as we can about the attack. We want to know what the attacker was doing in the office.'

'I'm afraid I can't help you. I wasn't there. The first thing I knew was when Steve came to tell me.'

'Yes, that's what he told us. Do you mind if I ask you what your relationship is with Mr Marlowe?'

'He's my lawyer. He's acting for me in my divorce.'

'That would be to Mr Giles Brightman, would it?'

'Yes, that's right. We're separated, and as soon as a year is up I intend to file for divorce.'

'I see. It appears the attacker was searching through some files when Mr Marlowe entered his office and disturbed him. The files he had out, and was examining, were relating to you, Mrs Brightman.'

'My files? I don't understand. What could he want with my files?'

'I was hoping you could tell us that.'

'I have no idea. They're papers relating to my divorce. I can't see how they could be of interest to an intruder.'

'I believe you had a break-in at your home recently, and that the intruders then were searching for some papers.'

Erin frowned at the memory. Could the two things be connected?

'Yes, of course. They tied me up and searched my house. They said they were looking for papers.'

'Did they find them?'

'No.'

'Do you know what papers they were after?'

'No. I asked them if my husband had sent them. They said...'she paused as she tried to remember the exact words, 'they said they didn't know who my husband was, but that their boss was powerful, and he always got what he wanted. And he wanted those papers.'

'Can you describe the men to us?'

'They both wore balaclavas but one was medium height and slim, and the other one was taller and more thick-set.'

'The description of the shorter one could fit Mr Marlowe's attacker, but as you didn't see his face, we won't know.'

'He had a European sort of accent.'

'They sound similar, but we can't be sure.'

The other detective, Maracini, stepped forward now.

'Mrs Brightman, you say you and your husband are separated. Forgive me for asking, but was that his wish, or yours? You're the one filing for the divorce, aren't you? Not Mr Brightman?'

'Yes, that's so.'

How does Mr Brightman feel about it?'

Erin frowned. 'Why do you want to know? What does that have to do with Aden's attack?'

'Perhaps I should ask first if you and Mr Marlowe have a personal relationship, as well as a business one.'

'As a matter of fact, yes, we have. We're good friends.'

'And how does Mr Brightman feel about that?'

'I have no idea. You'd better ask him.'

'I'm not just being curious. It wouldn't be the first time someone has been harmed because of jealousy. We're examining all possibilities.'

Erin's insides churned. She remembered the times Giles had hurt her. Would he have had Aden attacked? 'So you think he might have arranged the attack on Aden?' she said slowly, turning it over in her mind. He would be capable of it, she had no doubt about that.

'We're just exploring all options. Do you think he might have done so?'

'I don't know that he'd go to such extremes,' she chose her words with care, 'but he does have a bad temper when he's crossed.'

'Thank you, Mrs Brightman. You've been very helpful. We'll leave you alone now. I hope Mr Marlowe recovers fully.'

'Thank you.'

When they left Erin continued to sit there. As she held Aden's hand she willed him to wake up. But his hand lay inert in hers, and she could see no change in his breathing. As time passed she drooped with tiredness, but she didn't want to leave Aden to go home. Her eyes closed and her head slumped on to her chest. She pulled herself up with a start. She was beginning to drowse. She would have to go home soon or she would fall asleep in the chair. She couldn't stay here all night.

She let go of Aden's hand and reached down to pick up her bag. As she did so she heard a faint sigh. She jerked upright. Aden's lips were parted, ever so slightly. She heard the sigh again, barely audible. It came from his lips. Her heart leapt. He was alive! She took his hand again, and squeezed.

'Aden, Aden my love. Can you hear me?'

She squeezed again, harder, and stroked his face with her free hand.

'Aden, wake up, wake up. Can you hear me?'

His eyes flickered for a second, and then closed. They flickered again. She heard a whisper, soft as the flutter of a butterfly's wings. 'Erin.'

Aden slowly opened his eyes. He turned his head, ever so slightly. He was awake! He was alive!

'Aden, my darling. You're awake. You're all right.' Tears fell then, unstoppable.

'Don't...cry.'

She shook her head, and swiped her cheeks with her free hand.

'I'm so happy.'

'Cry... when you're...happy.'

'Yes. I've never been so happy. You're safe.'

'Love...you.' She had to lean close to catch the words

'And I love you too.' She kissed his cheek, and smoothed the hair back from his forehead.

'Need...to talk...my... briefcase...'

'Not now. You need to save your strength. Tomorrow we'll talk.'

'Tomorrow...'

'Yes. Now you must rest.' Erin pressed the bell.

A nurse appeared in seconds. 'Well now, we're awake, are we? Wonderful.' She turned to Erin. 'You can go home now and have a good night's sleep. The doctor will be here in a minute and we'll look after him. He'll be all right.'

Erin kissed Aden gently. 'I'll be back in the morning, and we'll talk then. Now you have a good night's rest.'

As she left she turned at the door. He was watching her, although his eyelids drooped. When she blew him a kiss, a faint flicker of smile lifted a corner of his mouth.

Erin rang the hospital as soon as she woke the next morning and was told Aden had spent a comfortable night. He was safe.

After she ended the call her mind turned to his attack. Who could have done this? Was it Giles? Or was the fact that the attacker had been looking at her files just a coincidence?

As she ate a quick bite of breakfast she thought about the few words Aden had spoken. Just that they needed to talk, and he'd mentioned his briefcase. As she ate she wondered why his case was important enough to mention as soon as he woke up. Had the intruder been taking it? Was he carrying something important in it? Why was he worried about it? Or had he just been rambling? She would ask him.

Perhaps he wouldn't remember.

CHAPTER FORTY EIGHT

Erin stood for as she second drank in the sight of Aden, propped up with pillows, but awake. Relief surged through her.

His face lit up when he saw her, and he smiled.

'Erin.'

She crossed the room with quick steps.

'Hello, my darling,' she greeted him, and bent to kiss his lips. As she made to move back he caught hold of her hand.

'Do that again,' he whispered, 'it's better for me than medicine. It's the best cure in the world.' His voice was weak.

She took his face between her hands and looked deep into his eyes. She kissed him again, gently.

'If love can cure you, you'll be better in no time.'

'I can feel it already.'

She sat in the chair by his bed, and when he held out his hand she took it in hers.

'How are you feeling? Are you in much pain?'

'No, not too much. They tell me I've got a deep cut, but I can't feel anything, except a bit when I move around. I think they're giving me something to stop the pain.'

'I'm sure they are.' She paused, wondering how much Aden recalled of the attack. 'Can you remember what happened?'

'Yes. When I went into the office there was a guy ransacking the place, and he had files pulled out and scattered around. He had your file out, but he hadn't found what he wanted.' He paused for breath. 'He said something about the Phoebus shares. He thought I must have hidden them because they weren't with the rest of the papers in your file.'

Aden paused to take another breath. He ran the tip of his tongue over his lips and closed his eyes for a minute. He was tiring. She mustn't let him talk too much.

But he opened his eyes and continued. 'He tried to persuade me to tell him where they were, and when he was getting nowhere he decided to jump me. Then, when he thought he was getting the worst of the fight, he pulled his knife on me, and that's when Steve walked in. I don't remember much after that, but the police told me what happened. I have Steve to thank for being here. Without him I'd have bled to death. He saved my life.'

As Erin sat listening to him recount the tale of the attack a kind of numbness spread through her body. The blood thundered in her ears. She had come so close to losing him forever. How could she ever repay Steve? If he hadn't been so brave... She bit down on her lip.

'Thank God he came in when he did.' She couldn't keep the tremor from her voice.

'Yes, I'm afraid it would've been curtains for me if he hadn't.' Aden patted her hand. 'But he did, and I'm here. I'm safe. So stop worrying.'

Erin drew a deep breath as she tried to put the horror from her mind.

Aden leant back again and closed his eyes, and the next instant he was asleep again. Talking about his ordeal had worn him out. She would not to speak of it again until he recovered.

Erin stayed there with him for the rest of the day.

Aden drifted in and out of sleep. Each time he woke he smiled at her, and they spoke a few words. But he was still very weak.

When the doctor came he told her the worst of the danger was passed, but Aden still needed careful monitoring, and he could give no definite prognosis for the future.

By late afternoon there was no change in Aden's condition. When Erin finally left it was to return home and spend the night tossing and turning as she worried if he would ever recover fully.

When Erin arrived at the hospital the next day she was told Aden had been moved to another room. When she went in she was delighted to see him sitting in an easy chair by a window, a pillow at his back and a rug over his knees. His face had regained some of its colour, and he was free of all the wires.

'Good morning, my darling.' He greeted her with a smile, and his voice was much stronger. When Erin leant towards him he pulled her face down to his and kissed her.

'How do you feel this morning?' she asked him as she pulled up a chair and sat next to him.

'I'm feeling pretty good, all things considered.'

'Have you seen the doctor this morning?'

'Yes, and he tells me that when the wound's healed I'll be as good as ever. I might just have to take things a bit easy for a while, that's all, but he doesn't anticipate any lasting damage.'

'That's wonderful.' Erin relaxed back against her chair and let the relief wash through her. He seemed to have bounced back remarkably well.

The door opened and a nurse walked in carrying Aden's briefcase. She placed it on a small table by his chair. 'A friend of yours brought this in to reception and asked me to give it to you. He said to tell you that Steve will be in later to see you.'

After the nurse left Aden sat forward and pulled the case up on to his lap.

'Well now, let's see if we can find out what everyone's been looking for. Our friend didn't find what he wanted in the office, but we'll see if we can find it.'

Aden opened the case, and extracted the large envelope with Phoebus Mining written on the front.

'Now, let's have a look.'

He pulled the sheaf of papers from the envelope After scrutinising the front page, he laid it aside.

'We'll go through the pages one by one, and see if we can find anything.'

'Surely Giles didn't want the shares just to sell them? There's not much money in them by his standards.'

'I doubt it. No, it has to be something else.'

Aden continued his perusal of the sheets, placing each one aside after he skimmed the contents.

'Hel...lo! What have we here?'

Erin leant forward to look at the paper he held. It was not the same as the others. From the front it looked like all the others, but it seemed thicker. When Aden turned it over she saw another sheet was taped to the back. This was a slightly smaller sheet of paper, and hand written.

'Does it have anything to do with the shares?'

'Nothing at all.'

'What is it?'

'It's a list of items. Of sorts. And instructions.' Aden spoke slowly as he continued reading the script. Hs brows drew together. 'If this is what I think it is, it implicates your husband, and Simpson, and Harvey, in activity that would land them all in gaol.'

Erin's eyes widened. 'Why would they get themselves involved in something illegal? They're all wealthy enough without that.'

'Sometimes it's never enough. For some, they still want more, and don't care too much how they get it.' Aden took a deep breath. 'Have you ever seen or heard anything unusual? Ever seen your husband with someone who didn't look...well, like his usual associates?'

Erin thought back. 'He didn't do any business at home, nor have people call there. And he never discussed anything about his business with me. But there was one phone call...' she tried to recall it. 'Yes. It was the morning we were discussing what to do on our fifth anniversary. He took a call that upset him. He raised his voice and swore, which he never did, at least in front of me. That's what made me take notice. There was obviously a problem, and he told whoever it was to fix it. And I remember he called someone 'fucking George', and said he'd better be able to come up with the goods, or it would be the worse for him.'

'You don't have any idea who he was talking to?'

'None whatsoever.'

'I'd better call the police. They'll be interested in this.'

It was the same two detectives who had called to see Erin before, Wells and Maracini, who arrived shortly after Aden's phone call.

After greeting them Detective Wells examined the paper carefully, holding it by its corners. First he checked the front, and then he turned it over and read the hand written sheet on the back. When he had studied it carefully he handed it to his colleague with a lift of his brows. 'Interesting,' was all he said.

''So this was concealed in amongst the rest of the Phoebus stuff, was it?' asked Maracini, when he had finished reading.

'Yes.' Aden went over the details of how they had gone through the sheets one by one.

Both men listened carefully, and then Wells turned to Erin.

'I'd like you to go over very carefully how these papers came to be in your possession, Mrs Brightman.'

'Of course.' Erin pulled her mind back to the day when she had left the house in Point Piper. She took a moment to gather her thoughts together.

'When I left my husband I was away for three nights, and then I returned, in the company of Steve Waterman, to collect my personal belongings from the house. With Steve's help I packed all my clothes into cases, and into some cartons he'd brought with him. There were some papers and books sitting on top of a chest of drawers and I gathered them all up, put them into a satchel, and put that in a case. The Phoebus envelope must have been amongst them, although I didn't notice it especially at the time. My husband had given it to me shortly after we were married, and it was always in with my other papers. It wasn't until I consulted Aden about my divorce and he asked me about certain papers, including a possible pre-nuptial agreement, that I opened the satchel again. '

'Where were you when you opened the satchel again, and where had it been before then?'

'The satchel was stored in a suitcase in a storage place in Chippendale that I have. I got it out to take it to Aden's office.'

'Did you open it before you were in his office?'

'I opened it just to check it when I picked it up, but I didn't look through what was in there.'

'Did anyone else have access to the storage area?'

'I have a key, and my partner Bobbi Harvey. And I suppose whoever was in charge probably had one too.'

'But no-one else?' he persisted.

'No.'

'When the satchel was in your room at Point Piper could anyone else have had access to it?'

'Yes. My husband and any of the staff.'

'Would your husband have known where you kept the Phoebus envelope?'

'I suppose so. When he gave it to me he told me to keep it somewhere safe, and I told him I'd put it with my other papers, in my satchel.'

He turned to Aden. 'Was it the first time you'd seen these papers, when the satchel was opened in your office'?

'Yes.'

'And the Phoebus envelope was in the satchel then?'

'Yes.'

'Did you look through the contents?'

'Yes. But I only gave them a cursory glance at the time.'

'And after that where was it kept?'

'In the file with the rest of Erin's papers.'

'Why was it in your briefcase on the morning you were attacked?'

'Because Erin wanted to arrange payment of her dividends and I needed her signature.'

He turned back to Erin. 'Let's get back to your husband's phone call that you overheard. Are you sure he used the name, 'George', in reference to someone who was causing him a problem?'

'Yes.'

'Then I think that's about all we need at the moment. Thank you both for your time. We'll be in touch if we need anything more.'

When they left they took the paper with them.

It was later in the day when Aden took a call from Mrs Crawford. When he finished the call he smiled at Erin.

'I have some amazing news. The good part of it will please you. The man who attacked me turns out to have been Annie's husband, George. He came before the court and he's been refused bail. He's been remanded in custody until he goes to trial in two month's time.'

Erin gaped at him. 'Annie's husband George. How amazing.' She turned it over in her mind. Why would Annie's husband attack Aden? But the good part meant he would be locked away. 'So Annie and Emma are safe. At least for the next two months.'

'For more than that, I believe. He'll be charged

with attempted murder, and he'll receive a stiff gaol sentence. He'll be locked away for several years.'

'What good news. I must ring Irene and tell her so she can pass it on.' Erin frowned. 'But what a coincidence that it was him who attacked you. I wonder why? If he was really after the Phoebus shares what could he want with them?'

'I can only suppose he was working for your husband.'

Erin thought back to when Bobbi had brought Annie back with her. She spoke slowly as she tried to sort it all out.

'Bobbi was in Simpson's office when Annie's sister, Suzi, approached her, asking for her help and advice about Annie's problem. And then Annie's husband told Bobbi that Suzi had been seen with her, in her car. That's why he thought Annie might be at Bobbi's house, and he called there looking for her. And Simpson, and Laurence Harvey, and Giles, all knew each other, and did business together. There has to be a connection.'

'Yes, you're right. It can't be all coincidence. I think we should mention it to the police.'

CHAPTER FORTY NINE

The next few days were an anxious time for Erin as she watched Aden's recovery. He was allowed out of bed as much as he wanted, and encouraged to walk around, but he tired easily. He was still on heavy pain-prevention treatment. Sometimes it seemed to her as if it was two steps forward and one step back. But she took hope from the doctor's prognosis that he should make a full recovery.

She wanted to be with Aden as much as she could, but she worried that Bobbi was spending so much time working on her own at *Serendipity*. There was still much to do before they would be ready to open and, while Bobbi was willing to spend more than her share of time at the shop, Erin felt guilty as she accepted her offer.

'This is no good. ' Erin said one morning as Bobbi arrived at the shop with the baby. 'You're spending too much time here all on your own, when you could be spending it at home with Tasha, just enjoying her.'

'No, it's all right,' Bobbi protested.

'It's not, and I've been thinking. Now Annie is safe, with her husband locked away, I think we should contact her and see if she can come and work with us now. It would be such a help. And you could discuss more with her about how she'd like to work with her designs.'

Bobbi was busy dressing a dummy in a *Valentino* gown that she had bought from a socialite friend when she heard a tap at the door. She was delighted to see Annie there with Emma in her basket. She greeted her with a smile and a hug.

'I was so excited to receive your call,' Annie enthused as she returned the greeting. 'I'd be over the moon to work here.'

'We hoped you'd still be interested. We can do with the help. But first, tell me...how have you been?'

'I'm fine, but it's been a strange few days. Firstly, to hear about George stabbing Aden, and then about him being locked up. It was only when I heard that he'd been remanded without bail that I was sure I could stop worrying about him harming Emma. And that I could believe we were safe.' Her face clouded. 'But also I've been so worried about poor Aden. How is he?'

'He's recovering. But Erin is spending a lot of time at the hospital. That's why we need you right now if you can come. Where are you living now?'

'I'm staying with Suzi, but her place is too small for us all, so we'd like to take a flat together if I'm working too. And I'd love to work here but I don't have anyone to mind Emma.' She fluttered her hands. 'I can't go back to my family. I want to be free for us to live our lives as we want, like normal Australians.'

'Until she starts to move around she can come with you, and by then we'll work something out. And the other thing is that we're interested in having some of your work to sell.'

Annie's eyes sparkled. 'You really think it's good enough?'

'I do. We both do. Perhaps before long we can set up a display corner called Annie's Designs, or whatever name you choose.'

'That would be a dream come true.'

'Do you have any more of that fabric?'

'No, but I'll contact my aunt and ask her to send some more.'

'Good, and for now let's get to work and finish pressing some more garments.'

Aden's improvement continued day by day. Finally he was pronounced out of danger and moved to a recuperation facility. Here he would have the remedial treatment he needed to complete his recovery.

Erin felt as if she could breathe freely again. She was able to concentrate once more on *Serendipity*, and its opening launch.

'I'm sorry I've been no help to you since Aden has been in hospital,' she told Bobbi and Annie as they stood together in the shop the next morning.

Bobbi shook her head. 'No worries. Aden has been more important. And with Annie to help we've finally finished pressing and hanging everything. I think we're almost ready to go ahead now and open.'

'Then let's set a definite date. How about a month from today?'

'Sounds good to me. What do you think, Annie?'

'I think it sounds wonderful.'

Erin had just finished fixing a sign to the door, announcing 'OPENING SOON', when Jim Stacey appeared He was accompanied by a young man with a pleasant face, a generous mouth, dark hair cut quite short, and skin the colour of milk chocolate.

Erin opened the door and invited them in. Jim

introduced his friend as Max Darley.

Max was dressed casually in jeans, and a shirt with a dark background over-printed with circles and scrolls in white and muted colours.

'Nice shirt,' Bobbi said. 'Looks like an indigenous print. Is it?'

'Yes, you're right.' Max smiled.

'That's why I've brought Max to meet you,' Jim explained. 'He's a rep too, and I know you're interested in unique designs. I thought you'd like to see what he has.'

'I represent the indigenous women in a fabric gallery in Alice Springs,' Max told them. 'They specialise in authentic Aboriginal and Australiana fabric printed on quality cotton. But they also have silk scarves, bandanas, table runners, table cloths, napkins, cushion covers, bags, and all sorts of pieces like that. Would you like to see what I have with me?'

'Yes, let's see.'

Max opened his bag and took several samples of cotton fabric from it. He spread them out on the counter top. Then he added some napkins, small bags, and silk scarves. He stood back to let the women examine them.

'These are beautiful,' Annie breathed, as she picked up two of the fabric samples. One was a bold design in vivid red, green and black, while the other was a softer pattern in muted tones of soft green, pink, turquoise blue, and lilac. 'I could do something special with these.'

'They're all made by local artists and craft people from Alice Springs. The designs are all from their Dreaming.' Max picked up one of the scarves. 'This is one of my mother's designs.'

'So do you represent your family?' asked Erin.

'My mother's people. I do this to help them gain recognition for their work.'

Annie picked up each piece, feeling the fabric and tracing the patterns with a finger tip.

'What do you think, Annie?' Erin asked. 'Would you be able to work with these?'

'Oh yes. I'm already thinking of designs.'

Max's face lit up. 'That's wonderful.'

'Then I think we'll be able to do business,' Erin told him. 'Bobbi and I will work out our budget, and we'll talk again in the next few days. Do you have a card with your phone number?'

'Yes.'

He handed over his card and Erin tucked it in her pocket.

At that moment Tasha woke up and began to cry. Bobbi walked over and picked her up. She immediately stopped crying, and Bobbi walked back to join the others.

Erin looked at her watch. 'It's time we were thinking of finishing for the day. Leave us another card and a price list, Max, and we'll place an order as soon as we work out what we want.'

'Can I drop any of you ladies off anywhere?' Jim asked.

'Thanks, but Bobbi and I have our car.' Erin turned to Annie. 'How about you, Annie?'

'I'll go home on the train. I'm living at Suzi's place.'

'Where do you live?'Max asked.

'Turramurra.'

'I can drop you off. It's not out of my way.'

'Thank you. That'd be great.'

CHAPTER FIFTY

'What's your baby's name?' Max asked as they walked out to his car.

'Emma.'

'Pretty name.'

'Thank you.' She smiled shyly at him.

He opened the back door of the car. 'Let me take that.' He held out his hand for the baby basket.

As he placed it on the back seat and strapped it in, Annie was surprised to see he had baby restraints fitted in his car.

'Oh, you have children too?'

'No, not me.' He laughed. 'But when I go to my mother's place some of my cousins always seem to have babies, and always seem to need a lift somewhere, so it makes it easy to have these fitted. '

With Emma safely strapped in he opened the passenger's door for Annie, and closed it after her.

They drove in silence for a while as he manoeuvred through the traffic to reach the Pacific Highway.

'So where do you live?' Annie asked, when they had joined the steady stream of cars heading up the highway.

He flicked her a quick grin. 'Newtown.'

'But you said Turramurra was on your way. It's nowhere near.'

'Well, it's not all that far. But far enough to need some refreshment on the way.' He shot her another grin. 'Perhaps we could stop on the way, and you'll join me for coffee.'

'But...but...I've got Emma...'

'I'll hold her.'

Annie swallowed. 'Anyway, I didn't know indigenous people drank coffee.'

His grin widened. 'I'm only half aborigine. It's my white half that drinks coffee.' His eyes twinkled with humour. 'Come on. Just coffee. There's no harm in that.'

'How do you know I don't have a husband waiting for me?'

'You said you're living with your sister.' He paused. 'You don't, do you?'

'No.'

'Then how about that coffee?'

'I...Oh, all right.' Annie laughed.

Max pulled the car into a spot near a coffee shop, and he was around to open the back door before Annie reached it.

'I'll get the baby,' he told her as he reached in and lifted out the basket.

He ushered Annie inside and guided her to a table in a corner. He waited until she was seated before placing the sleeping Emma alongside her.

After the waitress had taken their order for coffee and the cake Max insisted on ordering, he leant back in his seat and gazed across at her.

'Do you like living with your sister?' he asked.

'Yes. Suzi and I get along well. And now that I've got a job we're planning on finding something bigger together.'

'But you are married?' He glanced at the ring on her left hand.

'My husband and I don't live together. We're separated.' She paused. 'You don't wear a ring. Do you have a wife?'

'No. I've never met anyone I cared for enough. Yet'

'Do you always live in Sydney, or do you just visit here from Alice Springs?'

'Sydney is my home now, but I grew up in Adelaide, with my father. I went to school and Uni down there, but I spent all my holidays with my mother, and that side of my family.'

'That must have been hard.'

'Not really. My parents are still good friends. They simply found the cultural differences too hard to cope with. Dad wouldn't ask Mum to leave all her family behind to come and live in Adelaide, and once his job up there finished, he had to return to Adelaide. Their marriage only lasted about two years.' He paused, shrugging. 'Long enough to have me. So I find myself with a foot in both camps, so to speak.'

As Max told his story, Annie relaxed, seeing him as a kindred spirit.

'Do you find it difficult?'

'Not now. I did when I was younger. In fact, I went to the California for three years, to get away from it.'

'What did you do over there?'

'Whatever I could find. I washed dishes, waited tables, anything.' He gave a wry smile. 'I had aspirations to be in films.'

'You wanted to be another Ernie Dingo?'

'Still do, I suppose. If it happened, which looking unlikely.'

'It's hard when different cultures have to mix. I know all about that.'

'But you're very Australian, accent and all. Were

you born here?'

Yes, but my parents still cling to the old ways.'

'And your husband?'

'Oh yes. Him most of all.'

'Is that why you separated?'

'Yes.'

His eyes were warm and concerned, and somehow Annie found herself telling him the whole story.

He listened without a word, and when she finished he leant across and took her hand. 'I can only begin to imagine how bad that's been for you. But thank goodness he's locked away now, where he can't do you and Emma any further harm.'

'Yes, and with my new job I can begin to make a new life for us.'

Their coffee arrived and he let go of her hand.

As they drank their coffee, he looked at her directly.

'You have talent, Annie. I'd be very happy to see you working with my fabrics.' He reached down into his bag and pulled out a handful of samples. 'What would you make with this?' He selected a swatch and spread it on the table.

Annie studied it. It had big, bold squares in deep teal on a background of black and white. 'It needs a big sweep of material.' In seconds she had her sketch pad out, and in a few strokes drew a long skirt with a tied waist. 'Like this. And to go with it...' a few more strokes of the pencil and she had added a halter top...'this.' She sat back and studied her work for a moment, then turned it around and pushed it across the table.

Max looked at it, then he pulled another swatch from the pile. 'How about this?'

Annie examined the bright yellow colour splashed with short black lines and small splotches of white and red.

'Definitely playtime.'

She drew brief shorts, a sleeveless top and sat back for a moment. 'And a cover-up top for when the sun gets too strong.' Another minute of concentration.

Max watched her. The pink tip of her tongue poked between her lips as she worked.

'Just like that!' He gave a slight shake of his head as he took the proffered sketch. 'I don't know how can you do it so fast, but they're both spot on. Perfect for the fabric. You're amazing.'

Annie's cheeks coloured. 'Oh no. It's just what suits the motif and the colours.'

'Does it just come to you, when you look at it?'

'Oh yes. I can see it how it looks.'

'And I can see you have a big future in designing.'

Her eyes sparkled. 'It would be wonderful if you're right. I could think of nothing better than to design clothes, and to actually make a living from it.

'I think it will happen.' He sat back in his chair, gazing at her flushed face and radiant eyes. 'You're very lovely, you know.'

Annie shook her head. 'Oh no. My nose is too big, and my mouth is too wide. I know I'm not pretty. Alongside Erin and Bobbi I feel like Plain Jane. '

'Your face has character.'

Annie screwed up her nose. 'That's not what a girl wants to hear.'

'Being pretty is not always a blessing. Take Erin, for instance, look where it got her. Jim told me her story. Her husband married her for her looks. He wanted someone to show off, someone to look good on his arm at his big social do's. She was a trophy wife. And very unhappy. No, beauty's not always a big deal.'

'It's what every woman wants.'

'Perhaps. But then you'd never know if someone was asking you out because they really like you, or because they want other guys to envy them for pulling such a pretty chick.'

At that moment Emma squirmed in her basket, screwed up her face, and emitted a loud cry. Annie stooped to pick her up, but Max was ahead of her. He scooped the baby up and settled her in his arms, where she lay silent as her eyes searched his face.

Annie sat back, wide-eyed. 'You look quite at home holding her.'

'Sure. Like I said, my cousins have babies, and I take my turn at helping. I'm used to babysitting, and lugging babies around. I like them.' He smiled down at Emma. 'We'd get on all right, wouldn't we, Emma? Hey?'

He chucked her gently beneath the chin, and she rewarded him with a gurgle.

'See? We get on fine.'

Annie regarded him thoughtfully. 'So you spend a lot of time with your mother's people. Is that where you feel you really belong?'

'Not really. I feel at home in both camps now, so to speak. At last I feel that I have the best of both worlds. I want to help my mother's people – my people – to achieve their rightful place in society, and to have their talents recognised, same as the rest of Australians. And I'm comfortable in that world. But I grew up more in the white world, with my father, and I enjoy being part of that world. I like the benefits of living in that world.' He shot her a quick smile. 'I can assure you I have no intention of 'going bush'.'

Annie laughed. 'No, I couldn't imagine that.' Her gaze swept over him. 'If it wasn't for your darker skin no one would pick your heritage.'

'You don't find it off-putting?'

'Of course not.'

'That's good. It gives me confidence to ask you a question.'

'What's that?'

'I like you, Annie. I like you a lot. Can I see you again? Outside of business, I mean.'

'Oh! But I...I'm still officially married. With a child.'

'But you will get a divorce?'

'Yes.'

'And as for the child,' he smiled down at Emma, 'we're getting on fine. So what do you say?'

Annie gazed at him, and looked into his eyes. She liked what she saw – warmth and understanding.

She smiled. 'Well...we could try it and see how it goes.'

His face brightened. 'Then if it's okay with you I'll pick you up from work tomorrow, and perhaps we could go out to dinner.'

'Instead of going out, you come home with me and we can have dinner at home. I'd like you to meet Suzi.'

'That would be great. And I'd love to see some more of your work, if you don't mind. You have such talent for designing the right style for a specific fabric. I'd love my mother and my aunties to see what you can do. Perhaps I can take some photos and email to them?'

'If you want.'

Suzi sounded a note of caution when Annie told her about Max. 'You mustn't forget about the family. They wouldn't be pleased if they heard you were seeing another man.'

'But after what George has done surely they won't expect me to remain married to him.'

'Emma is still their grandchild. I think they'll make excuses for George and expect you to remain in the family, even if he is in gaol. At least until he's sentenced by the court. They might even believe you and the baby should go to live with his family while he's in gaol.'

'I'll never do that.'

'Of course not. I'm not suggesting that. And if you like Max then I'm not saying you shouldn't see him. Just be careful about being seen together, at least until George is sentenced and securely locked away.'

Annie agreed to be careful, but she thought Suzi was being overly cautious, and worried that she would be critical of Max when they met.

But Suzi greeted him with a smile when they arrived the next evening.

'It's good of you to have me for dinner,' Max told her as he handed her the bottle of wine he brought to go with their meal.

'Not at all. Annie's been telling me about the wonderful fabrics you have. How they're created by a group of women artists in the outback areas of South Australia.'

While Annie took Emma into the bedroom, Suzi set about preparing their meal.

'What can I do to help?' Max asked. 'I'm used to being in the kitchen.'

'Can you shell peas?'

'Sure thing.'

Suzi placed a bowl of peas on the table and indicated the chair. 'Then here's a job for you. Sit down and shell these for me.'

As Max sat at the table Annie came back into the room.

'Emma is settling down to sleep.' She opened the refrigerator and took out a plate with three steaks on it, and carried them towards the kitchen bench.

At that moment there was a knock on the door. Suzi crossed the room to open it. As she unlocked it, the door was pushed wide with such force that she stumbled backwards.

Annie screamed as a man pushed his way past Suzi and into the room.

'George! What are you doing here? You're supposed to be in gaol.'

In three strides George crossed the room and grabbed Annie's arm.

'I've got a smart lawyer and he arranged bail. I've come to take you and the baby where we all belong. We're going back to my country. Where we'll be safe from interfering do-gooders trying to tell me what I can do with my family.'

Annie tried to free her arm from his grip, but George shook it fiercely.

'Go and get the baby. Hurry up. There's no time to waste. We're booked on a flight away from this cursed country.'

'What are you talking about? You can't leave the country. You're going to be tried for attempted murder.'

'I'm absconding, that's how. My brother helped me and he's got us new papers with new names. And he's booked us seats on the next flight. Now hurry up! We haven't got much time.'

'No!' Annie screamed again and cowered away from him, struggling to free herself from his grip. 'No! I'm not going anywhere with you.'

He shook her savagely and slapped her face. 'Do as I say. Get the baby. Now!'

Max pushed his chair back and sprang to his feet.

'Leave Annie alone. She doesn't have to do anything she doesn't want to. If she doesn't want to go with you, she stays here.'

George swung around to face Max, but kept his grip on Annie's arm.

'Who are you?' He snarled.

'Never mind that. Let go of Annie's arm.'

'You keep out of it. She's my wife. She'll do as I say.'

'I'm telling you once more. Let go of Annie.'

George turned back to Annie, scowling. He ignored Max, and shook her again. 'Get the baby, I said. Do it! Now!' He attempted to shove her towards the door. Annie stumbled, but went no further.

Max moved swiftly and grasped George's arm above the elbow, digging his fingers into the muscles.

George screamed, and let go of Annie's arm.

'Bastard!' He rubbed his arm, and began yelling at Max in his own language. 'I'll teach you to interfere!'

He swung a wild punch at Max, who stepped aside, grabbed his arm and twisted him around. George kicked wildly behind him, but the kick went wide. Max released him and he spun around, cursing.

He swung another punch, aiming for Max's jaw.

Max grabbed his shoulder and with one deft movement turned George around and threw him to the floor, where he landed face down. Max twisted his arms behind him and sat on his back.

The whole episode took only seconds.

Max looked at the two women, who were standing watching, uncertain what to do.

'What do you think I should do with him,' Max asked.

'I don't suppose you could kill him?' Suzi asked with a shaky laugh.

'Nah, sorry, 'fraid not. There are laws about that.'

'Then in that case, I suggest you ring the police.'

'Can we check his pockets?'Annie asked. 'In case he has the false papers with him. I'm sure the police would be interested in those.'

'Good idea. I'll hold him firmly while you two check his pockets.'

George squirmed and kicked, mouthing obscenities, but Max held him firmly while the girls checked his pockets.

'Here! Look at this.' Annie held aloft booklets and papers she pulled from his pocket. 'Passports made out in different names. And airline tickets.'

George raised his head and glared at Annie. 'I'll kill you for this,' he hissed.

Max pushed his head back down, and twisted one arm further up behind his back. It brought a yelp of pain from George.

'No you won't,' Max growled. 'Karate's my game, and I'll be looking out for Annie from now on. You try to hurt her and I'll snuff you out like a candle. Now shut up.'

Suzie had her phone out and was already dialling the police. Within minutes there was a rap at the door, and she opened it to admit two uniformed officers.

'So what's going on here?' asked one, taking in the scene in the room.

Max dragged George to his feet. 'You better take care of him now. He's a prisoner on parole who's absconding and planning to leave the country. He came here to try to force his wife and baby to come with him.'

'Who's his wife?'

Annie stepped forward. 'I am. But I've left him, and he's trying to force me and our baby to go away to his old country with him.' She held up the papers. 'These are false papers his brother got for him.'

'And who are you?' he asked Suzi.

'I'm her sister. Annie and the baby live here with me.'

He turned to Max. 'And you?'

Max gave his name. 'I'm a friend who's visiting.'

'I'll take those.' He held his hand out for the papers.

Annie handed them over and, after perusing them, the officer looked at George.

'What's your name?'

George glared at him silently.

After a pause Annie answered for him.

The officer pulled out his phone and tapped in the details. After a short conversation he replaced the phone and looked them over. 'I think you'd better all come down to the station so we can sort this out,' he told them.

Annie went into the bedroom and returned with

Emma in her arms. The police ushered them all out to the waiting police vehicle.

After interviewing them one at a time, and hearing their stories of the events of the evening, George was led away.

'He won't be bothering you again for a long time,' a senior detective told Annie. 'Whatever the outcome of his trial for his other offence, this escapade will see him locked up for a considerable time. We don't look kindly at parolees who try to flee the country with false papers.'

By the time they all finally arrived back at the flat it was almost time to feed Emma again, so they decided to settle for a quick omelette instead of the dinner they had planned.

As Max was leaving Annie accompanied him to the door.

'I hope we can have our dinner another night soon,' she said.

'Like, maybe tomorrow?'

She smiled. 'If you can make it, yes.'

When he pulled her into his arms to kiss her goodnight she made no protest.

CHAPTER FIFTY ONE

Erin visited Aden every day, and one morning she walked into his room to find him up and dressed.

'Today's the big day,' he told her. 'I've been given the all-clear. I'm out of here today.'

Her heart leapt as he wrapped her in his arms and hugged her, then tilted her face and kissed her.

When they parted later, Erin realised they had still not discussed their future. Aden told her he loved her, but what did he have in mind for them? He'd made no commitment to a permanent relationship. Nor had he mentioned his wife, or what he intended to do about her in the future.

The day of the opening dawned bright and sunny, and Erin woke full of nervous excitement. Would today be a success? They'd received a large number of acceptances to the invitations, but would they all turn up? And, more importantly, would they come to buy, or just to look and enjoy a party?

Too nervous to eat, she headed to the store. She knew Bobbi was at home, busy with Tasha, so she was happy to go early and spend some quiet time alone before the busy day ahead.

Unlocking the door she switched on the lights. The chandeliers shone brightly, one at ground level and the others up on the mezzanine. There was no doubt they set the tone of elegance. They had been worth every cent. Standing still inside the doorway she let her gaze roam. This was her creation. From the day when she first had her idea for *Serendipity* it had slowly evolved. Oh, she'd had help along the way. She thought back over the long conversations with Bobbi. About how Aden helped her take measurements and put her plan on paper, and advised her. She was grateful for it all. But the inspiration had been hers. And spread before her was the culmination of it all.

Walking slowly through the ground floor she scrutinised each item, ensuring that everything was as it should be. She plumped up a cushion here, moved a figurine from one spot to another, eyed it critically and moved it back. She checked that the clothing hung evenly in the racks. She walked around each dummy, ensuring each hem was level, each garment hung correctly. She adjusted a scarf here, a necklace there. Finally she was satisfied. Yes, it had all turned out as she had imagined it. Smart, stylish and elegant.

Then she took the few steps up to the mezzanine and inspected each alcove. How well the padded chairs, with their silken fabric and delicate floral design, enhanced the rest of the decor. In the powder room she checked to see that the fresh towels and perfumed soaps were all in place. When she was satisfied everything was right she walked downstairs again. She went back to the store area that was to be the dressing and change room for the models, and checked once again that all the garments were hanging ready. Finally she checked the PA system that had been placed in readiness for the compere, Megan, whom she had hired for the day. She would introduce each model and describe each garment.

When Erin was content that all was as it should be, she returned home, with plenty of time to be ready and return before the caterers and the models arrived.

As she stood under the shower she luxuriated in the warm water as it streamed over her. It eased her tension. When she stepped out she dried herself on one of the big, fluffy towels, and smoothed on body lotion before spraying on perfume. Erin chose her clothes carefully for the important event. She must look elegant and stylish, but nothing too flashy or over the top. Over her *Simone Perele* lacy underwear she slipped on a white crepe *Carla Zampatti* fitted dress with a scooped neckline, and *Manolo Blahnik* heels, white with a silver trim. Around her neck she fastened a fine silver chain with a single black pearl. She completed her outfit with black pearl ear rings, a silver bracelet of two snakes entwined on one wrist, and a dainty *Classique* watch with a white enamelled band and diamonds in the face on the other. Twirling slowly in front of the mirror she examined herself critically. She was ready to face whatever the day might bring.

As Erin stood by the door ready to receive the first guests she was unable to still the butterflies that fluttered nervously inside her. Bobbi stood at her side, dressed in pale blue *Courreges* pants and short jacket, and *Ginger and Smart* high heeled sandals.

All was in readiness. The models were on standby out the back with the dresser she had hired for the day, and the caterers had the food and drinks under control.

Annie, who looked exotic with her dark colouring complemented by one of her own creations in canary yellow, stood by to help in any way she could.

Aden offered to stand by the glass topped counter nearby, ready to process the cards or take money for any sales. How handsome he looked in a *David Smith* patterned shirt teamed with a suede jacket and dark cotton chinos.

But a little niggle of worry reminded Erin that nothing had been settled between them.

As the first guests began arriving she forgot everything except making them welcome. Irene arrived first with a group of friends.

As Irene kissed Erin on both cheeks she whispered her delight at the outcome of their venture, and pressed her hand in gratitude before moving inside.

Waiters were ready and waiting with trays containing fluted glasses of champagne, as well as Mimosas and Margaritas, with Perrier water for those who didn't want alcohol.

Next to arrive was Jim Stacey with a party of four, including Max, who looked handsome in a suit with an aboriginal print tie.

Soon there was a crowd waiting outside the door, and Erin and Bobbi were so busy greeting everyone that Erin had no time to think of anything else.

Inside the shop everyone was mingling. They exclaimed over the decor and the designer garments. They surreptitiously checked the discreet price tags, and partook of the drinks and finger food that was now appearing – platters of little Greek meatballs, tiny pizzas, spring rolls, and canapés of several kinds. For the sweet tooth there were strawberries dipped in chocolate, and petit fours.

At the height of it all Evie Tate walked in with a photographer, accompanied by her husband and several friends. Evie stood for a moment gazing around with a shrewd eye before turning to Erin.

'This is all very impressive,' she told her. 'What a shame your husband is so tied up with the enquiry and his legal advisers that he couldn't be here to share in your success.' Her gaze flicked to Aden. 'But I see you have admirable support from the very capable Aden Marlowe. Very nice.' She gave a knowing smile, and her eyes twinkled. 'I wish you every success, both in your new business and anything else new in your life.'

She patted Erin's hand and moved away to mingle with the crowd. Soon she was posing the well known, and the not-so-well known, for shots, and recording little snippets into her hand held Dictaphone.

When it was time for the fashion parade Megan took up her position at the PA, and as the first model came out she introduced her.

'This is Mandy, and she's wearing a *Sea Sparrow* dress by *Camilla and Marc*, and her high heeled sandals are by *Ginger and Smart*.'

Mandy made her way to the steps and walked up to the mezzanine, where she twirled elegantly, showing off the dress to a round of applause. Then she came back down the steps and moved slowly in among the crowd, so that everyone had a close up view. As she disappeared behind the scenes another model emerged.

'This is Cleo,' Megan introduced her, 'and she is wearing a skirt by *Dark Angel*, teamed with a top by *Nicola Finetti* and footwear by *Jimmy Choo*.

And so it went on, with each model and outfit

receiving plenty of applause, until they came to the finale. Megan turned towards the dressing room and made a theatrical gesture as the last model came through the door.

'And here we have Rowena, wearing an absolutely wonderful bridal gown by *Vera Wang.'* Gasps of admiration came as Rowena moved slowly forward in the creation of white crepe and floating tulle. When she stopped and turned at the top of the steps thunderous applause broke out.

'This is a one-off creation,' Megan continued as Rowena came down the steps and moved among the guests. 'As are all the garments you've seen here today. And that concludes our fashion show for today.' She paused and smiled out at the crowd. 'Thank you for coming here today, ladies and gentlemen. We hope you've enjoyed seeing our fashions. May I remind you that all the garments you've seen here today are for sale. Please ask Erin, Bobbi or Annie for any information, and we hope you'll stay and continue to enjoy yourselves.' With that she replaced the microphone and retired.

The waiters emerged from behind the scenes and began offering refreshments again. A buzz of conversation broke out as the guests took glasses from the trays and wandered. Many of the guests were already removing clothes from the racks to examine them.

Erin, Bobbi, Annie and Aden had watched the parade from the front of the shop, where they could see everything. As the parade ended the three women mingled with the crowd. Immediately Bobbi and Annie were joined by Jim and Max, as they circulated among the crowd, chatting and answering questions.

By the time Erin returned to the counter she saw Bobbi had already folded a garment in tissue paper and was placing it in an oyster coloured carry bag with *Serendipity* printed on it. Aden was recording the sale and taking the credit card payment.

'Our first sale,' Erin whispered with a smile as the woman walked away with her bag. It was the first of a steady stream. Until the last guest left, much later, they were kept busy wrapping purchases and taking payments.

Finally the last guest left, carrying her *Serendipity* bag, and the day was over.

As they stood looking around the empty shop Bobbi turned to the others, her face alight with enthusiasm.

'Today has been nothing short of amazing, and it's only the start. I'm sure there would be a demand for baby designer ware, and probably we could add a men's fashion section, too.'

Erin turned to Annie. 'And I think you had better start designing and sewing. Do you want to use Max's fabrics?'

'Yes, I like them very much.'

'Then I think we'll make a special section for your designs.'

'That's wonderful.' A smile wreathed Annie's face.

'Well, girls, I think you've arrived,' Aden told them. We can't say that today was anything less than an absolute success. I think that *Serendipity* is now part of Sydney's boutique scene.'

CHAPTER FIFITY TWO

A headline in the Sydney Morning Herald screamed its message...

BUSINESS MOGULS CHARGED WITH DRUG MANUFACTURING.

Well known business entrepreneur Mr Giles Brightman and solicitor Mr Robert Simpson were arrested today and charged in the local court with manufacturing the drug methamphetamine. Both men have denied the charges and the case was adjourned to a later date. They were granted bail and ordered to surrender their passports. They will appear in the District Court on the fifteenth of next month.

It was the day after the opening, and Erin and Aden were sitting on Erin's terrace, relaxing under the shade of the frangipani tree. The air was laced with sunshine, the bees buzzed, and the scent of roses and frangipani hung in the air.

Aden handed the paper to Erin. 'I've been expecting this since my last talk with Detective Wells.'

Erin took the paper and began to read the article. When she finished she put the paper aside and shook her head. 'How could they become involved in such a dirty business? I find it hard to believe.'

'It's amazing what people will do for money.'

'Yes, but they have so much.' She continued reading. 'They don't mention Laurence Harvey. I'm pleased for Bobbi's sake. She wouldn't want Tasha having to believe her father was a drug dealer as she grows up.'

'And how do you feel about your husband being tagged as a drug dealer?'

'I'm amazed he would become involved with drugs, knowing how much harm they cause. Why would he want to do that, with all the money he already has?'

'Greed, I'm afraid.'

'What a fool. But how did that piece of paper come to be in with the Phoebus shares?'

'It was too dangerous to keep anywhere in his office, and he'd have thought it was a safe place, tucked in between the other sheets in a satchel in your bedroom.'

'And if he hadn't attacked me, and caused me to decide to leave him in such a hurry, it would have never been found.'

'That's right. And the same applies if he hadn't sent his tough man, George, to search my office, and I walked in on him.'

'And was it George's confession that finally led them to the manufacturing plant on that remote land they'd bought on the mid coast?'

'Yes. When they told him I was in danger of dying, and that he would be charged with murder, he opened up and told them everything he knew in order to gain leniency for himself, and they began the investigation from there.'

'It's strange the way things work out. If you hadn't had the Phoebus papers with you, he would have found them in my file at the office, and he might have been gone before you arrived. You wouldn't have been harmed, and none of this would have happened.'

'And you wouldn't have the Phoebus shares, or the

dividends from them.'

'And we wouldn't be able to go ahead with buying Arundel.'

'All true. Well, at least you won't have any hold-up to your divorce. I doubt your husband will be contesting it. He'll have more things on his mind. So it seems as if everything is working out well for you. *Serendipity* is a success, and you and Irene have Arundel to do your good work with.'

Aden stood and offered his hand to Erin, tugging gently until she stood alongside him. He took her in his arms and kissed her, long and tenderly.

Erin felt a familiar stirring inside her. Kisses weren't really enough, but, conscious of his wound, she'd kept things light between them since he came home from hospital.

'My darling Erin,' Aden murmured, when they finally parted. He pushed a tendril of hair back from her face. 'We need to talk. I want to ask you a question that I shouldn't really ask you now, but I need to know.' He paused. 'Two questions, actually.'

Her shoulders tensed.

'The first is, will you marry me?'

Erin's heart soared. She wanted to laugh as joy flooded through her.

'Yes. Oh yes, my darling.'

He took her in his arms and his lips sought hers again, hungrily. She pulled his head down to her, and melted into him. She loved the feel of his mouth. Loved the feel of his body. Loved the smell of him, manly and spicy.

Finally she pulled back, breathless. 'So what's the second question?'

'Will you have babies with me?'

Her heart went into overdrive. 'Yes.'

A slow smile spread across Aden's face.

'There is something else.'

'Yes?'

'I'm not quite sure it's the correct thing to do, but do you suppose two people can get engaged while they're still technically married?'

Erin smiled. 'Oh yes, I think that's quite in order.'

Aden reached into his pocket and brought out a small box. He opened it. An emerald surrounded by diamonds winked up at them. He reached for Erin's left hand and slipped the ring on her finger.

Erin turned it this way and that to admire it. 'So now we're officially engaged?'

'Yes.' He drew her into his arms and kissed her again, long and slow.

Erin felt a hot rush of passion. She drew her head back, her breath coming fast. 'Talking of babies, how many do you have in mind?'

'I think four is a good number. How do you feel about that?'

'Sounds good to me.'

He tightened his arms around her. 'Do you think now would be a good time to start trying?'

Her senses swam as she gave a shaky laugh. 'Well, it's probably a bit too soon, but maybe we should have a few practices before we try in earnest. What do you think?'

'I think it's the best thing I've heard all day.'

He pulled her to him again, and the intensity of his kiss set her on fire. Then he swept her into his arms and carried her inside.

EPILOGUE

Erin and Aden sat in the shade of the frangipani tree on a quiet summer Sunday. The scent of its blooms hung in the air, and the fairy-wren serenaded them from the bottom of the garden. They lingered over their coffee, enjoying the mid-morning peace.

Erin's heart swelled with love as she watched her husband playing with the baby. Avril, now five months old, gurgled with delight as her hands reached for the stuffed rabbit that Aden was nuzzling into her chest, pulling it back, going in again, time and time over. It was a game they both enjoyed, and played endlessly.

The gate in the fence between the neighbouring houses opened, and Tasha toddled through, trailing a large stuffed Panda behind her. A toothy smile stretched ear to ear as she dropped the toy to the ground and clambered on its back.

'This is my birfday present.'

Erin called out to her. 'Happy birthday, Tasha.'

Aden tore his attention away from his daughter. 'Yes, happy birthday, Tasha. You're a big girl now you're two, aren't you?'

'Yes, I'se two.'

'Who gave you the Panda?' Erin asked.

'Uncle Jim. And he gave me some shoes too, wif all sparklies on dem.'

'Uncle Jim?' Erin and Aden smiled at each other. 'He's very good to you, isn't he?'

'Yes, and he's good to Mummy, he brought her a present too. He brought her some pretty flowers.'

'That's lovely. And is he coming to your birthday party?'

Tasha's eyes shone as she rocked back and forth on Panda's back. 'Yes, and Annie and Max wif Emma, and Aunty Irene too. I got a birfday cake, and ice cream, and lollies.'

'What a lucky girl you are.'

'Yes, I'se lucky.' The toothy smile was back as she rocked some more.

Bobbi appeared at the gate. 'Come on in,' she called, 'the others are here already, and the festivities are about to start.'

Aden put Avril into her pusher and they followed Bobbi through the fence, with Tasha still trailing her Panda.

Bobbi's patio looked festive with hanging balloons and paper ribbons. A birthday cake with two candles in the middle took pride of place in the centre of the table.

Emma toddled up to Tasha and planted a resounding kiss on her cheek.

'Happy birfday,' she said. She reached for the Panda and tugged at it.

'No. Mine!' Tasha wailed, tugging it back.

As a tussle started Max swooped in and picked up Emma. Annie offered her a stuffed elephant. After a last look at Panda she clutched the elephant and covered it with kisses.

With peace restored and greetings over, Jim poured drinks and Bobbi offered nibbles around.

When they were all comfortably settled Jim held up a newspaper. 'Have you caught up with the latest news?' he asked.

'What about?'

'About your ex-husband, Erin, and his mate Simpson. The trial's finished, and the judge has handed down his verdict.'

Erin sat up straight. 'What's the verdict?'

'They've both been found guilty of manufacturing amphetamines, and they've been fined three hundred and eighty five thousand dollars each. And...' he paused for the full dramatic effect, 'and they've both been sentenced to five years imprisonment.'

Erin let out her breath, and sat back in the chair.

Irene shook her head, her lips tight. 'They deserved more. I've seen enough of the harmful effects of drugs to wish they'd been given a much harsher sentence.'

'And they're very lucky they didn't get it,' Aden observed. 'It could have been fifteen years. Their counsel did a very good job for them.' He took Erin's hand. 'Are you upset?'

'No.' Erin shook her head. 'He deserved what he got.'

'Why would a man with all that money become involved in such a thing?' Jim mused.

'To some people money is everything, and they can never have enough,' Aden said. 'Wealth brings power.'

Erin thought about her previous marriage. Giles, suave, impeccable Giles with all his wealth and possessions. On the outside he was a generous, friendly entrepreneur. But scratch that facade of bonhomie and behind lay a ruthless, scheming mind. He was happy to give her anything she wanted, as long as it could be bought with money. He called that love, and many of their acquaintances envied her life with him for its material pleasures. But he gave Erin nothing of himself. His time, his thoughts, companionship. He shared none of those with her. All the things she had now with Aden. This was love.

She turned and smiled at Aden, who still held her hand.

'Are you all right?' His voice was anxious.

'Yes. I have you, our baby, and our friends. What more could I want?'

A sudden squeal brought everyone's attention back to the children. Emma and Tasha were squabbling over the Panda again.

'Time for the birthday cake.' Bobbi's voice rose above over the ruckus. 'Come on girls, watch me light the candles. And then you can blow them out, Tasha. And when you do you can make a wish for something nice.' Bobbi lit the candles. The girls watched wide eyed, Panda forgotten. The adults crowded around.

'Now, big blow,' Bobbi told Tasha.

Tasha sucked in a huge breath. She puffed out her cheeks and blew. The flames wavered and died. They all clapped and started to sing 'Happy Birthday to Tasha'.

Erin caught a whiff of the smoke trickling from the gutted candles. She was transported back to an incense-filled room with Grace sitting opposite her, predicting her future. Many of her predictions had come true. Lucky guesses? Or was it Fate?

'It's amazing how things happen, and how they can grow.' Erin spoke slowly as she turned it over in her mind. 'If I hadn't lost my mother when I did, I wouldn't have moved to Sydney, I wouldn't have met Giles. And if my marriage to Giles had been happy, we wouldn't all be here today. I wouldn't have met Aden, and we wouldn't all be friends.'

Aden smiled. 'You and Bobbi wouldn't have made your cheeky plans to start a business.'

'And what a business that's turned out to be,' Jim added. 'From your original concept for an up-market, re-cycled.

'Pre-loved,' Bobbi corrected him.

'Of course. From a pre-loved designer boutique it's grown to an eclectic emporium that includes Annie's Corner design garments, hand-made items from the women staying at Arundel, and aboriginal arts and crafts.'

'If you hadn't left Giles there would be no *Serendipity*.'

'That *is* serendipity!' Bobbi exclaimed.

'Yes, it's like throwing a stone in a pond, watching the ripples affect more and more as they spread. One thing leads to another.'

Aden raised his glass. 'I propose a toast to serendipity.'

They all raised their glasses.

'To serendipity.'

The End

****

About Kate

Kate Loveday grew up in a seaside suburb of Adelaide, South Australia. Her two passions as a child were to spend as much time as possible at the beach, and to curl up with a book. Her love of books never left her.

She always wanted to write, and dabbled a bit, but it was not until an extended caravan holiday around Australia with husband Peter that she began writing in earnest. She started with travel articles about places they visited. When these were accepted for publication by travel magazines she began to write fiction.

She now writes Australian contemporary and historical women's fiction/ romance.

When she is not writing she enjoys reading, listening to music, and spending time with husband Peter and her family and friends. She loves chocolate, good food and wine, dogs, music, and seeing new places.

****

Connect with Kate Loveday

I really appreciate you reading my book! Reviews can help readers find books, and I am grateful for all honest reviews.

Thank you for taking the time to let others know what you've read, and what you thought.

Friend me on Facebook:
https://www.facebook.com/kloveday

Follow me on Twitter:
https://twitter.com/LovedayKate

Favourite my Smashwords author page:
https://www.smashwords.com/profile/view/PL

Subscribe to my blog:
https://kateloveday.wordpress.com/

Visit my website: http://www.kateloveday.com/

__*****__